Stan Wolf

# GEMS OF DOMINION

## MYSTERIOUS MOUNT UNTERSBERG

▲

Volume 1

**novum** pro

Bibliographical data of the German National Library:

The German National Library records this publication in the German National Bibliography. Detailed bibliographical data are available via Internet under http://www.d-nb.de.

All rights of distribution, also through movies, radio and television, photomechanical reproduction, sound carrier, electronic medium and reprinting in excerpts are reserved.

© 2011 novum publishing gmbh

ISBN 978-3-99026-118-7
Translated from German by:
Globale-Kommunikation,
Owner: Felix Teske
Cover Image: Stan Wolf,
Kriss Szkurlatowski | stock.xchng
Coverdesign, Layout & Type:
novum publishing gmbh

Printed in the European Union on eco-friendly, chlorine-free and acid-free bleached paper.

**www.novumpro.com**

AUSTRIA · GERMANY · HUNGARY · SPAIN · SWITZERLAND

DOMINION HAS MANY FACETS
PURSUIT OF DOMINION IS OUR FATE
MOST POWERFUL DOMINION IS FOUND IN
HIDING

▲

# Preface

▲

Many things are too unfathomable to write them down like that. Perhaps they even should stay hidden, for the human mind accepts only what it is familiar with. Therefore I am writing this book in the disguise of a novel.

It is up to each reader to decide what he will acknowledge as true.

# Acknowledgements

▲

My gratitude is primarily due to Linda who accompanied me with big patience and perseverance on my journeys and adventures and always carried a bottle of water.

My gratitude also to Werner, Apollo and Gero who have supported me vigorously in my research.

Above all, however, I praise Bard, the artist from Farafra, because in his modest, charming attitude he has made the connections clear to me.

Raghab the fisherman took me at last to the right place at the right time.

Sheik Mohammed Abdul Yussuf, may Allah save him, showed me the way to the Mountain of Visions.

For helpful support I express my gratitude to Franz, the manager of the Sheraton hotel Soma Bay in Egypt.

The General finally provided me with evidence of the impossible ...

# Chapter 1

▲

## GREECE, OCTOBER 1941

A rainy day of October came to an end in the Aegean Sea. Low clouds hid the sky over the coast of Greece. The whitecaps of the turbulent sea and the bleak spume of surf reinforced the gloomy impression of unpleasant autumn weather.

Lights were already burning in the barracks of the small frontline airstrip of Kalamaki, not far from Athens' harbour of Piraeus, when mission order was received for the two Heinkel HE 111 fighter bombers of the 4th Unit of the 26th Bomber Wing of the German *Luftwaffe*. As its emblem the Wing bore a seated red lion with the motto *Vestigium leonis* – The Lion's Track –, for that reason it was also known as the Lion's Squadron.

Now just thirty minutes were left for the pilot, Leutnant Jansen, to discuss the route with the airman of the other plane. Their first stopover was scheduled to be the recently established airstrip of Iraklion. Additional fuel tanks would be fitted there and the planes refilled, for this time, their range had to be increased to maximum. As their target was named the Red Sea, south of the Canal of Suez. For according to just recently received reports of the military intelligence service, the *Queen Mary* was there, having aboard enormous amounts of supply for the Allied troops in North Africa.

At that time the *Queen Mary* was the largest passenger-ship of the world; but for war purposes the Brits had re-equipped her as a troop transporter. That night of October 6, 1941, the two German planes were ordered to sink her with special torpedo bombs.

Jansen started the huge engines of his aeroplane. Roaring loud its mighty propellers came up to speed, and after the other bomber had also started its engines, both planes rolled closely behind each other to the left end of the airstrip. The twin-engined Heinkel 111 with their five-men crew each had take-off on schedule, and after little more than an hour they already arrived at the barely illuminated runway in Iraklion on the island of Crete. Within short distance to each other both machines touched down on the levelled airstrip and rolled to the already waiting tank lorry. In the air surveillance barrack the two flight commanders received the current weather report for their flight course. And within shortest time the additional tanks were fitted under the wings and the planes refilled. They departed South and set course for the Egyptian port of Alexandria.

Just before reaching the African coast, Leutnant Jansen ordered to cease all radio traffic, lest the enemy might home in on the bombers. Over the north of Egypt the sky was cloudless, and in the moonlight the coastline of the African continent stood out crisply. Now Jansen altered, as agreed before, his course to 110 degrees, and the second HE 111 followed in close distance. At an altitude of 10,000 feet they passed North of Cairo, and just after midnight they were approaching the Red Sea South of Suez. Now they had very good visibility and descended to 300 feet above sea-level. Within the next thirty minutes they should encounter the *Queen Mary*.

A calm sea shone below them in the pale moonlight. Both planes followed the coastline of the Sinai peninsula South. Yet there was no trace of their target.

'If this ship won't get into view soon we'll have to turn around!' Leutnant Jansen, already a bit nervous, wiped sweat from his brow. He looked first on the fuel gauge and then his watch. Their fuel supply would just last for about twenty further minutes South, latest then they would have to turn around so that they could still safely get back to the Cretan airstrip. And still there was no trace of the *Queen Mary*.

Then, suddenly, an anchoring convoy of the Allies appeared before them. The largest ship was a freighter of more than 120 metres length; behind there anchored a medium-sized cruiser and many smaller escorting ships. Jansen broke the radio silence, ordering immediate attack on the large freighter: 'Release and fire at will!' Almost instantaneously the 20-millimetre guns of the planes began to chatter loudly. Now everything had to work out very fast. They didn't have a lot of time, for as soon as they were revealed at this low altitude, they would certainly be sitting ducks for the naval guns.

The first bomb released by Jansen's plane made already a direct hit. The large freighter was torn open like a canned food tin. Obviously it had a lot of ammunition on board, because explosions went on for several minutes like huge fireworks before the ship finally sank into the Red Sea before the coast of Sinai with a red glowing stern. This unexpected success had made the pilots careless: Now they also were determined to sink that cruiser which meanwhile fired back with all its guns. Taking a steep turn port Leutnant Jansen tried to arrange his plane in release position for another bomb. And then a sheaf from the naval guns of the cruiser punched their right wing. The other plane was hit in the fuselage. Black smoke trailed after it when it tried to turn away and unmistakably managed it. Jansen's own plane was still maneuverable, and he also wanted to fly back, when he noticed that one of the tanks had been shot leaky. This loss of fuel would prevent their return to Crete.

'We got a hit in the right tank! Return flight to base unpromising. Trying to land in the desert behind the mountains on the other side of the Red Sea. Lots of luck to you, mates', after this final radio message to the crew of the other machine he veered round to the open sea, hoping to cross the Red Sea with what fuel was remaining in the left tank and then to get over the mountains of the Eastern Egyptian Desert, so that he could attempt an emergency landing in the level, sandy area of the Nile Valley. From there he might get somehow with his four members to Cairo. Half an hour of flight time should be enough – if the fuel would last and the plane keep up that long.

Leutnant Jansen observed tensely the control displays of the engines. The sound had changed, and this meant bad news.

'The left engine is damaged, it runs only at half performance. Prepare to leave! I don't think that we can still make it over the mountains.' Now Jansen had trouble keeping the plane up in the air. Slowly the hand of the altimeter was turning left, indicating steady drop.

Meanwhile it was two o'clock in the morning. They were still above the mountains when suddenly the plane began dropping faster. The right engine of the HE 111 started to stutter, and then it ceased completely. Jansen stared, transfixed, at the silent propeller. Instinctively he put the blades to feathering pitch to prevent descending even faster. Yet they rapidly lost height. It was obvious that they would not reach the plain desert to the north of Luxor any more.

Jansen considered that only for a short moment. 'All hands, prepare to jump off! Take care to get out of here fast, otherwise you will jump from too low. Meet you at the plane.' He screamed into the board microphone and pulled up the machine one last time so that his members might easier leave. In rapid succession the four soldiers jumped out of the plane. And soon afterwards, when the height was already alarmingly low for risking a skydive, flight captain Jansen also left the heavily damaged aeroplane. Dangling at his parachute he could observe his aircraft dropping steeply and finally crashing into the foot of a high mountain.

An immense explosion followed. Burning wreckage eerily illuminated the mountaintops of this remote rocky desert.

Jansen touched ground in a gravel trough between two minor mountain peaks and was able to quickly get free of his parachute. He supposed that his members had come down about one kilometre away. The burning plane should indicate to them where to go. Jansen groped his way down through the darkness, and the glow of the fire guided him. Silently he hoped to find still something useful in the debris, such as an operable compass, because finding their way in the desert would otherwise be hard. Till Cairo it was at least 500 kilometres.

Jansen wondered where they might be. From the southern tip of the Sinai peninsula where they had attacked the convoy it was about fifty kilometres as the crow flies to the Egyptian coastline, and high mountains such as these were only up to eighty kilometres inland. They should definitely have reached already the lowlands of the Nile valley. Unless, that was, the north-wind had been stronger than anticipated, not an unusual thing at this time of the year.

Suddenly, when he came closer to the burning aircraft wreck and saw the mountain at which the plane had crashed, he realised where they were. No other elevation of the Eastern Desert at about Luxor was as high as this one. This would be the mountain of Gebel Semna, raising gloomily to more than one-thousand metres. At its foot there blazed the flames from the debris of the crashed aeroplane. So this meant that the north-wind had shifted them more than 100 kilometres South.

Jansen had to grope his way through the darkness over pieces of rock that were razor-sharp. He watched out for his men. The first one found was Obergefreiter Krüger. He as well had survived the skydive unhurt and was obviously glad to find his leader safe, reporting: 'All right, sir, Obergefreiter Krüger is back!' Then, behind a small rocky hilltop, they met two other crew members. These did not seem so well. Gefreiter Huber had sprained his ankle and struggled to limp over the sharply edged rocks toward the wreck. Feldwebel Körner even had a gaping wound at his left arm that he had gotten during his descent from the mountain slope on which he had touched ground.

Any help was too late for Unteroffizier Berger. His parachute had been entangled high up at a ledge. When trying to cut himself from the ropes the poor soldier must have fallen down and broken his neck. They found him lying on the bottom of the valley.

'Soldiers', Jansen said, 'as sad as it is that we have lost a mate, we can feel lucky that death didn't take all of us. It meant taking a big risk to skydive into these mountains in darkness and from minimum height. Let us bed Unteroffizier Berger on his final resting place.'

They took from the dead soldier his identity disc and stacked rocks on the lifeless body as a simple burial mound. Then they continued on their way, guided by the light of fire.

After a while they arrived at the wreck and discovered that the mighty explosion seemed to have caused a rockfall. Not far above the slowly dying flames they saw a stone porch rising halfway out of the scree.

It looked like some ancient, buried gateway. When they came closer they noticed that a sort of greenish smoke or haze crept out of the half exposed entrance.

'I will have a look at this', Krüger suggested. At Leutnant Jansen's nod the Obergefreiter climbed up the scree to the gateway.

'What is this green haze, sir?', asked Huber. He looked as if was somewhat under shock.

'Smoke from burning parts of the plane, maybe, assuming a greenish colour from hydraulic oil?', Jansen suggested.

'Sir, that is possible. But I don't think that's smoke', Huber said, 'It looks to me as if it came out of the porch up there.'

Meanwhile Obergefreiter Krüger had arrived in front of the stone porch, approached it straight. And as soon as he reached the greenish haze wavering on the ground, he suddenly disappeared from the eyes of his dismayed mates. The haze was not that thick that it could hide him, no, it only crawled along as a layer of a few centimetres above the ground. But one second Krüger was there, and the very next second he was gone.

Terrified, the other three stepped back, understanding nothing of what was going on before their eyes. They called for their mate, but he remained vanished. It seemed incredible. Finally, they tried to recollect themselves and looked near the wreck for a place to establish a night camp. Huber got his ankle bandaged, then they slept under a ledge, completely exhausted, for as much short time as there remained till dawn.

▲▲▲

Slowly, Krüger went on toward the old porch. The greenish haze on the ground was really only a thin layer; he did not think twice about it as he passed through. Then he stood just before the gateway of stone. Before it were lying some boulders, and he found it difficult, squeezing himself between them. But when he finally made it and passed through the gateway into the mountain, he arrived in absolute darkness. Fear took him. There was something unknown that he could not classify. Quickly he took his *Luftwaffe* lighter from his flight jacket, it dropped from his shaky hand. Krüger bent down and felt for it in the darkness on the ground.

Finally, his fingers touched the round item of metal.

He lifted and lighted it. In the glow of the small flickering flame he noticed that he was standing in a narrow, coarsely made passageway. Curious he went on. At the end of the passageway he found a life-size relief of the ancient Egyptian god of death, Osiris, that was chiselled there into the wall. Krüger turned aside – and was terrified. For on the right side of the wall, the image of a lion-headed deity was engraved into the rock, gazing down at him with fierce eyes. Then, before the image of Osiris, he could barely descry a cube of rock, about the size of a table, the next moment the flame of his lighter flickered out. All was pitch-dark around him.

Panic struck: He had to get out of there quickly! Krüger groped attentively his way through the darkness back toward the entrance. Stumbling over a rock, he fell flat down. Rapidly he struggled back on his feet and now ran towards the exit. From there, bright light shone, and he was completely surprised to find that dawn had broken outside. He felt as if he had been in the passageway for only some minutes – had he possibly fallen unconscious and laid in the cave for hours? In the desert, dawn could sometimes break rather fast, he thought, especially in such a mountainous area. But Krüger was even more surprised when he had finally crept out of the stone porch and saw the sun high up in the sky. It seemed to be midday already.

He could not interpret this. Immediately he began to search for his mates. When nobody answered his loud calls he started looking for their traces, but except for the coarse burial site of Feldwebel Berger, nothing was there. Nearby the wreck of the plane was lying, now fully cooled down. Sand had already been blown into the destroyed cockpit. It looked as if the relics of the crashed bomber had been around there for weeks already.

Krüger had only his *Luftwaffe* canteen and a knife, and that was it. He set out west, toward the Nile, the sun being his only guide. But Krüger was horrified. How often had he already being facing death during flight missions: Three times he had jumped out of a burning plane with his parachute and each time survived unharmed. But now, in this remote desert of rock, he was in extreme peril.

He was aware that if he did not meet people within one or at the utmost two days, and if he did not at least find water somewhere, then he would miserably die of thirst in this lonesome region. And he did not bet on high wages for himself any more. Krüger laid down in the shade of craning rocks, waiting for the sun to set. In the cool night he might get at least get further than in the heat of the day.

He had, though, not reckoned with those many small rocks on the ground that provided harsh trouble when walking in darkness. However, Krüger was extremely lucky. For the next morning he descended already from the gulches by the extensions of a wadi and reached the flat, sandy desert. And there was a bedouin's tent, inhabited by some old Arab. The guy gave him water and food. Then, in the evening, a group of riders showed up at the tent, and the next morning they took Krüger along on horseback to the Nile. Two days later they got to the river. Quickly, a felucca was found, a boat that would take him to Cairo. For just as it had been agreed about with his mates on the evening of the crash, he intended to get from the capital of Egypt straight through the zone occupied by the Allied Forces and to the German units in Libya.

Yet after his arrival in Cairo, the blonde Krüger was discovered by the English while trying to acquire Arabian clothes, and he was arrested. Thus he fell into British captivity. This was the end of the war, as far as Obergefreiter Krüger was concerned.

When Leutnant Jansen awoke, it seemed to him as if he had had a bad dream about the attack on the British convoy, the skydive in the mountain desert, the death of Unteroffizier Berger, and finally Krüger's disappearance in front of the old porch under the rock face.

When daylight had come they re-examined the spot where Krüger had disappeared, keeping away from the gateway. Still that greenish haze hovered everywhere around the porch, although it was now not as clearly visible as in the night before. But they found no trace of Obergefreiter Krüger. In the end, they decided to look for things that might come helpful from the wreckage of the crashed plane, and indeed they found a bag of maps that had been cast out of the aircraft during the collision. Everything else was burnt.

Jansen, studying the map, told his mates: 'We are here at the mountain of Gebel Semna, and the Nile is more than 100 kilometres away. Our supply of water will last for one day. If we intend to get to the Nile Valley, we will first have to pass a hardly penetrable, mountainous rock desert'. He kept aware that without water they could impossibly make it across that distance. 'But here, in the Southern mountains, there are some wells or watering places marked on the map. Turning to there will mean a detour of two days, though.' Jansen passed the map to his mates.

Feldwebel Körner seemed to be most doubtful. 'Sir, what shall we do if the wells have silted or don't exist any more?'

'In my opinion we have no other choice. We do need to put our hope into those wells!'

'I agree with our leader's opinion', Huber said. His sprained ankle still caused him strong pains.

Not losing any further time, the three got on their way. The injury of Gefreiter Huber slowed them down considerably, but after a walk of eight hours under blazing sun they got into a settlement that was fallen in ruin, and it had a well that was silted. A few small trees surrounded it. With bare hands and the help of stones they took turns digging and finally found in low depth the urgently needed water. The next day went similar, and on the third day they came to a sea of debris. Inmidst there was a large, deep well with a staircase spiralling down down all the way into the shaft. They climbed down on the stairs hewn into the rock. Every few metres there was to the inside of the staircase a small breakthrough through which dim light shone from the shaft. Then, arriving at the bottom, they indeed found fresh water.

After they had refilled their water supplies and established a camp for the night, the three soldiers explored the surroundings of the well. What they found took them by surprise. All around, the rock faces were decorated with ancient drawings, carvings, and hieroglyphs. It seemed that unknowingly they had followed from the site of their crash an ancient path of the Pharaohs, and now they had found the remains of a settlement from that era.

The next day they hit close-by on a gravel road, leading west to the plain of the Nile Valley. Again and again their talking returned to Krüger's mysterious disappearance. What had really happened there two days ago? And if they got home, how would they explain? Who would believe them? Yet right now there was no time to think about that. Huber's ankle had gotten slightly better and now they made progress more quickly. In the end they left the mountains of the rugged rock desert behind. An almost endless plain of gravel, permeated with some spots of blown sand, now lay before them. But there was at least a kind of road that they could follow. According to Jansen's map, it should take them to a town at the Nile. Maybe they would even meet people before.

Indeed, in the afternoon they encountered a small caravan of bedouins and some camels who took them along to the Nile. There was at last a small town named Kift, too unimportant for the English to establish a permanent control post there. Facing thus no danger from this side, and with the Arabs being friendly and helpful – for these simple peasants hardly knew or cared for whether Brits or Germans were the occupying forces –, the three soldiers acquired Arabian clothes from the locals so that they might not immediately be recognised as Germans if they happened to encounter some English. An old captain of an as old sailing boat, taking goods from Cairo to Upper Egypt with the north-wind's help, agreed to take the soldiers to Cairo. And when two days later they passed by the city of Assyut, they could barely breathe. For their felucca swam very closely along an English gunboat.

But because of their bedouins' clothes nobody took notice of them.

Unchallenged they reached Cairo six days later. With much luck they found their way during the next weeks, off the traffic routes, through sandy deserts to Tobruk, Libya, where they met an armoured unit of the German Africa Corps, and so they were safe at last. Their report on the disappearance of their mate at Gebel Semna was however taken with extreme reservation. And a dispatch to that extent was sent to the army intelligence service.

# Chapter II

▲

## Mount Obersalzberg, Germany, November 1941

Icy north-western wind was racing across the terrace of the Berghof. But no one was of course exposed to the freezing cold outside within this luxurious abode of Adolf Hitler on Mount Obersalzberg near the town of Berchtesgaden, in the farthest south of Germany. The Führer stood in front of the giant retractable window, lost in thoughts, looking across at Mount Untersberg. Sombre clouds above the Alpine range announced more snowfall.

The Reichsführer-SS, Heinrich Himmler, entered the large study. 'My Führer! We have just received a remarkable dispatch by the army intelligence service, concerning the Panzergruppe- Afrika. October 30, three crewmen of a missing HE 111 of the 26th Bomber Wing have shown up in Tobruk. The plane commander, one Leutnant Jansen, has told a hair-raising tale about a vanished Obergefreiter. He claims this man entered some green mist and then was suddenly gone. Both his subordinates confirm his story. They claim it happened at a porch of stone in the mountains of the Egyptian East Desert.'

'Green mist and one vanished soldier.' Hitler still stared musingly out of the window. 'This reminds me of the tales about Mount Untersberg. Something similar also seems to have happened here once. – Select the most capable man for a trip across the Libyan desert! Also send two agents to this porch! I want to know what is going on there and whether there is something hidden.'

Quite curious whether there was any truth to this story, Himmler raised his right arm to salute. Exclaiming 'Yes, my Führer!', he left.

At Mount Obersalzberg, Adolf Hitler had set up a feudal Alpine stronghold, including plenty of bunkers. The idyllic mountain range near the Greater German town of Salzburg had already attracted him many years ago. Yet his preference for mountains was not the only reason. As well he was drawn to the mystic tales of Germanic history, mentioning Mount Untersberg; in particular he was most interested in the legends of the Holy Grail that also the composer, Richard Wagner, had exploited for his opera 'Parcival'.

This lore inspired Hitler to arrange for a search of the Holy Grail, that lost treasure of the Knights Templar. The Reichsführer-SS, Heinrich Himmler, was his loyal minion during this quest, himself being much attracted to mystic affairs. In 1939 his search had focused on Southern France. There, in the mountain range of the Pyrenées, at Mount Montségur, there had once been the largest castle of the Knights Templar.

The extensive wealth and power of the Order of the Templars, said to have been in possession of the Grail since the conquest of Jerusalem in 1120, had been a painful thorn in the side of the medieval Catholic Church. 200 years later, the castle at Montségur and many other sites of the Templars got therefore destroyed by the Holy Inquisition, and in the aftermath almost all Knights Templar were executed. But this mysterious object, the Holy Grail, was never found.

Near his Berghof at Obersalzberg there was something else which attracted the Führer almost magically. Mount Untersberg, situated between Berchtesgaden and Salzburg, is the northernmost solitary mountain of the Calcareous Alps, rising like a triangular spearhead that is turned towards the east. This mountain inspired many tales and legends about shifting time, apparitions, green mists and one miraculous gem which was supposed to be hidden in the mountain. Hitler therefore left it as undefiled as he could, he even prevented a ropeway from being installed up to its summit. On the terrace of his house he had set up up a telescope by the aid of which he, time permitting, observed Mount Untersberg.

Hitler of course was as familiar with that old traditional tale deriving from the 13th century which claimed that once, a crusader brought a black gemstone from the Levant to Mount Untersberg and hid it there in a cave. In the ruins of mesopotamian Niniveh this knight had had a vision: a female apparition, later called *Isais,* revealing to him the Gem, an orbed black stone, and instructing him to take it to the 'Mountain of the Ancient God' in the land of his forefathers where he must conceal it deep inside the mountain. The crusader recognised that the described location was Mount Untersberg near Salzburg, and after a long journey he brought the black Gem to the mountain. There he found a safe hiding-place, a small, concealed cave, and deposited the Gem therein. Later he had a commandry established, a Templar base similar to a small monastery, near the hiding place. Some centuries later this commandry became a Catholic pilgrimage church, in particular because apparitions of *Isais* happened there over and over again. The Christian populace considered Isais an aspect of the Holy Virgin Mary, the mother of God. It was then that legends and tales about disappearing people began to spread in this area. Often, the vanished people reappeared after a long time and claimed to have stayed only briefly in one of the countless caves of the mountain.

Much later, in the early 20th century, a National Socialistic brotherhood was founded in Vienna that dedicated itself to the exploration of the Isais tale, named *Die Herren vom Schwarzen Stein (DhvSS)* – The Lords of the Black Stone.

The *Ordo Bucintoro*, another order that was from the 16$^{th}$ to the 18$^{th}$ century located on the island of Murano near Venice also dealt intensely with these data. It was said to possess old documents and objects which would explain them.

Could all these tales be connected to that Gem which legend claimed was hidden in Mount Untersberg? And could this phenomenon in Egypt involve another such Gem, a sibling that might have caused the disappearance of that soldier? This should be examined as fast as possible, because if there really was such a Gem in Egypt, Adolf Hitler desired to possess it at any cost!

Still, Hitler gazed across at Mount Untersberg. He remembered his paternal friend and mentor, Dietrich Eckhart. The Führer recalled that until his death Eckhart had also owned such an orbed black Gem which he referred to as *My Kaaba;* he believed it to be a meteorite. Hitler did not know enough about Eckhart's Gem and what happened to it later. And he could not ask his friend any more, Eckhart had been deceased already nearly twenty years ago. But perhaps there really was a link between the Gems and these peculiar phenomena.

Meanwhile, Himmler had focused already on a man who seemed fit for the task: Leutnant Almasy, a former Hungarian count, test pilot and desert explorer. He knew the Egyptian Sahara better than anyone else. Himmler chose him to take two German agents from Libya to the Nile near Assyut in Middle Egypt. The agents should then try alone to access the foot of the mighty Gebel Semna, retrieve whatever was behind that porch of stone, and bring it to Greater Germany. Two submarines were immediately deployed. They had order to pick up the two agents at the end of their mission near the coast of the Red Sea, and then to return them to Germany on a long journey all around Africa. For a return of the agents through Egypt seemed too hazardous, considering the presence of the British armed forces.

# Chapter III

▲

## OPERATION SALAAM

The preparations for *Operation Salaam*, as the mission happened to be called, were quickly accomplished, and the three men taken by a long-range reconnaissance aircraft via Sicily to Tobruk at the African coast. There they took to two cars provided for them that were suitable for desert drives, carrying along a big stock of fuel, water, food and some spare tires. Almasy had driven this route twice already. He had been the first man to cross the Great Sea of Sand in its entirety by vehicle. Many months he had already spent in this desert to find relics of the army of a Persian king, Kambyses, who disappeared 2500 years ago. However, Almasy's search had been in vain. Not the slightest clue to this lost army was found.

The dunes of the Great Sea of Sand rose up to one hundred metres. Sometimes they were three hundred kilometres long. So the three men had to cover a distance of more than one thousand kilometres before they encountered human settlements again. Until then they were all alone. They had not taken a short wave transceiver, because it would have allowed the enemy to home in on them and endanger their mission.

The journey across the sandy desert did not turn out as being very difficult, owing to Almasy's excellent familiarity with the area. Also Major Clarsen, the older one of the agents, was not in the desert for the first time. During a mission in Sudan the year before he had already gathered some experience in remote desert areas and was already acquainted with the huge differences of temperature prevailing in the Sahara.

Hauptmann Mahler, the other agent, was a trained archaeologist and had already taken part in excavations near Baghdad before war came to Iraq. None of the three men thus minded much the hardships of this long desert journey, and they reached the oasis of Kufra in less than seven days. From there they continued on tracks of sand to the southern reaches of the sparsely inhabited Kharga depression and arrived in the town of Assyut at the Nile another two days later. There Almasy left the agents and returned with one of the vehicles on the same way.

The two men who fluently spoke the Arabian language hired a peasant who rowed them south of the town on his boat across the Nile. There they acquired from the locals two horses and a little bit of equipment for a few days, and so they set out as fast as possible into the East Desert, towards the Gebel Semna. There were no English far and wide outside the larger towns and off the main roads, only local peasants and bedouins who took hardly notice of them. Clarsen and Mahler tackled the first eighty kilometres in the plain country quite quickly, and in the evening of the second day they came to the edge of the mountain desert.

Their precise maps allowed them to get the next day to the deep well already and to the valley of the hieroglyphs and the rock drawings that Leutnant Jansen had described. There they refilled their supply of water, and in the next evening arrived at the crash site of the German bomber. The wreck of the HE 111 was by then covered almost completely by drifting sand. Yet it was unambiguously identifiable as Jansen's aircraft.

And the porch of stone, half exposed by the explosion of the aeroplane, was clearly there. However, the green mist was not.

During the mission briefing they had been told that a similarly described mist at Mount Untersberg near Salzburg appeared only when the air was extremely dry, and on such occasions, people were already reported to have disappeared. This was claimed to be connected with some magnetic field shift or so and a temporal anomaly. Sometimes the victims reappeared after days or weeks and pretended to have been away only for minutes, or so it was said. The special department of the SS could not tell them more, for any temporal phenomenon at Mount Untersberg had never been exactly specified. Just as little was known about the origins of the magnetic field shift, only that it was most frequent in extreme dryness. Therefore the two were left with puzzling speculations.

In February, nights in the Egyptian desert were the coldest. Temperatures could drop to the freezing point. During daytime it turned however quite warm in the sun, and so, in the morning hours there was always a haze that quickly dissolved, but after all suggested a certain amount of humidity. Therefore the agents waited for daybreak and then went up to the porch. Major Clarsen suggested that water could not mean any damage. He flung his filled, open water bottle straight into the half-a-metre wide opening of the old stone gateway, and with a clatter, the Bakelite bottle fell on the floor of stone inside.

They waited for another while, and then, removing boulders and scree, they tried to widen the opening that had since the crash been partially refilled by falling stones. When the passageway was finally large enough, Hauptmann Mahler was first to creep through the opening inside.

Clarsen took out his flash-light and followed his colleague. The low passage took them to a small, squared chamber. Its walls were only roughly smoothed, and no decorations or inscriptions were there. Only right in the centre of the chamber there was an ashlar of stone, about the size of a table, and behind, the shape of Osiris, god of death, embossed with vivid features. The two agents almost overlooked the small, black orb of stone, shaped and sized like a flattened orange, that was deposited right in the centre of the stone ashlar in a slight deepening not unlike a bowl. It almost seemed that the image of Osiris was watching over this gem.

Was this tiny black piece of stone really responsible for the green mist and the disappearance of Obergefreiter Krüger? For there was nothing else in this coarsely made chamber. Clarsen and Mahler continued investigating for some time, but ultimately they removed the Black Gem, wrapped it as a precaution in wet cloth and stowed it away in an ammunition box. They almost failed to notice the image of the lion-headed creature at the end of the wall.

'This would be Sekhmet, goddess of war. The breath of death she brings', Mahler gasped. He, being archaeologist, was of course also very well versed in ancient Egyptian mythology.

'Nice coincidence', Clarsen commented. 'On the crashed plane there is also a lion depicted.'

'Indeed, you are right! A remarkable coincidence, I say. It was a bomber of the Lion's Squadron, as far as I was told.' Mahler pulled his camera and made a series of images to take home for documentation purposes.

And so they set out on their way back. Outdoors it had become already quite hot by now. In the shade of a craning rock Clarsen examined the maps while Mahler fed the horses.

Their destination was now the coast of the Red Sea, north of the small town of Al Quseir. That meant for them two days of riding along the wadis. They did not need to fear any English in this forsaken mountain desert; not even bedouins got there. Eventually they reached the coast where the submarine was supposed to pick them up. The agreed signal was a campfire that they made on the beach at night, followed by blinks of a flashlight. They had to wait for another two days, but these passed without incident, and at the third night, after they had given signals by campfire and flash, they saw the tower of the submarine rising only one hundred metres off the coast out of the pitch-black floods of the sea. A small rubber dinghy retrieved the men from the shore. Immediately after they had been taken on board, the submarine dived again and headed for the Horn of Africa.

Fourty-one days at sea took it to the port of Brest in France. The two agents had meanwhile all the time kept the Gem in the ammunition box wet, just to be absolutely sure that no unwelcome temporal phenomenon might happen. After arrival at the submarine bunker of Brest, Clarsen and Mahler were brought at once to the airfield where a completely manned Junkers JU 52 aeroplane was waiting for them, ready for take-off.

'This Gem must be of special value. Otherwise we wouldn't be retrieved from here with our own plane', Clarsen mused. He did not even know where the flight was heading to.

The three-engined plane set down the agents and the Gem in its box on the Alpine airfield of Ainring, in Southern Germany. A car, escorted by the Waffen-SS, took them up to the Führer's Berghof on Mount Obersalzberg, only a few kilometres away. And finally, Hitler personally received the agents in his great hall as if they were honourable guests.

Clarsen raised his hand to salute. 'My Führer, I report humbly that the mission is accomplished. Requested object secured!' He handed over the ammunition box with the Black Gem to Hitler.

The Führer took the metal box and slowly opened it. Almost reverently he held the Black Gem in both hands as if he was feeling emanating power. In any detail, and several times, the Führer ordered the agents to describe the porch, the passageway and the image of Osiris. Mahler passed to Hitler the camera with the roll film on which he had taken the images of porch and surroundings.

'Gentlemen, by your bold action you have in these grave hours paid a great service to the German People! Its significance you cannot be aware of today.' On Hitler's request an ordinance entered, bringing a cushion on which lay two medals. And then Major Clarsen and Hauptmann Mahler were each decorated with the Knight's Cross with Oak Leaves, Swords and Diamonds. They were taken over to the Waffen-SS and promoted to the rank of Obersturmbannführer.

Adolf Hitler was firmly convinced that this Gem was an enigmatic tool of Dominion. And it was in his possession now. He already knew where to keep the Black Gem.

Already in 1938 he had established a subterranean vault not far from the Berghof on a level forest clearing. That he had arranged for after his fruitless investigations into the mythical Gem of Mount Untersberg. This place was not another bunker, not at all, it was rather a sort of cross vault, supported by six strong and sturdy columns and almost reminiscent of a crypt. Above it, a large wooden beehive was set up as camouflage. This construction had been placed by the metre precise on the continuation of an imaginary straight line that set off at the pilgrimage church of St. Mary at Mount Untersberg and passed to Hitler's Berghof on Mount Obersalzberg. That was proof that Hitler knew about the Knight Templar said to have hidden the Black Gem near the pilgrimage church, inside of Mount Untersberg.

The Führer came quite often to this subterranean construction. However, nobody knew what really was going on there. Hitler frequently went for long walks on a road through the forest that had been made for his use alone, and this road took him just past the vault. Then sometimes he was spending hours in that sombre structure that may have had a fireplace and a toilet; however, no electric power. Torches at the walls rather eerily illuminated it. And nobody was allowed to enter. Not even Martin Bormann, the Führer's Assistant and commander of Mount Obersalzberg, had ever been in these chambers below the 'beehive'. Only Hitler went there, and sometimes Himmler joined him.

So the Führer had found a site that was worth of the Black Gem. There it was to be kept, right in the centre of this subterranean enclosure. Hitler readily identified the Gem with the Holy Grail. He felt sure that by the aid of its power he might the easier achieve Dominion of all the World.

But he knew not how and when the Gem might show forth its power.

# Chapter IV
▲

## General Kammler

It happened also in the year 1942 that the Reichsführer-SS, Himmler, appointed a competent, highly intelligent engineer to the SS. Dr. Ing. Hans Kammler became chief of the armament technology factories. Most of these facilities were built underground and now subordinated to his staff. Within the following months the development of jet aircraft and rocket missiles were as well subjected to Kammler. Everywhere in the Reich, giant manufacturing halls were installed underground; and there, completely shielded from the Allies' hail of bombs, new high-technology weapon systems were made. Thousands of prisoners from many concentration camps were exploited for building those facilities and then for making the *vernichtungswaffen*. Kammler had the rare skill to understand very quickly, and to gain control of them, even areas which were outside his field of expertise. Nuclear research, long-range missiles for an attack on the USA, and large-scale technical production of synthetic propellants were quickly advanced. Since Dr. Kammler was always very well informed about all these projects he gained ever increasing competences, and finally he gained entrance to the intimate circle of the Führer. This sober technocrat of course could not fail to remark on the mystic affinities of Hitler and Himmler. For such 'hare-brained nonsense', as he called it, he had no sympathy. Only that was of concern to him what could be proven actually. He also thought that it was absolutely possible to win the War with those recently developed 'wonder weapons', as they were often called, but not with Hitler and his occult fantasies in charge. Kammler's had already advanced to the rank of *obergruppenführer* of the SS, which was equal to a General in the *Wehrmacht*. He was looking now for an ally, and found him, finally, in Albert Speer, his former superior, the Minister of Armament and the Führer's personal architect. Speer was also chief of the Fighter Staff and thus closely cooperated with Kammler in development and production of the new Messerschmitt ME 262 jet aircraft. These two men even contemplated removing Hitler and seizing power themselves.

Kammler visited the Führer on Mount Obersalzberg several times. And of course he learned from Hitler about the legends of Mount Untersberg and the connected temporal phenomena. But Kammler was only interested in some quarries at the foot of Mount Untersberg, for there, beautiful red marble was exploited. Everything else belonged to Fairie, as far as he was concerned, yes, fairy tales and fancy stories that only simple-minded people could find pleasure in. It was of course well-known that the Führer and Himmler were receptive to such stories – well, one more reason for Kammler to consider Hitler a fool. But after all Hitler was the Führer, and nobody must dare to disagree with his orders even the slightest way.

While planning and beginning to build the motorway from Salzburg to Carinthia, it was noticed that in a tunnel through the Alps the flow of time seemed to take odd turns. Workers disappeared and showed up again after days, yet they claimed to have spent only minutes in one of recent tunnel excavations. Then, Himmler told of similar incidents around the Wewelsburg, a castle in Northern Germany that the Reichsführer-SS was rebuilding to become his residence and palace. Of course, Kammler believed nothing of that, he was after all a rational engineer; yet he concluded that these phenomena, if they existed, better had to be investigated. Maybe something showed up that could be useful for the War.

Investigations and experiments in the motorway tunnel proved that what the workers had told was true. There was indeed strange evidence which inspired Kammler to have an instrument made in a subterranean facility in Thuringia that might twist time. Disguised under the code names of *Lantern Bearer* and *Chronos*, a device in the shape of a large bell was constructed there. The very structure of space and time he intended to change with that, applying an enormous acceleration of mass. But although Kammler was on the right track, he lacked the time to complete this engine. Many of the engineers who worked on the Bell died. Kammler, seeing that his attempts to build a 'time machine' would remain fruitless within any foreseeable future, recalled again Mount Untersberg. Well, if such temporal shifts as he wanted to create were really occurring there naturally, then it was worth to look for them.

Of course, he took into account that the Führer would never tolerate excavations and blasting to harm this mountain. Therefore different tests were run on the north-west side of Mount Untersberg, that was facing away from the Berghof. And thus it was quickly found that there some peculiar places on the mountain really revealed a slowdown of time. The maximum factor of the slowdown was determined to be about 1: 300, translating into one minute of staying at such a place vs. three hundred minutes or five hours of lacking behind the outside world. Kammler indeed had an unspecific idea why this might occur just here at this mountain. But that was only speculation. The actual reason no one could tell.

The exact locations of temporal phenomena occurring were quickly investigated and precisely marked in maps.

Meanwhile, Kammler was aware already that the War was virtually lost. And so he gave order to install a comfortable bunker up at the mountain, a base comprising food and fuel that might last for years. He could work out himself that in case he was caught by the enemy, his rank as *obergruppenführer* and the power connected to it were sufficient to take him to a tribunal. For some time he still toyed with the thought of ransoming himself somehow by handing over the secret weapons and the documentation of his latest research to the Allies. But shortly after he rejected that. He was not the scientist behind, sorry, he was in fact only coordinating the research of others. This did work well, but as soon as the Allies were in possession of all the plans and documents, and of the corresponding scientists, he would be of no concern for them any longer.

A refuge then, a shelter that would allow him to spend a few months inside, waiting for the next one-hundred years to pass outside: this was the proper hiding place. For who would still show interest in him, after such a long time, if at all?

Suitable roads that lead to the old marble quarries were developed and applied for the construction vehicles. Kammler even made use of an old railway track high up on the mountain that once had been built to carry down the blocks of marble that were quarried there. The residents were concisely told that red marble was now quarried again, and oh, besides, this area was now restricted SS territory. Anyway, the people in the village downhill took scarcely notice, for too severe was already their need that cruel war inflicted. Only foreign labourers were forced to the task and disposed of without further ado as soon as the site was completed. Thus there was no one who had heard about that secret building project which would provide Kammler with a unique escape route into the future.

The entrance to the base under the earth was set up just at a spot where time shifted, and for that reason it could only be found if someone stood immediately before it.

At that time the collapse of the Greater German Reich was imminent.

It was now April 1945, and Kammler was increasingly aware that there was no way left to win that war, not even with the recently developed high-technology weapons that were just about not yet operational. In one last struggle he arranged for more than five hundred members of the 'intellectual elite' that was labouring in rocket-missile development at Nordhausen to be evacuated to Southern Germany. Other, highly qualified scientists who knew about his confidential research and experiments with the Bell were quickly fetched by SS-units with lorries from Bohemia. They must not get into the hands of the Red Army. For Kammler, he had a plan ...

In April 1945, events rushed. Kammler drove once more to the underground missile and propellant factory Zement, near the town of Ebensee, Austria. There he chose some reliable, high-ranking SS-officers for his purposes and discussed with them all the required precautions. They were meant to join him in his refuge. Then he quickly proceeded once more to that stronghold of the Reich's technology, Prague, to the factories of Škoda, and he himself retrieved the most important plans and documentation of the recent research. That was just a few hours before the Soviet troops invaded.

The last place where the Waffen-SS General, Dr. Ing. Hans Kammler, was seen – in company of his adjutant, Obersturmbannführer Stark – was the Benedictine monastery of Ettal, near Oberammergau, Bavaria ...

# Chapter V

▲

## LINDA AND WOLF, 2006

They were very late at the airport of Munich. Almost too late – in the very last minute they arrived at the check-in counter. Quickly they cast their suitcases on the conveyor belt and rushed with the tickets to customs. Linda had to open her bag and lo! the customs official made a find. In his hand he had a tiny metal object. He bent his head slightly aside and told Linda:

'Unfortunately, you will have to leave this here.'

'So you forgot to remove the nail file from the hand luggage? Anyway, I hardly believe that this time you'll need it', Wolf said. But immediately he gave in again: 'I'll buy for you another one at the hotel.'

'Now cut that out, will you? Hurry up rather, so that we'll get to the gate before it is closed.' Such was the not quite as charming response by sleep-deprived Linda while she rearranged her handbag.

'They won't leave without us. We already have the boarding passes, so they do know that we are here.'

'Don't count on that and keep moving!'

'The final two passengers of flight 668 by Condor to Hurghada are requested to immediately proceed to gate 34.'

'I think that means us', said Wolf as they hastened along the glass wall. Gate 34 was very far behind and on the left. So this was the result of not reckoning with the traffic jam on the motorway. They were indeed the last passengers and scrutinised with disgruntled looks by the other travellers sitting in the plane. The engines were already running. They had just fastened their seatbelts when the Boeing 757 took off towards Egypt.

The two of them had visited the country at the Nile many times before, and each time there had been new wonders. Wolf spent his professional life almost exclusively at the desk; but when journeying he transformed into an adventurer even though he did not look like one at all. He was slightly overweight, his hair was sparse, just suitable to his fifty years of age. Wolf was a private pilot with a licence for two-seaters, a passionate gemstone collector, and he felt an affection for ancient artifacts. He was not the rash daredevil's type, his journeys were always well-prepared, yet for him nothing ever went according to plan.

On this journey they planned to drive for the first time with a rental car – all alone and without support – across the rocky desert from the Red Sea to the Nile. Wolf had spent a long time sorting out what contradictory information on foreigners driving was available. Usually tourists were only allowed to drive across the desert in a convoy that was accompanied by police, no matter whether in a taxi, bus or rental car. Anyway, rent-a-car was only available in three Egyptian towns at all. Would that work out? Would the policemen let them pass at the checkpoints?

What then about the other checkpoints?

Thoughts like this kept revolving in Wolf's head while the plane accessed its cruising altitude above the Alps. Their flight would still take nearly four hours. Linda leant comfortably back against the seat and listened to Rachmaninov on her headphones.

Tired Wolf gazed out of the window. The long drive to the airport, so early in the morning, and the hectic rush inside had taken their toll. He observed the scenery deep below passing by and got lost in thoughts. Past voyages to Egypt he remembered, knowing that in this country hardly anybody ever kept to precise regulations, so it should be somehow possible to explore the remote parts of the East Desert on their own and without a taxi driver. Maybe some baksheesh would do? It often worked wonders in Egypt. But did policemen accept baksheesh at all? Wait and see, they would find out.

Weeks ago he had already phoned Aladdin, the car rental company, and ordered a neutral car, if possible with a license plate of Lower Egypt. This would confuse the posts at the checkpoints a little and perhaps make them believe that Wolf and Linda were residents of Egypt rather than suspect they might be tourists.

Ever since their first trip to Egypt many years ago Wolf and Linda had been fascinated by the temple of Queen Hatshepsut, the Lady of the Two Lands, as she was also called. Even more, however, they were impressed by the queen herself. This great woman on the throne of the Pharaohs had sent expeditions into the legendary land of Punt. According to tradition it was supposed to been located in modern Somalia. In order to get there, Hatshepsut had ships built at the Nile which then, disassembled into several parts, were transported across the rocky desert to the Red Sea. There the ships were reassembled and then they cruised along the coast, far down toward the south. Inscriptions and reliefs in the funerary temple of Hatshepsut at Luxor spoke of more than four thousand people participating in this expedition.

Such stories had inspired Wolf already years ago to trace the footsteps of Queen Hatshepsut and to find the way that these people had taken through the mountains.

# Chapter VI

▲

## GAZELLE'S STEW

Nowadays two asphalted roads wound their way from the Nile to the Red Sea. Yet this route, which a vehicle could pass within a few hours, was certainly not the one that the Egyptians had used at the time of the Pharaohs. For back then, people would have taken more than one week to cross these more than 250 kilometres. However, water was mandatory for passing the rocky desert, and water was available only at a few places in the mountains. For that reason a substantially longer way had to be taken into account, one that passed by wells within a day's trip each.

Wolf intended to find this road, for very little was known about it, and the egyptological reference books gave only sparse hints about possible courses it might have taken.

At the coast of the Red Sea, near the small port of Quseir, he had already discovered ruins dating back to Pharaonic times. Even up to fifty kilometres inland, in mountains on the edge of a wadi - a dry course of a river - there were remnants of buildings and ceramic shards from that time.

Wolf remembered a journey he had made four years earlier by a Land Rover that he had rented together with a Nubian driver, Muhammad. By means of computer-printed satellite maps and GPS he had researched into one possible course of the Pharaonic expeditions and thus directed the jeep driver across rough terrain deep into the interior of the Egyptian East Desert. Several times they had to turn around at the end of what had seemed to be a wadi, because high rocks obstructed their way. After half a day of driving, they came on a railway track that was not marked in the official maps and which might have been built at any time within the last few decades. It served just the transport of phosphate which was mined at many places in Egypt. This track led from the oases to the west of the Nile across more than 1000 kilometres to the Red Sea and the shipping ports there. The driver wanted to follow the railway track and simply steered the car onto the high embankment. There he drove along the sleepers until after some kilometres the rails bent off into a very narrow ravine.

An uncomfortable feeling grasped Wolf. If a train approached them between these rock faces, there was only left the possibility to drive the vehicle very quickly down the steep, ten-metre-high embankment. None of them dared to think of the consequences. However, trains might pass there probably rather rarely, maybe about once per week, Muhammad suggested. And then, at the end of the ravine, they finally left the embankment down a ramp and felt clearly relieved.

After some more openings through the oddly shaped mountains they came to an abandoned mining settlement. From far away they saw two dogs roaming around.

'There should be people', said Muhammad. Indeed they found behind an old slag heap a small, paltry hut, with two dark-skinned Egyptians sitting before it and drinking tea. Wolf and Muhammad stopped the Land Rover before the dwelling of the Arabs, and with a torrent of Arabic welcome phrases the two men approached the car. To Wolf, who could only speak a few words of Arabic, it was mostly gibberish of which he understood close to nothing. Muhammad however interpreted that these two men had shot a gazelle two days ago and made a stew out of it. Wolf and the driver were kindly invited to join their meal.

The two guards of the old mine did not really inspire confidence, regarding their looks. Wild fellows they were, otherwise seen only in adventure films. Yet these two were real. One of them re-enforced with a few pieces of wood the fire that had been smouldering under the soot teapot, and he placed above it another clay pot in which was swimming a hardly interpretable mass of gazelle's meat, potatoes, and other vegetables.

After Wolf had asked how they had hunted down the animal and after Muhammad had interpreted this, the older one of the two Arabs suddenly pulled a big dagger from his galabiya and waved it wildly in the air. Wolf did not get worried, but it looked somehow menacing. The gazelle's stew did not look very appealing, either; however, he found it had an excellent taste. For drinking there was water, but it certainly had been standing around in the open clay pots for a long time and probably was no longer really suitable for a European digestive system. Wolf asked whether he might have some tea. Its water was heated in that soot pot, but at least it was boiled and he could drink it.

Later all four of them sat around the steaming teapot, and the guards told in florid Arabic quite a few imaginable stories out of their long solitude in this godforsaken area and hardly compliant to any kind of truth. Non-stop Muhammad had to interpret. They were talking about mine tunnels of the Pharaonic age, of pits in which djinni or spirits were living, and of entrances into which some of their relatives had disappeared. Wolf knew about the imaginative power of the Arabs. If one would give only faith to half of their narrations, then that was still too much.

The most mysterious story that the older of the two guards mentioned, however, was that of Osiris' Gem.

None of his kin had ever seen this Gem that was not deemed to be particularly large, yet old tales claimed that everyone who came close to it would vanish into thin air. It was a superstition of a kind that Wolf considered typical for most Arabs, and he did not ponder such stories any further for now.

After an exuberant parting ceremony and many wishes for Allah's benediction, Wolf and Muhammad drove on with the Land Rover. They were now somewhat rested of the cumbersome, long drive and deliciously amused by the simplicity of those two mine guards. The trip now continued toward the west.

In the late afternoon, when the sun was already standing rather low, they took a gravel road and reached the connection to Luxor which they followed back towards the coast and the Sheraton hotel. The reddish light of the setting sun painted an impressive mood over the mountains, observable only at this time of day. The reward of the trip was however less impressing. Except for a small decayed settlement in the mountains and a few pieces of clay they had not found on this cumbersome trip anything of what Wolf was actually looking for. Only this item that had kindled his attention. Osiris' Gem of which one of the guards in the phosphate mine had spoken …

An announcement of the flight captain tore Wolf from his thoughts – they had reached the Adriatic Sea. Very soon, their meal would be served: chicken with broccoli, and mashed potatoes or lasagne.

Wolf chose the chicken for himself and for Linda the lasagne.

She had fallen asleep while listening to the music.

# Chapter VII

▲

## ABYDOS

Wolf, as mentioned, was also a pilot himself, but only for small private planes. Two years ago he had together with Linda chartered a seaplane in Luxor: an old 6-seater Cessna 206 with gigantic swimmers. He had intended a flight to Abydos, and this came close to failure because of the oriental bureaucracy of the Egyptians. However, after telephone consultation with the Ministry of Aviation in Cairo and various fax broadcastings, permission was in the end granted. Yet they had to wait two days for that.

The safety pilot was one Per, a German who used this old plane to offer round-trips for tourists high above the temples of Luxor. Per was only 32 years old, but already an experienced pilot. He specified to Wolf the peculiarities of the old plane, and after a breathtaking flight over Hatshepsut's temple and the Valley of the Kings which was directly under their flight route, they landed one good hour of flight-time later near the small city of El Balyana on the Nile. Two police rubber dinghies escorted the Cessna after the landing to an exit point where the plane was moored on the bank.

Hundreds of onlookers were on the roofs of the houses and lining the bank of the Nile. They marvelled at the seaplane as if an UFO had just landed. The policemen accompanied the three visitors with several vehicles, flashing blue light and sirens to the Great Osiris Temple of Abydos nearby.

'You know that some stories place the grave of Osiris in the very rear of this temple?', said Wolf to Linda.

'That Osiris whose figure you got at home in the glass cabinet?'

'Indeed, this very Osiris who is standing behind my black stone from the Pyramid of Cheops.'

When they arrived at the temple, they were treated as state guests. The officials had no idea who those three guys were who had arrived with the aircraft. Casual tourists, if any, came always by bus and sometimes by taxi. So these had to be in their view some higher-ranking, important people. Their impression was reinforced by Per who was wearing his captain's stripes on shirt cuffs as if he was Wolf's and Linda's private pilot.

The temple was quickly evacuated by the police. An individual guide was dispatched for the three guests. An entire bus of tourists had to wait in the parking lot until they had left the temple.

The return to the Nile and the landing of the small aircraft was similar. As soon as their small escort was caught somewhere in the narrow, dusty, unpaved streets of the city because of an ox cart or a crowd, the sirens were turned on and the policemen waved their Kalashnikovs like mad. Within a moment then the road was free again. The policemen brought them with their rubber dinghies back to the aircraft and helped them climbing on-board on the water. The two rubber dinghies then escorted the Cessna to the take-off position in the middle of the Nile. Wolf pushed the throttle forward, the engine roared, and only almost a kilometre later the plane lifted from the water. After an additional lap over the small town they were heading back to Luxor.

The next day, the Egyptian daily newspaper Al-Ahram featured a report on the first landing of a seaplane at Abydos since the end of the Second World War.

The stewardess brought food: chicken in sauce with mashed potatoes and a chill German beer. Also Linda had woken up again and enjoyed her lasagne. When the stewardess had cleared the trays, Wolf leant once more against the window of the plane, and his mind strolled off again. To Egypt.

# Chapter VIII

▲

## Major James

Impressions of his earlier trips to Egypt passed across the imaginary screen of Wolf's mind. It had been three years ago; they had just come back by taxi from Aswan to Luxor. It was the eve of the Islamic Feast of Sacrifice. Before the houses in Luxor, sheep and turkeys were tied to almost every doorstep, moaning eerily, for they were to be slaughtered the next morning. The two of them were taken by the taxi driver to a large Bedouin tent which was specifically set up for purposes of tourism. They were the only guests. It was February and very cold at night. Tightly wrapped in her parka, Linda sat on a bench in a tent, Wolf was attempting a *shisha* – smoking a water pipe. They both were drinking hot and fresh peppermint tea when suddenly a well-dressed, elderly gentleman entered the tent and sat down at a neighbouring table.

It was not long before he asked in good German with a slight English accent whether he might take a seat at the table with Linda and Wolf. The gentleman was about sixty years old, his hair streaked in grey, and his shape was athletic. He was a retired British major and had been for a long time in Iraq and Jordan with the Royal Navy, so he told the two. But his final years of service he had spent in Wiesbaden, Germany, which explained his very good German.

They quickly got into contact with him. Archaeology was the hobby of the English, and he told about his many small finds in the desert. The Major also spoke of secret hiding places which the Pharaohs had created far away in the mountain desert. To date, only a few of them had been discovered.

It was a very interesting conversation, and they agreed to meet again next evening in the bazaar of Luxor, to be precise, in the Lotus Restaurant. It was a hard-to-find tavern on the first floor of a nondescript house. Its kitchen, the Major claimed, was excellent, however. The Englishman was already there when they came upstairs. Again he spoke about his research, and for both it was interesting to listen to what he had to tell.

This time, they discussed the long survival of the Egyptian culture. Major James, as the English called himself, was of the opinion that the rulers of that time seemed to have had some unknown (to us) means for preserving their dominion for such a long time and for successfully facing any enemy during this period. He himself, he said, had achieved no ultimate result by his musings, but there were quite a couple of indications that the Pharaohs had been in possession of very powerful tools, indeed.

Major James sported a hypothesis which currently he could not yet support by conclusive evidence. Maybe it was possible, he said, that the lords of ancient Egypt had possessed relics of a bygone era, objects of Dominion which they kept hidden from the common folk. He then made a suggestion about the Holy Shrine of the Egyptians that might have kept such a secret object. It was claimed to be Osiris' Gem, whatever that might be.

Wolf stopped short, for this term he had heard somewhere. Yes, the two old Egyptians who had guarded the phosphate mine had spoken about Osiris' Gem, too. Major James went on, comparing this Holy Shrine with the Israelite Ark of the Covenant. The Israelites had after all spent enough time in the land of the Nile before their exodus from Egypt. Maybe they had come in some way into possession of such an item. Maybe that was why they succeeded in escaping from Egypt? Or were these only legends? He had no answer to these questions. Sometimes, when Major James was horse-riding in the Western Desert, in the mountains behind the Valley of the Kings, he kept looking for traces of the Pharaonic age. Many beautifully painted pottery shards and also fragments of slabs inscribed with hieroglyphs he had found, but nothing else.

Also he talked about the time he had spent in Iraq. There he had served as a news officer in the Royal Navy and during that time come frequently into contact with archaeologists who run excavations in the ruins of Nineveh, near Baghdad. Ever since then, he had been fascinated by the relics of the local high cultures. But only now, in retirement, he could fully dedicate himself to this activity which had become his true passion.

Linda listened enthusiastically. The gentleman had the gift of vivid and very suggestive story-telling.

They ordered lamb chops, and the Major chose a steak. Dinner in the bazaar was really good, and a glass of red wine might have added a special touch; but here in the souk of Luxor, wine was not available. Alcohol was only served in the big hotels in town. So they just drank freshly squeezed lemon juice and soda.

▲▲▲

The stewardess came once again and brought drinks.

Wolf looked at his watch. Still about two hours to go until touchdown in Hurghada. 'Well, do you finally have overcome your fatigue? In two hours we will be in Africa. What do you think: Will it be quite hot when we leave the plane?'

'Let us wait and see! Winter jackets I will definitely not need', laughed Linda.

▲▲▲

For her, this was already the sixth time she travelled with Wolf to Egypt. Always this turned out to be another adventure, every time. Nothing went according to plan, but most of the time there were some exciting events that were not always without danger, but certainly had a charm of their own.

Linda had grown up as a well-protected only child. She was the daughter of a respected architect and herself had graduated in a convent school. Her profession as a teacher in an elementary school had been tailor-made for her. She was rather shy, and her petite figure, her blue eyes and blonde hair matched her character perfectly.

To Wolf, she was always the good spirit of their joint ventures and provided him with good advice whenever necessary. Sometimes even when it was less necessary but she deemed fit. Her teaching profession drove her to that, and Wolf sometimes mad.

However she was a hands-on type, always caring for sufficient water supply, for example, which Wolf by consequence almost every time forgot about. Thus this couple complemented each other on their travels, even if they did not always agree.

# Chapter IX

▲

### THE WHITE DESERT

'I would like to get a coke and an orange juice for the lady.' The flight attendant acknowledged the order with just a nod, but she served the drinks really quickly. Wolf sipped his cup and was now thinking of their latest trip, in February of the year before.

▲▲▲

This time it was the White Desert: far to the west, at the Libyan border, was their destination.

With a rented bus plus driver they left Luxor and drove past the oases Kharga and Dakhla to Farafra: eight hundred kilometres across the barren landscape, completely devoid of vegetation.

After three hundred kilometres of desert and a visit to the ruin field in Kharga, their small bus remained stuck in the sand. At one of the historical sites the driver had simply dared to advance too far into the treacherous sand. After two hours of desperate, bare-handed digging by the driver, an Egyptian policeman called for a heavy excavator, and this device without further ado lifted the entire bus out of the sand with its shovel. How very Egyptian!

The next day they reached the oasis of Dakhla. Taking a bath in a spring that had a temperature of forty degrees centigrade and reddish brown water tasting of blood, that was a real omen.

While preparing their trip, Wolf had learned that Dakhla was the birthplace of the mythical god, Seth, the brother and eventual murderer of Osiris. In the early morning of the following day, when they paid a visit to the oasis, the two of them came near the ruins of a large fortified granary. An old, blind man was sitting there in the dust, offering clay images of Seth in the shape of a dog for sale. When Wolf was passing him, the blind suddenly picked up one of these ugly figures, felt for Wolf with his stick and then pushed the clay figure into Wolf's hand, mumbling some unintelligible Arabic about Allah's blessing or something like that. He did not want to get any money paid for the clay dog. Wolf took the figure and wrapped it in napkins. He did not quite grasp the meaning of this.

The Egyptian driver then enlightened him. 'The blind man said you were a guardian of Osiris' Gems and therefore committed to receive, actingly, the Dog-Shaped Seth. As an offering to Osiris, you might say, so that the blind will suffer no harm from selling images of Seth the Fratricide.'

Linda too had a hard time trying to understand that. What was supposed to connect Wolf, Osiris, and those black gems? Moreover, the old man with his eyes extinct could not even have perceived Wolf. Well, those Arabs often had a very fertile imagination, she thought.

Wolf laughed: 'After all, there is this original statue of Osiris in my cabinet and the black orb from the Great Pyramid, too. This old man must have sensed that; he has a feeling for a truely big mind!'

'Big head, I take it! Or, matter of fact, this business about bigness is more consistent with your waist', Linda returned, somewhat sneering.

After an extremely long and dull drive along tracks on which they met not a single person they came the following evening at last into the White Desert. A Land Rover that they had ordered days before was waiting for them at a police station at the edge of the last oasis. Their luggage was unloaded. With the four-wheel vehicle they continued far into the desolation which looked to them like a landscape on the moon. Great numbers of sculptures made by nature stood in glaring white like mushrooms, high as houses. Some of these rocks of limestone looked like animals or heads of men. Wolf's camera clicked incessantly. After several hours of driving through this wonderland the driver stopped the car and began to establish a camp for the night. They intended to sleep in this desert under the stars. The rising moon was large and otherwordly. Wolf desired to observe this countryside in peace.

'I know that wolves incline to howl at the full moon', said Linda when she found him sitting on a limestone rock, away from the camp, gazing into the impending night. 'But you may want to get down from your rocks and back to us. Abdul has finished supper!'

Wolf climbed down to the camp. He eyed Abdul mistrustfully who took the pot from the fire and placed it on a mat that he had spread out on the sand. 'Thank God it's already dark and we're hungry. At least you don't see what you eat, and yet it tastes well.'

'I know. Have you noticed, by the way, that plastic container with the brown broth inside over there?' Linda asked out of a desire to curb Wolf's appetite somewhat. Eating less would hardly mean harm to his waist size.

'Yes, why? Isn't that the spare can of diesel fuel?' Wolf looked inquiringly at Linda.

'No, it just looks like. Matter of fact, that's the water for the very tea which we are drinking right now', she returned in pretended equanimity.

He did not flinch, the mint tea was good after all. The campfire gave its warming light, and when he wanted to have some mineral water after dinner, the Egyptian driver remembered that he had forgotten the bottles in the oasis. Meanwhile it was completely dark, as gathering clouds were shrouding the moon. Abdul allegedly knew where other SUVs were standing, and he went on his way into the desert to fetch some water. He took no lamp along. After just a few steps, darkness had devoured him.

Linda felt now a bit uneasy. Many times there had been reports of scorpions and snakes in the desert. Was there not a howl from somewhere? Indeed, it was said there were jackals, golden jackals, in whose shape the ancient Egyptian god Anubis had been formed. Wolf took another cup of hot mint tea from the fire when that eerie sound was heard another time. Now, even though Linda was otherwise not easy to be scared, she approached Wolf closer. And then again they heard something. But this time it sounded like whistling and hissing.

In the next minute they knew what it was. A sand storm!

Within shortest time, none of them could keep there eyes open. Sand was everywhere. Was Abdul at all able to find his way back in this storm and in total darkness? The ignition key of the Land Rover stuck. But where might they look for that poor fellow the next morning, if the storm had ceased at all till then?

As quick as possible they rearranged the loading area of the vehicle into a sleeping area. Now they kept pressing cloths over their mouths, because breathing in this dust storm was close to impossible. Linda had a shawl made of pashmina wrapped around her head and looked hardly distinguishable from a Bedouin woman. Only her bright blue eyes that could be seen through the narrow slit allowed for recognising her.

The wind had blown out the fire and it was completely dark when Abdul reappeared at the car one hour later, bringing six bottles of mineral water. Linda and Wolf sat in the Land Rover, and a swig from the whiskey bottle – each time Wolf bought one from the duty free shop at the airport – washed not just their fear but also the sand down their mouths.

After midnight the storm faltered as suddenly as it had come. The clouds cleared again. Eerie silence, a star-studded sky and the bright moonlight transformed the night that just before had been raging, dark, into a scenery of a kind the two had never seen before. It was a fairyland, a winter landscape, far from any civilisation, indeed like an alien planet. A plethora of those large, white structures was sticking up in the desert, casting strange shadows in the moonlight. Almost reverently they looked out of the car window.

'Do not move, keep very still!' Wolf tried to tell these words very calmly. Yet Linda, only half awake, became terrified. With a swift movement Wolf opened the tailgate of the Land Rover from inside and pulled off Linda's foot a large black scorpion that fell out of the car in a wide arc.

'Now this might have turned out worse! We seem to have laid half the night with that scorpion in the car.' Linda, who had not at all noticed the animal nor was aware of the hazard, said mockingly:

'It wanted to have a warm place, too.'

The next morning there was breakfast, and Abdul was visibly cheered when Wolf told him that they had been worried about him.

'What dust storm? This was but a little wind, wasn't it? Something like that happens all the time here', he said. In a real storm, the Land Rover would probably not have been visible any more next morning. '*Hamdulillah*', he added, meaning something like 'Thank God', and with that he poured the peppermint tea in the cups that he had rubbed clean with desert sand.

After an extensive Arab breakfast the camp was dismantled, and after driving back a few hours they reached the oasis of Farafra, a small village, six hundred kilometres from Cairo and almost eight hundred from Luxor. The hot shower in the only hotel was a real treat after this icy, sandy night.

After the meal Wolf intended to visit Ali Abdul Moghny Bard, an artist. This fellow was making very beautiful works of art in stone, so he had read.

# Chapter X

▲

## Bard the Artist

With the Land Rover Abdul took them to the house of Bard. It was a building with many stairs, chambers, and corridors, and everywhere the artist's works were displayed. Bard was a bearded, well-educated middle-aged man; he worked as a sculptor of stone, but also painted pictures. His works were well known and he had even had exhibitions in Europe. Bard looked himself for his stones in the desert, and for this reason he accessed very remote parts of this already desolate area.

His journeys took him till the Great Sand Sea, the vast desert near the Libyan border. When he saw that Wolf and Linda showed interest in his works, he obviously was not so much focused on selling any more and began to tell.

Bard described how he chose his stones, where they were found and what qualities they had. For him the stones were living entities, and he ascribed to them certain characteristics and effects. The artworks which he had created really had an expressiveness that acted directly on the observer's psyche. He quickly noticed that the two visitors seemed to understand him, and with Arabian hospitality he invited them to dinner. His wife had meanwhile kindled fire in a kind of open hearth, and they all sat down to a very low round table with thick padding on the floor.

Wolf told Bard of the gems that he had at home. For years he had been collecting ground gemstones, and

Bard could only confirm that these crystals, whether sapphire, ruby and diamond or amethyst and topaz, had a strong power on some people. Bard was aware that he had a like-minded guest here, and he was obviously glad now that the two had come to visit him.

Wolf asked him if during his drives to the Great Sand Sea he had also seen the famous desert glass. Then Bard rose without a word, walked to a chest and took two pieces of this extremely rare meteorite glass out of it. They were the only samples he had ever found, he said, and he picked the smaller of the two glasses and gave it to Wolf as a gift. No one had ever asked about that yet, said Bard, and he began to tell.

'A few years ago, when I was on my own, seeking in the desert for stones, well over a hundred kilometres from the oasis, I found these two yellow-green fragments of silica glass at the edge of a high sand dune. At this spot I set up my camp for the night, boiled some tea and crawled into my sleeping bag when it was cold. The starry sky at night in the Sahara, as always, offered a magnificent spectacle. The stars seemed so close I might touch them. Deep in wonder I looked up to the sky and was already bound to fall asleep.

'Then, a very low noise made me listen. I saw a fennec, a desert fox, with his big ears. The fox was curious and came closer. It had sneaked up at me till two metres distance only when it jumped and ran steadfastly to a ledge at the edge of the dune.

'I thought that in the dark I saw a greenish haze on the ground, right there beneath the rock, but then rejected the idea. Where would here in the barren desert haze arise from? Moreover, a greenish one and only at a small spot? Well, the fox ran straight towards it and was gone the next moment!

'I rubbed my eyes and crawled out of the sleeping bag. In the light of my lamp I was looking at the trace that the beast had left when approaching me. I slowly followed the small fox prints in the sand, and when I halted a few meters from the green haze at the rock, I could see that there was nothing more. No trace of the fennec, and the trace broke off at once. It was strange, I realized that the green haze rose from a small crack in the rock, just as wide as a finger. Back in my sleeping bag, I could not sleep for a long time, for persistently I had to think about this oddity.

'The next morning there was no more haze. There were only the crack in the rocks and the traces of the fox.

'Why and where the fox was gone, I cannot tell at all.'

Linda and Wolf listened, spellbound. They took only a sip of peppermint tea at times.

'But I just remember a parallel case to this one', continued Bard. 'More than two thousand five hundred years ago, a Persian king named Cambyses marched with his army from the east through the desert, desiring to conquer the oasis of Siwa. In Siwa at that time there was one of the richest and most famous oracles of classical antiquity.

But there, in the Great Sand Sea, about two hundred kilometres south of the oasis of Siwa, any trace of Cambyses and his army was lost. Once it was said that a huge sand storm had buried those five thousand people. It sounded reasonable and would have been quite possible. But a few years ago the army was researched for. Aircraft and satellite studies were carried out, and they absolutely brought no result. Attempts were made, by means of magnetic field meters that even deep in the oceans could locate metal objects, to find the shields and spears and armaments of this army. But nothing was found, and so, the disappearance of Cambyses remains an inexplicable phenomenon. Just as with the missing little fox', laughed Bard.

'In the months after I asked Bedouins whom I sometimes encountered in the desert whether they had ever had strange experiences in this area. Then, ordinary people told me of peculiar black gemstones, orbed and as big as a somewhat flattened orange.

'According to their old traditions, such gems have often been the cause of people disappearing. These Black Gems – which none of the Bedouins themselves had ever seen – were said to occur only in the same region where the desert glass was found. It was the same area in which Cambyses' army and the little fox had disappeared.

'The desert glass', Bard said, 'had been highly appreciated in ancient Egypt at least since the Pharaoh, Tut-Ankh-Amun. A scarab in the amulet of the young Pharaoh was made out of this beautiful glass.'

Thus it was obvious that the people of that time had known about the sites of desert glass. Was it not also possible that they had also found such a black gem, or even several of them?

If this was so, and there was much evidence in its favour, no doubt they also knew about the strange Dominion that these Gems were emanating.

None of them could tell where these stones, if they were real, might have come from, whether they were connected to the yellow-green desert glass, or whether both were possibly of the same origin. Had they been created by the impact of a meteor or in a huge explosion of great heat?

But what might have kindled an explosion, thousands of years ago? Questions, questions to which there was just no answer. Bard then mentioned the story of the god Osiris whose legend told how he was murdered by his brother, Seth, then dismembered and scattered throughout Egypt. Isis, Osiris' wife, gathered the pieces back together. Thus the might of the god of the dead had been restored. Bard also told them that Isis had long before conceived a daughter by her brother-in-law, Seth: a secret child, named Isais. This was a little bit more than Wolf could swallow at once.

What on earth had Isais, a Mesopotamian goddess, gotten to do with the Egyptians? She was supposed to be a daughter of Isis and Seth then? And the Osiris legend was just a metaphor for the black orbs hidden throughout Egypt? But how had the pharaohs made use of the power of these Gems? What had they been used for? Bard said that there was another ancient tradition which circulated among the Bedouins: If several of these extremely rare Gems were placed together, this could mean a large-scale upheaval of things.

Bard wanted to keep to established facts, however. He said that on many reliefs in tombs and temples just such round objects were to be seen.

'These are solar discs', Wolf replied, 'everyone knows that.'

'Ah, but it is also known that the ancient Egyptians represented everything in their pictures and reliefs in two-dimensional depiction. Thus it might quite well be possible that the putative solar discs were in fact flattened orbs', said Bard.

'What the High Priests of the pharaoh had kept in their sacred shrine we do not know. But if it was something like such a Black Gem, then this might address many unresolved questions today.'

Bard's wife brought a large plate with oriental appetizers and a bowl of *aish baladi*, the pita bread.

Bard, who had studied in Cairo, looked thoughtfully at the fire in the fireplace, put some pieces of wood into it and began again to tell.

'During my studies at the Al-Aksar University in Cairo I met a Coptic priest who told me peculiar tales about the plateau of Giza. The Great Pyramid, he said, was millenia older than the egyptologists might conceive of, and the entire area was a giant subterranean maze, he said. One night, the priest took me behind the little pyramid of Menkaure. About two hundred metres away from it there was a small, old descent right inmidst the rubble, and there he led me deep into the earth. Passageways, chambers, some of them embellished with strange, quite ancient hieroglyphics I saw, and in between them many very deep shafts. Of all this you will hear nothing in egyptology, even though this entrance was freely visible and actually accessible to everyone. Only there was usually no one going down. After hours we returned shortly before dawn to the surface. Since then, I was aware that many things from ancient Egyptian times are kept under lock. The priest also told me of the King's and Queen's Chamber in the Pyramid of Khufu from which there are departing twenty centimetre wide and more than fifty metres long shafts, each towards the north and south side of the outer wall. The shafts in the King's Chamber are leading directly to the outside, but those in the Queen's Chamber end many metres before the pyramid's outer surface. However, inside, in the chamber itself, these shafts had not been visible until two-hundred years ago, for they came to light only after the outbreak of the walls, after two spots had sounded hollow there. There, in the exposed shaft of the Queen's Chamber, there was a Black Gem, about the size of a flattened orange. But no one could say why the Gem was there and if it had to mean something.

This Gem is now in the British Museum in London.'

# Chapter XI

▲

## A SHIFT IN TIME

**B**ard's wife brought fresh tea, and the artist went on with his tale.
'I think the egyptologists have known about the secrets of the pharaohs for years. But they are withheld from the people, now as then.'

In the background music by Mozart set in abruptly. His wife had inserted a CD, and the artist said that he was a great admirer of Mozart and had already twice visited Salzburg in Austria.

During his stay in the city of Mozart he had also taken the cableway up to Mount Untersberg. This mountain seemed to him to emanate something comparable to that dune where the little fox had been. He could not explain that exactly, but he suggested that Mount Untersberg might evoke similar phenomena as this location in the Great Sand Sea where the fox had gone.

That was a cue for Wolf to tell about his own excursions to Mount Untersberg:

'More than twenty years ago I was with a large group on Mount Untersberg, just on the top, in the shelter. We had a party and then slept well on the mountain. In the evening, four strangers, a man and three women from Munich, arrived as well and inquired the landlord for stories about temporal phenomena which according to old legends might occur there. The four felt decent, and from the landlord they heard a few of the old stories.

'I then talked to these fellows, and the man told me that he had researched for many years into the reports on time shifts on Mount Untersberg.

'A few years after, radio and newspapers reported that August 15, four German hikers had gone missing on Mount Untersberg. For many days after, about a hundred men kept searching for them and even several helicopters were involved. They found no trace of the fellows. Their car stood on a parking lot at the foot of the mountain, even the passport of one of the three women was in the car. The German police searched the apartment of the guy from Munich and found numerous documents, sketches and calculations on the temporal phenomenon at Mount Untersberg. His company considered him absolutely reliable, and according to information from his employer and his bank, there was also no reference to financial or other problems. Eight weeks after the search had been cancelled, in October, the four fellows unexpectedly reported from a ship in the Red Sea, and then they told the following story that was also published in the newspapers and magazines:

They left their car on August 15 at the foot of the mountain, though not for climbing it but for getting to the nearest bus stop from which they rode ten kilometres to the Salzburg train station. There they got tickets to Villach in Carinthia and took the train. From there a bus took them fifteen kilometres further to the foot of the mountain border to then Yugoslavia, the Karavanke. This they crossed and hitch-hiked a lorry to Greece, where they left from Piraeus to Alexandria by ship and finally came through the Suez Canal to the Red Sea. There, they reported on marine radio via the Norddeich radio station to their families, and in consultation with the German Embassy in Egypt they received tickets for the trip home.

Many people in Salzburg who secretly had hoped for some mysterious fairy-tale were then a bit disappointed about this rather trivial outcome.'

Linda picked up a piece of pita bread, dipped it in white sauce and listened attentively, although she already knew the story. Wolf went on to tell:

'I saw myself the car of the four fellows from Munich at that time on the small forest parking lot, and I immediately thought of those guys who during our party on the mountain had asked for temporal phenomena. By the car-plate I could then identify the name of the holder. He was indeed, as it turned out, that computer scientist with whom I had spoken on the mountain at that time, the very one who for years had been tried to research in time shifts on the Untersberg.

'During one of the following summers I also wanted now to investigate this phenomenon. I took my then sixteen-year-old daughter, Sabine, and we made a short excursion to the foot of the mountain. In order to control in a simple manner whether there existed any time shift, we set a few days before the seconds' hand of our watches exactly the same and compared them again and again. There were virtually no differences. For, if one of us should find that time would pass faster or slower, we should have been able to register this from tiniest discrepancies between our watches. Thus on a beautiful summer day we went through the mountain forest across steep meadows and bushes several hundred meters up the mountain, and all the time we kept a distance of about ten to twenty metres to each other, climbing across the rough terrain. We came to an old, overgrown path, and shortly thereafter approached a dilapidated railway track in a ravine. Following the tracks, we reached after a time an old, abandoned quarry that probably had not been operating any more for many decades: Between large blocks of marble grew grass and bushes. We climbed further up the mountain.

'Suddenly, Sabine was no longer there. I loudly called many times her name, looked around for her and could not find her anywhere. After about two minutes, she stood a few metres away from me and asked, puzzled, as to why I was calling out so loudly. She had heard me call but once. And then she claimed to have lost me from sight just for a few seconds. An immediate comparison of our watches revealed a discrepancy of almost two minutes!

'So there really had to be a time shift!'

Wolf hesitated. There was one other aspect about it that seemed to him too weird to retell. Immediately after Sabine had appeared again, they had seen on the other side of a very steep trench that there was standing a man, clad in a dark robe and hood like a monk. This strange fellow, he might have been about forty years of age, had gazed right across at them. But when they had crossed the ditch he had been gone as if he had dropped off the face of the Earth.

'Then I remembered the incident with the four Germans and decided to explore this matter at last. From the residents' registration office I could locate the address of the computer scientist. So I just drove to Munich and visited him. I reminded him of our first meeting many years ago in the shelter on Mount Untersberg and told him what had happened above the old quarry to my daughter, Sabine. Initially the guy did not want to talk; he told me that everything had been just the way it had been printed in that magazine. But I did not settle with that. I told him that I was determined to continue research. He looked at me intently and then told me his story, which sounded a little different from what had been written in the newspapers many years ago:

"That year, August 15 was a foggy and rainy day. It was not suited for a mountain hike. But just this date, August 15, we had scheduled for our tour. For according to the traditions the temporal phenomena did most frequently occur that day. We got up quite early and left the campsite at seven o'clock. About half past seven we arrived at the parking lot named Rositten at the foot of the mountain. Still somewhat tired, we chose the right one of the two steep paths to the top, the Reitsteig, but only for a few hundred metres, then we continued west on an old hunting trail. The weather was, as I said, not very good and it was drizzling slightly. Therefore we decided to look for a shelter from the rain under a rock overhang and had a snack there. When half an hour later we wanted to proceed, we felt suddenly very cold and concluded that a chill wind was dragging through the forest. So at last we decided to go back to the car. When we left the coniferous forest and entered the mixed woodland, we noticed that there were hardly any leaves on the trees and many brown leaves were lying on the ground. Also there were no travellers on the road. Everything felt different from before. Arriving at the parking lot, we saw in horror that our car was not there. Stolen, perhaps? A dreadful fantasy seized us. We set out for about a kilometre on the road towards the city of Salzburg, taking at an intersection a daily newspaper from a booth. Our terror was huge when we saw the date – it read October 21! In addition, it had to be late afternoon, soon it would be dark. Without noticing we must have fallen victim to a massive shift in time.

"If we reported to the police now, we would likely be sent for examination in psychiatry. Ditto if we called our relatives in Munich. After all, we must have been regarded as missing for almost two months. Probably they had been searching for us. Now good advice was dearly needed. Our clothing was more or less proper for summer temperatures but not for damp late autumn. Also we did not have a lot of cash, and there was no point in returning to our camping tent at Berchtesgaden or trying to draw out money with the credit card. So we came up with the idea of travelling to the warmer south the cheapest way – by bus and train. However, at the border with Yugoslavia there would have been our last stop, for Kerstin, one of the two friends of my wife, had left her passport in the car. Therefore we crossed the uncontrolled border from Austria to Yugoslavia on foot across the mountains and went to Greece with a driver who hid Kerstin in his truck behind the load. There we found a ship in Piraeus that for a bit of money and without further formalities would take us to Egypt and through the Canal of Suez into the Red Sea. From there, we could safely call home and pretend to have made a joke. Actually, we had to report from there even then, for by now we had run out of money, and contacting the German Embassy in Alexandria was inevitable."

'Manfred, that was the computer scientist, looked at me thoughtfully and said that in his view it was certainly better if the official story was left as it had been reported in the newspapers, rather than telling the truth about it. He had experienced the temporal phenomenon firsthand and would have warned everyone else, because it occurred without warning and the victim did not even notice it.

'I told him when leaving that I would still try to investigate into the causes of these temporal phenomena. And if I could find out more about them I would tell him.'

Bard was not very much surprised to hear Wolf's stories, it almost seemed as if he had expected something similar and felt encouraged in his previously expressed suspicion against Mount Untersberg. He repeated his view that this was somehow connected to the Black Gem. The phenomenon of the temporal shift was just one of its effects, he said. The Gem might even achieve a lot more if it was used properly and especially stored properly.

He then told about the Black Stone that once the Prophet, Muhammad, had found in the Arabian desert, a meteor fallen out of space that he believed was a tear of Allah. The exact history of the effects of Muhammad's Stone was not recorded anywhere, the only certainty being that the prophet was so much convinced of the Dominion which the Black Stone provided that he installed it in the lower left corner next to the door of the Ka'ba, the greatest sanctuary of the Muslims in Mecca. Only a small piece of the Stone is sticking visibly out of this corner, and it is rimmed with a silver edge. Bard, who himself was Islamic and had already seen the Stone during a pilgrimage that any faithful Muslim is expected to do at least once in his life, said that there really was a kind of powerful Dominion to be felt about it, but he could not say whether it directly emanated from the Stone or from the huge crowd of pilgrims.

It was further said that five hundred years after Mohammed some Crusaders were searching for hidden treasures in the subterranean passageways of the Temple Mount in Jerusalem, and there they found another such black gemstone in a chest that was shod inside with thin foil of gold. These crusaders, who subsequently called themselves the Knights Templar, brought the Gem supposedly to France. According to tradition, they carried it in a chalice, believing this was the appropriate vessel for such an alleged gemstone. Another tradition says that the gold-shod wooden chest simply was too large and striking, and that is why the cup was used. In addition, a chalice was a sacred symbol for the people of that time, in short, a taboo that not anyone might touch just like that. So it was a safe vessel. It might have been that for this reason the Holy Grail was since supposed to be a cup. The fact was, however, that the Order of the Knights Templar from that date on acquired untold wealth and dominion, and only centuries later it was overthrown and destroyed by the Roman Catholic Church.

It was also reported that the Curia in Rome was and is in possession of another Gem. This black stone, now believed to be inside the Vatican, was said to have been taken to Rome by Emperor Augustus shortly after Christ's birth, out of Egypt, to be precise: out of the oasis of Siwa. It had been found there in the empty tomb of Alexander the Great.

'I am an Arab, and I do not find it hard to believe that the Israelites who in the Pharaonic age were living together with the Egyptian people may have taken some of these Gems to Palestine where they might have gotten into the hands of the Zionists later. It is said that the Zionists to this day more or less dominate the financial markets in the world. Who knows, maybe these Gems contribute to the enormous dominion of this Jewish movement.

'In short: Whenever and wherever in the world an extraordinary, massive increase in power, dominion, and money was to be noted, this might sometimes indicate the presence of a Gem. But as I said, this is just a hypothesis.

'There was in ancient Egyptian mythology the ibis-headed god Thoth, the keeper of wisdom and knowledge. The Greeks later called him Hermes Trismegistos, the three-times largest Hermes. According to tradition, from him originates the so-called Tabula Smaragdina, the Emerald Tablet, a very old script describing the proper handling of the Philosopher's Stone. Whether this is a reference to the Black Gems I do not know; but it might sound fitting.'

Bard pointed to a small pendant that Wolf wore at a leather belt around his neck and asked:

'Where did you get this stone? I have been noticing it for quite some time already.'

'This pendant is a gift by an old professor who was participating in excavations near Baghdad. When the Gulf War began, the researchers had to leave head-over-heels and did not even find the time to return to the Archaeological Institute in the capital. Due to sudden fighting they were taken directly from the excavation site to the airport in Baghdad to be flown out as quick as possible. Many more such small items they had in their luggage.'

Wolf took the pendant from the neck, handed it over to Bard and said:

'For many years I have been friends with the professor. He knew that in my spare time I occupy myself with antiquities and antiquity, and so he gave me this Babylonian seal in the shape of a black, pierced hemisphere, featuring on the flat side an engraved, twelve-rayed sun. He thought it was more than 5200 years old and dedicated to the Babylonian goddess, Isais.' Here, Wolf pondered again that the Egyptian Isis might have been connected to this much earlier Isais from Mesopotamia; or that they were perhaps one and the same goddess.

Bard turned the pendant in his hand and said:

'You do attract things, you know. They come to you, just like the desert glass which I have previously given you. As well the tales of the Black Gems I have not told to anyone yet like I did to you. It seems to me that you are the intended recipient of this. Moreover, what ring have you gotten there on your left hand? I saw a reflection on its stone in the firelight, were these twelve rays?'

'Indeed', said Wolf, 'this is a twelve-pointed, black star sapphire of thirteen carats, a gem that I bought a few years ago from a dealer in the mountains of Sri Lanka.'

Wolf slipped the ring from his finger and gave it to Bard. He put on his glasses and re-examined the stone in the firelight very closely.

'The dealer in turn had acquired the sapphire from miners in the jungle. It was ground right there, in the jungle, by hand. He said it was a fairly rare variety of the normally only six-pointed star sapphire. In Salzburg, I asked a jewellery shop to insert the gem into this ring of white gold. I have worn it since quite every day.'

'The twelve-pointed variety of star sapphire is indeed extremely rare. And it seems significant that just you got such a gemstone. It matches perfectly your twelve-rayed pendant from Mesopotamia. As I said: You do attract things.'

Linda then told of the encounter with the blind man at the fortified granary in the oasis of Dhakla, and that this old man had called Wolf a guardian of Osiris' Gems. Pensively, Bard looked at Wolf and said:

'There is something in you that this blind man in the oasis Dhakla as well perceived. I cannot tell you what it is, but I perceive it too.'

'Oh well, now, because you are telling such things', said Wolf, 'I remember that about thirty years ago I saw in the window of a pawnshop a very nice Egyptian bronze figure. I went in and could purchase the statue for little money. Many times it had been offered for auction and never anybody had bid on it, so the price had been set down each time and finally it was cleared for direct sale. I showed this figure later to a museum director who I am friends with, and he was able to confirm that it is a genuine artifact from the 17$^{th}$ or 18$^{th}$ dynasty. This Osiris is now in my glass cabinet and "keeps guard" over my old Egyptian "finds", that is, my little painted and glazed pieces or plates which I have brought home from each voyage.'

Bard grabbed his black beard, looked at Wolf and said:

'I'll tell you now, because it just fits, I think. In Cairo there is an imam, a scholar of our religion, who once told me something very interesting. He spoke of a talking head from the Sahara. This head is made of stone and was found in a mountainous area between present-day Tunisia and Algeria, allegedly. It was a kind of ram's head, so I was told. There, near the mountain oases, there was once located an ancient culture, much older than that of the Pharaohs. And this head would be from the same material as the black Gems of Osiris. The Templars are said to be in the possession of this item, and they kept Baphomet's Head like a sanctuary and worshipped it. Also your Western culture is telling many stories about that?'

Wolf was now curious. 'Where exactly are these mountain oases?' he asked Bard.

'I do not know, but I can tell you the name of the imam who has told me this. He may perhaps provide you more accurate information', said the artist, 'he now lives in Kairouan, which is the fourth holiest centre of our faith, surpassed only by Mecca, Medina and Jerusalem.'

Wolf knew that Kairouan was in central Tunisia, he had passed through it once many years ago during a round-trip.

But even if he should go to Tunisia, how would he find this imam there in the city so easily?

Bard perceived Wolf's glance and anticipated his question:

'Go to the Sidi Oqba Mosque and ask for Sheik Muhammad Abdul Yussef. Every Muslim around knows him.

'And if you ever get there, have a look into the mosque. The imam's prayer stool originates in Mesopotamia, and it has twelve levels, which reminds me of your twelve-rayed solar seal from Baghdad around your neck. The imam by the way is speaking very good English, and he will certainly give you information as far as his power might. You can then take to him my kind regards, for we are good friends and he will assist you in your research.'

Wolf's curiosity was aroused once again, and he wrote down the name of the imam.

'Anyway, you will certainly still have to add some things. You need only show your interest, everything else will fall into place', said Bard. 'I also think that you will in one way or another have to face Osiris and his Gems', he added promisingly. 'And if you should one day discover the secret of the Black Gems, I would ask you to tell me about it.'

By now it was quite late already. Wolf and Linda said goodbye warmly to Bard and his wife and promised to visit them again.

▲▲▲

A gong's sound tore Wolf out of his memories. The sign for buckling the seat belts flashed, and the flight captain announced the imminent landing at Hurghada.

# Chapter XII

▲

## CAIRO, THE PYRAMID OF ABU ROASH

Yes, he would tell Bard if he himself would ever understand the mystery of the black Gems, if there was any mystery at all. Wolf suddenly had to think of another conversation, with an Egyptian in Cairo whom he had met some years ago. Ibrahim had been his name, and he was earning his money as a taxi driver. Actually he had been a mechanical engineer and spent many years in London where he had been working for an oil company. But when he had returned to his family in Cairo he bought a car and became a taxi driver. To continue his job he would have had to work on one of the oil platforms in the Red Sea, hundreds of kilometres from his family, and that was no longer what he desired. Therefore he preferred a modest living in Cairo, after all, he was at home there.

It was already dark, and they joined him sitting in a small café at the Alexandria Road. Ibrahim had taken Linda and Wolf before to an excavation site at the outskirts of Cairo. Wolf knew this place from an earlier visit and had directed Ibrahim unerringly across the gravel roads.

At Abu Roash, about fifteen kilometres north of Giza, there were the remnants of a pyramid situated on a hill. On holidays there was no work at the excavations, as Wolf did know for sure, and so they were able to examine the site thoroughly. They stayed till sunset. Gradually the colour of the sky changed to orange as the sun went slowly down in the distance. Then stunned and motionless they observed the wondrous show. That speed at which the solar disk was dropping down they did not know from home. All of a sudden, from hundreds or maybe thousands of mosques and their minarets in the city of Cairo the calls of muezzins were heard, calling the faithful to prayer. It was a moving scene, sculpted in the last light of the setting sun in the desert.

Within minutes it had turned dark, and the steep path down to the highway they had to drive back rather slowly. And now they were drinking tea with Ibrahim who was smoking a shisha.

Ibrahim was a man of many interests, educated, occupying himself as well with the Pharaonic past of his home. Wolf's enthusiasm for these matters encouraged him to tell some tales, as the conversation turned to Dr. Hamam, an Egyptian state archaeologist. Dr. Hamam had once been an archaeological excavation manager in Cairo. For many years he had performed a secret research under the Great Sphinx and the Pyramid of Khufu. But in Egypt, secrecy is a subject of strange qualities. Very soon plenty of tales had been circulating which posthumously were dismissed as imagination of the simple folk. Ibrahim told them that for example rumour spread about a large chamber, deep below the Sphinx, in which Hamam were said to have had discovered records on the Pyramid of Khufu. Subsequently, he had the small southern shaft in the Queen's chamber examined by a German engineer with a little robot that carried a video camera on-board.

This robot found that at the end of the shaft there was a door. Then at once, Hamam cancelled the project and sent the German engineer home with some pretexts. But at the upper end of the Grand Gallery he ordered a tunnel to be driven through the pyramid blocks, so as to access that door which had been seen on the video images. And during this time the Pyramid of Khufu was simply closed for visitors 'for restoration purposes'.

Around the same time, in a subterranean crypt which extended three levels down below the Temple of Dendera near Luxor, images were discovered which were so controversial that even egyptologists must not know of their existence. In a cloak-and-dagger action these images were chiselled out. Simple workers were applied to the removal of the plates of stone who, it was believed, would not understand anything of what they had seen. One of these workers had been a distant relative of Ibrahim and told him about it. As a result of these reports Ibrahim was convinced that Hamam had found something very important which was not to be reconciled with the teachings of egyptology, however.

At that time, in 1997, the terrible terrorist attack at Hatshepsut's temple near Luxor, killing fifty-seven people, showed to be a splendid opportunity for Hamam. The highest authorities then established a so-called Convoy Police of more than 40 000 members who set up checkpoints all over the country for the protection of tourists and reducing free travel of visitors to a minimum. All tourists, whether by their own car, by bus or by taxi, were now allowed to travel only with these police-escorted convoys and only on defined routes.

'Strangely enough', Ibrahim said, 'only the roads in upper and middle Egypt and in the Eastern Desert are affected by this convoy regulation. Just there where many hidden things are yet suspected to be. But anyone may travel without further notice to the remote oases of the Western Desert which are actually much more dangerous to approach and may bear greater risk for tourists.'

The coals in Ibrahim's shisha were now extinct and it turned very cold. They thanked the taxi driver for his interesting reports and asked him to take them back to the hotel.

# Chapter XIII

▲

## Safaga/Raghab the Fisherman

Gently the engine touched down on the runway in Hurghada. Within a few minutes Linda and Wolf would feel again the dry, warm air of the Egyptian desert. Getting straight out of the European winter cold into such a completely different ambient within a few hours was every time again an impressive matter.

▲▲▲

Wolf thought that he should again visit Raghab, that old fisherman. Raghabs eldest son Ahmed had two weeks before phoned him to tell, half in Arabic, half in English, that his father wanted to show him something in the mountains. For the fisherman knew that Wolf was keen on artifacts from the Pharaonic period.

Years ago he had met Raghab on his first trip to the Eastern Desert. With his daughter Sabine, Wolf had at that time gone by taxi into the mountains. The driver, Osama, a dark-skinned Nubian from somewhere around Aswan who was little familiar with the roads – rather tracks – into these remote areas, was willing to drive the two around there, though he would never comprehend what some tourists might want to find there. But even back then, Wolf had had already certain ideas about the ways of the ancient Egyptians which he was looking for.

Sometimes they had to turn back because suddenly some mountain made onward travel impossible. Then, it was just on Christmas Day, they saw a man walking at a long, straight road with a box on his arms. And Sabine said to Osama:

'Stop there! We will take this man along. There is enough space inside. Who knows how far he still might have to go? There is nowhere any house around here.'

Osama stopped and asked the old man in Arabic to enter the car. In the box he had fish, freshly caught in the sea just a few kilometres distant, which he intended to take home to his village. Yet it took still quite a while until they arrived in the small settlement of Umm Uweitat. There was a simple dwelling in which the fisherman was living. As a token of his gratitude he invited Wolf, Sabine and Osama for tea with him and his family.

Raghab, as the fisherman was named, did not understand any English or German, therefore Osama had to be their interpreter. They were all sitting on a carpet on the earthen floor of the house and drank a glass of mint tea. In the morning Raghab had been fishing in the sea, throwing out his net while standing up to his belly in the water and retrieving it after some time. Until a few hours later he had caught this way nine small fish. That had been a good day for him, and he praised Allah. Now, in winter, it was difficult to catch anything. The fish came during this season rarely close to the shore, but for now, he said, he had caught enough. Wolf and Sabine, though, were embarrassed by the poverty in which Raghab and his family were living and yet professed a serenity of satisfaction.

He wanted to show them something pretty in the vicinity, he told Osama. They got up and took the car into a mountain valley where Osama had never been before. It was no longer possible to conceive of any road there, there were only a few tire tracks visible before them. A barren area this was, yet standing out with a peculiar craggy beauty; mountain peaks rose there all over. After a while Raghab pointed to a narrow, steep valley and said they had to turn this way. Osama stopped the car next to the gravel road, and all four of them went up the rocky path. Before long, they were facing a small wonder of nature.

Out of a gap in the rock there sprang a trickle of water, gathering in a natural pool that had been carved into a slightly washed-out rock. Raghab bent and drank from it to demonstrate that this was pure water.

A strange thing it was to ponder where this water might have come from. The surrounding mountains were not high, and rain fell only once per year, and then only by a few drops, for a few minutes. A real rain, according to Raghab, occurred only every fifteen or twenty years. Then the water would really beat down for hours. Something like this he had seen himself only once in his life. But then, he said, the wadis would turn really dangerous. As a result of years of drought, water did not seep into the ground very quickly, so the mountain valleys would become fatal traps for man and beast. Anyone who was not able to find a safe shelter in time would then be simply swept away by flooding and usually be destroyed in knee-deep, rushing water.

Raghab tried to explain via Osama's interpretation that the water which sprang from the rocks was pressed upwards from the lower lying valley floor. An artesian well this was then, where groundwater got to the surface under pressure. The Bedouins called this well a tear of Allah and considered it a miracle.

# Chapter XIV

▲

## CAIRO/GARC

The director of GARC (the German Archaeological Research Centre in Cairo), Dr. Robert Hüttmann, was just through a conversation with his employee, Clemens Müller.

Müller had for a long time been conducting excavations and research projects in upper Egypt for GARC. Now he was appointed to accompany two groups of archaeologists with four-wheel vehicles from Luxor to the rocky desert between the towns of Safaga and Quseir. According to reports from Bedouins, a shaft or an entrance of a tomb had been discovered in the mountains. Hüttmann gave Müller a few instructions, for it was actually suspected that Said Hamam, the Egyptian state archaeologist, had also sent his men to this area in order to verify the reports of the mountain-folk. Hüttmann wanted his archaeologists to be there first. If there really was something behind this story, it would mean big news.

It was said that people had vanished from the site of the finding. Well, by all likelihood these were as usual some exaggerated tales of the Egyptians. They liked so much to floridly adorn their tales.

Still, there were ancient records concerning the area which these reports of the Bedouins were indicating. After all, some years ago in the halls beneath the Sphinx, and also in that corridor above the Great Gallery in the Pyramid of Khufu that was not known to the public, papyri had been found. They were telling of black gemstones. If these Black Gems of Osiris, as the old records claimed, were really existing, then maybe a unique discovery was waiting for them. And this time, GARC would at last be first to imvestigate the site! Müller and three employees were ordered to take two Land Rovers to the towns of Assyut and Qena and on into the mountain desert, so as to make inquiries at the described location.

That same evening the two vehicles left Cairo.

# Chapter XV
▲

## SHERATON HOTEL, ABU SOMA

When at last all the formalities required for their visa had been accounted for at the airport and after their luggage had been retrieved from the conveyor, Osama the Nubian approached them with a broad smile that his face was displaying from afar already. He was now one of many limousine drivers at the Sheraton Hotel. '*Abu dip*, Wolf, madam, *marhaba in Masr*, welcome to Egypt': Those were dark-skinned Osama's words of greeting. He stowed their suitcases into his car, and they drove the fifty kilometres from the airport to the hotel in the air-conditioned limousine.

Osama told of his two-year stay in the Emirates where he had been working as a taxi driver. His stories made the half-hour trip to the Sheraton Hotel pass by like nothing, and at once they seemed to turn into the avenue of sphinxes that marked the hotel entrance. These twenty sphinxes were copies of those at the Temple of Karnak near Luxor; matter of fact, the entire Sheraton Soma Bay Hotel had been built in the style of a reconstructed Egyptian temple, and it was one of the top names in Egypt. A stylized nine-leafed lotus blossom was its emblem.

When they arrived in the aristocratic, beautiful hotel, Franz the manager most warmly welcomed them. Franz was Austrian like Wolf and Linda, he had international experience as a hotel manager and was running the house in admirable way. He had reserved a suite for them. And

Franz knew that Wolf would again roam the wilderness of the mountains on another expedition this year.

'What will you find this time?' was his very first question.

'Osiris' Gem!' was Wolf's short-cut response, for he really did not know what else to say.

The hotel manager somewhat forced himself to a smile, for of course this reply meant nothing to him. But Wolf had brought a few times some lovely finds: ancient amphorae, to be precise. He was sure that Wolf again had a real goal in mind. Franz might just wait and see: Certainly after their return the two of them would have some exciting stories to tell.

Wolf and Linda went down the wide staircase made of red Aswan granite and entered the restaurant. In front of the entrance there was standing a huge Horus falcon, made of stone and with no less skill than its original in the temple at Edfu.

After a delicious dinner that also included a bottle of Egyptian wine they made a walk around the sophisticated facility. Crystal-clear water trickled over a pyramid of red granite into the well-tempered pool, at the end of which huge sphinxes were lying like watchmen on pedestals of stone. Behind them there was a clean sandy beach with palm trees, and the calm sea reflected the moonlight. This hotel in this wonderfully quite location was really a pearl of a kind. Wolf had spent already many vacations there. For him it was the base-camp for his exploratory trips through the Eastern Desert.

Linda and Wolf drank a cocktail at the bar, listening to the pleasant music. Then they went to rest, for the next day was likely to take quite some time.

In the early morning the car that they had rented in Hurghada was already waiting in front of the hotel. It was a nice middle-class vehicle including air-conditioning. They took no luggage, because it was supposed to be only a one-day trip.

But first, Wolf turned to a petrol station. Egyptian rental cars were always transferred with the tank nearly empty.

# Chapter XVI

▲

## THE PORCH

They continued on the desert road toward Raghab's hut. But first they had to pass through Safaga, one of the few Egyptian towns at the coast of the Red Sea. In the morning there was a market, as always in this small port town. Live goats and chickens, vegetables and fruit, household items, everything was there for sale along the dusty gravel road. Tourists there were virtually none. In one of the tiny shops that lined the road they bought six bottles of drinking water.

Forty minutes later they arrived at the simple dwelling of the old fisherman at the edge of Safaga. Great was the joy of reunion. Wolf and Linda distributed gifts to Raghab's children, and he himself received, as always, a sizeable amount of money that would make his life a little easier for a while. After the usual Arab welcome greetings and good wishes Raghab called his eldest son Ahmed, who spoke a little bit of English, and had him interpret:

'You know, in the mountains, far behind the ruins of the old mining settlement of Umm Uweitat, the state phosphate company has a few weeks ago blasted away some part of a mountain, for they were suspecting further deposits of that mineral sought after. The usual approach to mine construction would have taken them too long, and because far and wide there are no dwellings nearby, a blast was quickly decided for. But then it was found that the yield was not as great as previously thought. Therefore the work was quickly stalled. But on the opposite side of the mountain, the violent trembling of the explosion had provoked a landslide. And this laid bare some ancient porch of stone from the early days of Egypt!'

Linda and Wolf heard of that with interest. And there was even more about it:

'Some Bedouins of that country who are so inquisitive of nature, as you know, tried to enter the passageway behind this porch. Some of them were gone then, it was told.'

He could not tell whether there were genies at work, as the Arabs called the spirits, or whether those people just let their imaginations run wild. Ahmed paused, and then he announced that his father would accompany them to there this very day. It just took them about seventy kilometres driving. By car and without a road in the desert, though, covering this distance would certainly take a few hours.

Wolf was looking forward to that in a rather excited manner, and he paid Raghab thanks in Arabic for the offer. They left with the previously purchased water bottles and three melons which Raghab's wife gave them as provisions.

For the first twenty kilometres they followed the conveniently paved coastal road along the Red Sea; and even beyond the road was still for a while quite comfortable until shortly before reaching the old mining village of Old Umm Uweitat it shrank to a track of gravel. They relied now only on the guidance of Raghab who knew this territory well. Through endless wadis and narrow passages between high rock walls they reached more than two hours later the embankment of the phosphate railway which was not depicted on any map. Raghab pointed at a mountain far to the right ahead. And Wolf steered the car carefully towards it when suddenly they saw a train approaching from the distance.

Wolf stepped the brakes. He took out his binoculars and realised that this was not a standard phosphate freight train. No, this was a diesel locomotive with a single wagon on which there was standing an army jeep.

The train slowed down and halted. Several uniformed men put ramps on the wagon, and the jeep was unloaded. Then it drove down the steep embankment into the wadi and went off, exactly towards that mountain that Raghab had pointed at before.

What was the meaning of this? Was it just coincidence, or were there others already in search of that ancient porch, too? Wolf preferred to stay there, wait and see. After all, tourists were absolutely discouraged from moving off the main roads without authorisation. If they were discovered this could mean significant inconvenience for all of them.

After a while the soldiers and the jeep left sight. Only a quickly dispersing cloud of dust was still visible in the direction that the vehicle had taken.

Wolf took a swig from a bottle. They drove on, following the gravel track. Then Raghab got an idea and pointed to a small valley aside. There was a knoll at the end where they could hide the car comfortably between large rocks. It would be invisible when the soldiers returned.

A short while later they arrived on the knoll at the end of the valley and left their car, climbing across steep slopes of scree. Dark clouds loomed slowly over the mountains, and a strong wind had now arisen. The sand was itching in Wolf's and Linda's eyes. Raghab had his scarf wrapped around his face, and in his blue robe he was now no longer distinguishable from a real member of the Tuareg people. His galabiya, the cape, was flapping in the desert wind, and he appeared like Moses at crossing the Red Sea.

After a brief climb they came to a minor ridge, and from there they could descry the dust plume of the off-road vehicle by which the soldiers had now almost arrived at the backside of the blasted mountain on which the acclaimed porch of stone indeed was plainly visible. The jeep slowed down. Wolf thought he saw through his binoculars a greenish haze on the ground before the ancient entrance. The soldiers drove straight on. And the next moment the vehicle was gone with all its occupants.

Wolf did not trust his eyes any more. He handed the binoculars to Linda, and then also Raghab was able to verify that a track of a vehicle was abruptly ending there, and the soldiers and their jeep were nowhere to be seen. The dark clouds from the west drew nearer across the fissured reddish mountain peaks. And the mingling of light and darkness made seem even more unreal what they had witnessed.

'Do you believe in genies?' Wolf asked Raghab in Arabic.

Raghab nodded and murmured, very confused, some praises of Allah and pleas for their protection. Only two hundred metres still separated them from the porch of stone. They climbed higher up the ridge, and then from afar they saw two more jeeps approaching the porch by the wadi on the other side. The vehicles were still about three kilometres away, and it would seem to take them yet a good while to arrive.

Wolf and Linda wondered if they should get nearer to the porch, even though the soldiers with their jeep had just vanished from there.

However, they were relieved from making a decision. For soon after they heard the thundering noise of rotors. A menacing army helicopter appeared behind the ridge.

Presumably the soldiers in the jeep had been in radio contact with their military base, and when the contact was disrupted by their disappearance, the helicopter had quickly been sent off to their last reported position.

Wolf had the topography of this region well in mind: He knew that the nearest desert airfield of the Egyptian army was at the utmost about fifty kilometres away, as the crow was flying. But this valley was so narrow that it prevented the helicopter from landing just before the porch. Therefore it peeled off with a sharp pitch to the port and descended toward the outer, more level part of the wadi. Slowly, because of the strong wind, the rotorcraft lost altitude about one kilometre off. At last the helicopter touched down in a huge cloud of dust that the increasing wind rapidly dispersed. Some soldiers were seen jumping out.

Now they were at their wit's end. The three of them had to be relieved that their car had not been detected from out of the rotorcraft, but then, the soldiers would get there within the next few minutes. And from the opposite side, the two off-road vehicles as well came closer and closer. The clouds of sand that they stirred up now demonstrated that clearly, even without the aid of binoculars.

Only fifty metres were left for Wolf, Linda and Raghab to the porch of stone. The green haze was hovering before it like a very thin cloud, just a few centimetres above the ground.

Right at that moment, a lightning flashed through the darkened sky, followed by a deafening roar of thunder. An instantaneous downpour set in. Within minutes, water gushed all over the rocks, down, like a rapid torrent into the wadis.

A surprisingly large quantity of water gathered in there. In no time the first flood wave rose one metre high and attained the army helicopter in the wadi. So mighty was the force of that body of water that the rotorcraft, its blades still turning, tilted to the side and tipped over. The three of them could observe how the soldiers in front were washed off their feet by the raging water and swept away. On the other side of the mountain, one of the two approaching Land Rovers was turned over by the assailing flood. Doomsday seemed near: The deluge rose at lightning speed. And the three adventurers had to get to a safe place immediately, lest they might be swept downhills, too. The only recourse was now the old entrance into the mountain. All of a sudden the green mist was gone.

# Chapter XVII

▲

## OSIRIS' GEM

As soon as the rain had started, there was no more trace of the green haze at the ground. As quick as possible the three ran to the porch. Without hesitation they rushed across the threshold. Behind it there was a roughly cut passageway leading about twenty metres slightly down into the mountain. Wolf switched on his small flash-light that he always carried along. As well Linda had taken her lamp from the backpack.

They illuminated the walls, but there was no trace of hieroglyphs, nothing at all. But they did not have to walk far until they got to the end of the passageway. And there they saw, carved into the rock wall, an embossed relief of Osiris, the god of death of the ancient Egyptians. And to the right there was a cartouche engraved, displaying the lion-headed goddess of war, Sekhmet. Linda, whose hand held the flash-light with a minor tremble, was not quite sure whether to marvel or just to fear.

Before the image of Osiris there was a cube of rock, almost a metre high, and on it there was lying a small black gem, shaped like a flattened orange. Wolf was intrigued. A stone of the same kind he had found years ago in the underground chamber at the Pyramid of Khufu!

But he did not have much time to think about it. With the passageway slightly sloping inward, the water that came flowing down from the entrance gathered in the mountain and already began to rise. The cube was halfway drowned in wet mud. Many beetles, insects and remnants of withered plants were washed inside. Wolf thought he had seen even a scorpion.

'We have to get out of here, quick!' Raghab was already running back towards the entrance through the dark, without light, in water that rose up to his knees. Linda was struck by a trace of panic, for if there was anything that she disliked it was such narrow underground passages, and if there was even water flushing into them, well, that was obviously too much for her. The muddy waters which she had previously seen, those that had carried away even the helicopter and the Land Rovers, meant a peril to the lifes of all three of them.

Luckily, the torrents of rainfall that came down from the mountain shot for the most part over the porch like a waterfall. Nevertheless, the level inside rose steadily, albeit slowly. They rushed to follow Raghab who was already waiting out in the open. And yet, as soon as they arrived in the fresh air, sunlight dazzled them which slowly emerged from retreating layers of clouds. As sudden as the storm had come, as sudden it was gone.

'Only once every fifteen or twenty years', Raghab had told them a few years ago at the well, 'it is raining in the desert, and then the wadis turn very dangerous.' Now Wolf and Linda had seen this rare display of natural forces, and, as if by divine grace, it had happened exactly at the proper time. Raghab's galabiya was now in two colours, the upper part being blue while the lower had assumed a dirty brown. But they were relieved to see that no more danger loomed.

Quickly they climbed back up the ridge. The cloudburst, hopefully, had not washed down their car. They were alleviated to find the vehicle a few minutes later standing unharmed behind a rock. Down in the wadi, however, things looked terrible. Everything was covered with mud and debris: there was no sign of the helicopter and the soldiers nor of the two Land Rovers and their crews. All of them had probably been torn away by the force of the water and swept some kilometres downstream.

At once they started the car which ignited without trouble. Raghab tried to tell Wolf that preferably they should return by another way. Certainly, the army would soon be out looking for that helicopter, and then it would be only a matter of time before they were discovered. In addition, they could not possibly drive their limousine on the mud-covered wadi ground.

Getting away from there quickly, that was the top priority. But to where? Because of his good knowledge of the territory, Raghab already had a bright idea in his mind. The course of which the fishermen thought was an ancient caravan trail through the rocky desert which was perhaps suitable for horses or camels, but hardly for cars. Well, they had no other choice.

At walking pace they headed south. But it was already obvious that they would not get before sunset to the major road that connected the Red Sea with the Nile Valley. And they had an even worse problem. It was not water which they would run out of this time, but petrol. There in the mountains, it was of no use trying to calculate the consumption by kilometres driven. Many hours of driving in first gear over sand and stone were the main cause for rapidly emptying the tank. And spare cans they did not have, anyway their use was banned in Egypt.

At dusk, they stopped at an overhanging rock wall. There was no question of going on driving.

Raghab made a fire out of some coarse pieces of timber and root that they had gathered along the road. The two melons which he had brought from home were their dinner. Linda took from her pack a few cereal bars, for this time she did not only carry drinking water. After they had discussed how far they were still away from the road and whether the petrol would last, Wolf and Linda flapped back the car seats and slept inside while Raghab rested at the campfire.

The three of them woke up shivering in the morning. Temperatures in February were near freezing at night; fortunately, the car would soon turn warm again inside when driving.

There was no breakfast that day. Raghab performed his morning prayer, mumbling and turning to Mecca. In the meantime Linda and Wolf examined the Black Gem from the passageway.

It was almost identical to the one that Wolf had found under the Pyramid of Khufu. No one else other than Linda he had ever told about it. That other Gem had not been of any particular importance to him, anyway. Now this one had the size and shape of a flattened orange, it was dark, extremely hard, and heavy. So what was its real significance? Was it tolerable to connect it with the disappearance of the soldiers?

The sun rose higher, and the cold of the night was quickly replaced by scorching heat. How far still was the main road? Two or three hours, maybe more? For more their petrol certainly would not last. And walking over hill and dale in this desert would not get them far, without water. Raghab murmured: '*Inshallah.*'

Wolf tried to drive so that they kept the straightest course South where possible. After two hours they reached a site where Pharaonic hieroglyphs were visible on the cliffs.

'We are on the old Pharaonic road', said Wolf who had been looking for these ways for years, yes. There he had once been. These were the trails that lead since Queen Hatshepsut's time from the Nile across the Way along Wells, through the mountains and to the Red Sea. From there the asphalt road was not much further ahead. And yet, the petrol gauge was already pointing at zero when they finally heard the horn of a lorry.

The last drop of petrol brought them back to the road, and there they waited for any car whose driver they might ask for a little bit of fuel. Several lorries passed, but their diesel was useless. It took quite a while until there came an old pick-up and stopped immediately when Raghab waved at the driver. With a small piece of hose this friendly Arab sucked petrol from his tank, and it was transferred with the help of an empty water bottle. This amount should last for one hundred kilometres till Quseir at the Red Sea. There there were two petrol stations.

Before they got there, however, they had to pass the checkpoint of the Convoy Police. No one could circumvent it. Unfortunately, their journey was not registered and tourists could not simply come out of the desert, especially not with an ordinary passenger car.

'We will see. Somehow that will work out', said Wolf who clearly felt better now with 10 litres of petrol in the tank.

Linda secretly shuddered at the thought of possibly having to spend a night in an Egyptian police station. And of Raghab only a few invocations to Allah were heard.

By late afternoon they arrived at the checkpoint of Quseir. Theirs was the only vehicle there. The police checked the documents and passports. Raghab tried to explain something in Arabic, but the officials did not seem particularly impressed. One police officer who spoke a little bit of English asked Wolf where they were coming from.

'From Luxor', he replied. But this the officer wanted to verify by phone.

Then suddenly another officer stepped out of the small concrete station next to the barrier and approached Wolf. When he saw him, he hugged him and greeted him in Arabic. '*Abu Dip ben Nemsa, Marhaba, issayak, hamdulillah*, welcome again, Mr. Wolf.'

He told that other policeman who had wanted to call the checkpoint Luxor that Wolf was quite sometimes journeying to the hieroglyphic rocks, that he knew him and that everything was alright.

Calling Luxor was not required.

The policemen were evidently not yet informed about the massive rainfall in the mountains and the accident of the soldiers. Mahmud, that was the name of the officer, had Wolf already met several times on his journeys and now insisted to invite the three of them for tea. And finally they parted with as intense hugs and blessings as at their welcoming.

So they could freely pass. In a moment of joy and relief Linda kissed Mahmud goodbye on the cheek, and that left him a little confused, for he could not quite interpret it.

Now the last barrier was passed. Wolf's sarcastic words, 'I told you so: Somehow it always works out', and his violent honks when leaving the checkpoint unintentionally increased his image of an adventurer with Linda, and this made her tender heart once again boil over.

'You and your *somehow it always works out* – no, my dear, lucky we were, incredibly lucky!' And that was all that she got over her lips.

Actually, Wolf had to admit that she was right, but luck was sometimes necessary. Especially as he was of that kind that repeatedly got into such dangerous situations.

Fifteen minutes later they reached the town of Quseir, refilled the car completely, bought at the Promenade a few bananas for their hunger had by now turned to cravings, and they drove without further stay up the coastal road to Safaga. Eighty kilometres were easily covered within one hour. Having the Red Sea to the right and to the left hand the craggy mountain peaks that appeared in the evening sun like pieces of scenery gave this last leg of their journey an almost romantic touch. At nightfall they reached Raghab's modest hut.

They were received with joy. His son said they had all been worried because they had heard of the thunderstorm. Raghab told them in Arabic of the soldiers in the jeep, the Land Rovers and the helicopter. Everyone was listening to him intently. Only Wolf and Linda sad quickly goodbye and drove the last twenty kilometres back to the Sheraton Hotel.

It was already dark when they placed their car at the hotel's parking lot. The vehicle actually did not reveal what hardships it had passed through. But Linda and Wolf did: their clothes clearly showed the traces of the last two days. Being acceptable for high society looked different. Their trousers were dirty from the water and mud in the old passageway, and their shoes were suitable only for being thrown away. Linda was clearly embarrassed having to enter the up-market hotel in such condition. And Franz, the hotel manager, was quite surprised to meet them in the entrance hall like that.

But after having a shower and putting on fresh clothes they went into the restaurant for dinner. Franz sat down with them, curious as to what they had found. Wolf and Linda took turns telling him of the difficult voyage through the gravel and rocky desert, of the torrential rain, the cold night outside, the hieroglyphs and the way back to the checkpoint of Quseir. But the porch and the missing soldiers, the helicopter and the Black Gem they withheld from Franz. After all, this felt too imaginary to be made credible to someone. The Black Gem, though, was neatly wrapped in sheets of toilet paper and lying in the minibar in their suite.

When after dinner they returned to the room and Linda had not yet turned on the light, Wolf noticed that before the minibar fridge a small green puddle had developed.

"This was the Gem! Do not step too close to the fridge, otherwise you will disappear!', Wolf cried in a frantic voice at Linda.

But without listening to him she had stepped already with one foot into the green substance and opened the door of the minibar. 'Too bad for that good absynth.' Linda set down the tipped bottle of green, high-proof liquor upright into the door compartment. 'Next time you put it back to the fridge, screw that bottle properly', she advised Wolf. And he stood quite bewildered, feeling betrayed of another mystery.

The next days were only used to relax in the hotel. Wolf granted to himself a Thai massage while Linda was floating in the well-heated pool like a fish. But to be sure, Wolf went again by car to Raghab and warned him via Ahmed his son that he should better not go telling around everybody about the porch of stone and the disappearance of the soldiers. For who might know what else the Egyptians might come up with if it were known that Wolf and Linda had been the first ones in the passageway and had retrieved the stone from there.

The next day they went home again. The stone being in the luggage and some experience stored in mind, Wolf and Linda rested in the return plane back to Munich.

So what would the Egyptian army do now, with their soldiers and one jeep gone? Would the people in Safaga believe Raghab the fisherman's story if he should ignore the warning and yet tell it around, or would they call him mad? And was the cause for the disappearance of the soldiers really found in the Black Gem? Or maybe rather in the geological conditions of these outstanding rocks and mountains?

What if Bard, the artist from the Farafra Oasis, was right and things really were as he suspected? They might see for that. In Wolf's living room, in that case of glass that kept the other black Gem from the Pyramid of Khufu and the statue of Osiris, in any case never a green haze had shown up, and no one had vanished from there, either, if he thought about it.

Wolf in any case was determined to explore the subject.

Two weeks after their return from Egypt he received an e-mail by Franz, telling of an accident in the mountains. 'How lucky you were that you had not come close to this thunderstorm – I guess you were quite nearby, and probably no one has survived that.' The Egyptian daily newspaper 'Al-Ahram' reported that several soldiers had been vaught by a strong thunderstorm during a maneuver in the mountainous desert, and some of them were still missing. Nothing was said about the search for the porch of stone.

Neither there was anything to be read on the website of Dr. Hamam's Egyptian Antiquities Service. But Wolf had not expected otherwise, anyway.

# Chapter XVIII

▲

## THE VAULT

During the time that followed Wolf scoured the Internet ever again, looking for useful information on the Gems. But what should he really pay attention to? Black stones, time shift, green haze? He was surfing on the Web whenever he found some time to do so, hoping to find anything that might give him a clue.

First, he hit on reports concerning TLotBG, that was: *The Lords of the Black Gem,* and links from there took him further to the legend of Isais. But all of this homed in rather on the southern side of Mount Untersberg at the small pilgrimage church of St. Mary Ettenberg, not on the north-east where many years ago those four Germans had vanished. Continuing research then focused him on the *Ordo Bucintoro* whose last residence had been on the Venetian island of the glassblowers, Murano.

Well, Venice was only a few hours away by car, and Wolf, after all, wanted to get to the bottom of the matter. On a rainy weekend he drove thus with Linda to the City in the Lagoon. They left their car in a parking house and chose a vaporetto, a boat serving as a kind of public bus, that took them through the Canale Grande straight to the small island of Murano, passing gondolas that were rowing tourists through the canals despite the misty, damp weather.

But this very autumn weather gave Venice an appeal that was incomparable to the hustle and bustle of the carnival or the tourist crowds in summer. *La Serenissima* revealed a different, almost mystic beauty. The boat rocked at each pier, and they marvelled at the picturesque view of the narrow canals and the old mansions alongside.

Would this excursion yield more information on the Black Gems? By early afternoon they arrived on Murano. Having grown hungry from the ride, they had a break in a small, elegant restaurant that served Venetian specialities. The accompanying wine was also excellent. The owner, who allegedly knew where to find the villa of the Ordo Bucintoro, described them where to go. And quickly they found the villa indeed. The local landlord was a small old Italian; he only told them that supposedly there was no one any more who could give information on the Ordo Bucintoro: likely he himself could likely not tell much about it or perhaps did not want to.

Wolf had already felt a step closer to the mystery of the Black Gems. Now he was yet somehow disappointed. At least it had been a nice trip, and they still enjoyed the return through the lagoon. But Wolf would go on searching, in the Internet much could be found.

One day he discovered during his web-search a closed forum that held remarkable reports on desert glass and as well on time shifts.

The administrator of this forum, nickname Apollo, got quickly interested in Wolf's reports on Mount Untersberg and what had occurred there. Apollo lived far up in northern Germany and now virtually had an informant on the ground. Several months later, he came with his girlfriend and Gero, a policeman from Berlin, to Berchtesgaden at the foot of Mount Untersberg for continuing his research in the woods, as he had often done. Wolf agreed to meet with them, and Apollo promised to show him an interesting place on the Obersalzberg that Wolf had never even heard of.

They drove up the panoramic road from Berchtesgaden, and after a while Apollo pointed at a diversion to a forest road. There they left the car and went on walking. Half an hour later they came into a very dense, hardly passable young forest. Apollo went ahead and pointed at a spot where from afar nothing extraordinary was visible. Yet when Wolf got closer to him, he could perceive an entrance, leading down below the forest ground. It seemed as if there had once been a stairway, though now they stepped steeply down on mossy, fallen bricks and pieces of the wall.

Ten metres after, the three of them were standing in a vault. Indeed, it was a real, beautiful vaulted ceiling, as otherwise it might be found in sacred buildings only. Steep light wells allowed some brightness from above to enter the dim space, so that they were not standing in total darkness.

Five mighty columns, made of red brick and probably once clad with marble, gave the vault a very queer ambience which Wolf could not interpret.

'Step between those four columns in the centre of that large squat space', Apollo said to Wolf. He went where indicated and halted. The domed ceiling above him seemed to exceed a pressure on his head. Or was this coming from below him? He could not tell. But there was something – and what it was he could not figure out. 'Now step four metres aside', said Apollo.

Wolf did as he was told, and at once the pressure in his head was gone. Gero the policeman told him that he had also felt this every time he had stood between the central columns.

Of course, Wolf had to ask what kind of a building this was and what it had been used for. But neither Apollo nor Gero could answer that.

Wolf was determined to introduce Linda to these ruins. Under any circumstances he would avoid, however, to tell her in advance of the strange space between the columns. For he was curious whether she as well would feel something.

Without further ado, they went one week later again up the mountain and straight on along the blocked forest road to the immediate vicinity of the vault. When Linda then stepped into the centre of said place, inexplicable panic seized her. She felt a pressure in the stomach which rapidly increased.

Immediately she had to back out of this for her so nightmarish subterranean vault. Hours later she still complained about pain in abdomen and chest.

As was Wolf's wont, he was eager to explore this. Equipping himself with Geiger counter, earth-magnetic field meter and various other technical devices, he returned a few weeks later to the subterranean vault, now in the company of Werner, the boyfriend of his younger daughter, Alexandra,. Werner, who was a policeman, had taken strong lights which would provide enough brightness down below to take photographs and video footage.

It was notable that there, in an area of some hundred metres across, the radioactivity background was about twice as high as in the further vicinity. There were, however, no significant magnetic variations.

In the debris inside the vault, which over the decades had piled up on the ground when wall plaster fell down, Wolf found a rusty bracket that might have been used to attach a torch. But nowhere there was a hint for why this vault had been built once.

Meanwhile, Werner explored the ground in the woods around the vault with a mine detector, but that provided no useful result, either. At last he took a small iron rod and simply stuck it like a probe repeatedly in the moss-covered ground, when he suddenly pushed against something hard. He had found this way a concrete slab, about one metre wide, laying underneath the forest floor and leading directly to the vault like an access way. With his little shovel he needed to dig a few centimetres only to lay bare a part of this concrete slab. It was well preserved and extended over several metres in length just below the earth. Was it part of a whole road that had been paved with concrete? None could tell.

There was still a lot left to be explored up there. Wolf chose in the following week a small plane, a four-seat Cessna 172, and flew over the area around the mountain a few times. It was then that he noted a wall on a rocky ridge above the Obersalzberg. It was not far from the Kehlsteinhaus, or, as the Americans called it, the Eagle's Nest. This building, together with an access road in the high alpine terrain, had been built with enormous effort as a birthday gift for Adolf Hitler. Only a few hundred metres behind it, there stretched this strange wall. It had the shape of a giant Y that extended for more than one hundred metres, and it was aligned due East to the degree precise.

Back at home, Wolf examined satellite images to find this wall again, and due to a vague inspiration he drew a line from the base of the Y to the place where the Führer's Berghof had once been. And lo and behold, the line passed exactly to the metre through the vault and on, straight through the pilgrimage church of Saint Mary at the foot of Mount Untersberg.

This could not be by chance any more! The huge ypsilon of stone looked just like a Germanic rune turned east.

This was clearly the signature of Himmler and Hitler!

# Chapter XIX

▲

## THE CRYSTAL OF THE MOON

Again it was the Internet by which Wolf received further evidence for the examination of these structures. A completely unknown person who read Apollo's forum wrote him that allegedly there had been a bee-house on the clearing which at that time had served to camouflage the vault above the ground. The vault itself had been Hitler's secret hiding place for some black stone that had been brought from the desert of Egypt to Germany. But later Hitler was supposed to have removed it into the inside of Mount Untersberg: into that very cave in which also the Black Gem of Hubertus the Knight was lying hidden. The unknown forum visitor also specified how this cave might be found. High up on the mountain the moonshine used to be focused with a mirror and a crystal, and by a light well it was directed down into the vault wherein it was deflected through another light well towards a certain spot at Mount Untersberg. At this spot the entry to the hiding place of the Black Gems was to be found.

The cave into which more than seven hundred years ago as well the crusader had taken his Gem was supposed to be near Saint Mary's Pilgrimage Church at the foot of Mount Untersberg. The crystal on the other hand was allegedly been set on a small platform built on a promontory at Mount Obersalzberg.

The location of this promontory was very well described by the unknown forum guest.

The writer in the web also claimed that Hitler had been so much impressed by Leni Riefenstahl's movie *The Blue Light* that he had ordered to elaborate such a device, so as to mark a spot by moonshine and crystals.

The whole matter sounded a bit quizzy. What had Hitler and Himmler then discovered about the power of the Gem, and above all, why should they hid it then in the cave in the mountain?

However, the crusader was supposed to have placed his Gem in the very same cave. Were there now both stones: the crusader's and the one that Hitler had received?

Wolf, being familiar with the territory, had no trouble locating the spot where the crystal seemed to have been placed. The facility set up then was no longer in existence, of course. He would have to use another powerful source of light. And how should that be achieved, technically spoken?

Wolf had a very powerful portable green laser beamer at home. This little device produced such a strong beam that it could set tissues aflame and make balloons explode. This beamer was ideally suited for his project. It would easily be able to emit a sharply focused ray across a few kilometres distance.

One night, with the aid of Werner, they aimed the laser beam at the southern light well of the vault. A smaller tree stood just in front and was promptly re-cut. Then the laser shone exactly into the centre of Hitler's underground structure and made it glow in an eerie, intense green. Thousands of small condensation droplets on the red brick walls sparkled in the intense laser light and provoked an unreal, fairy-like view. Well, for one night this was enough.

In the following weeks, preparations were made to deflect the laser beam by some mirror or crystal in the vault and aim it thus at Mount Untersberg. This way they hoped to locate the spot where the hidden cave with the Black Gem was supposed to be.

Again, Wolf and Werner drove in a dark night up to Mount Obersalzberg. This time, Linda went with them. Werner was to operate the laser at the mountain top. Wolf, who wore safety glasses, would position the crystal in the vault so that a visible point of light would result at Mount Untersberg. Linda's task was to confirm the impinging of the laser beam with special binoculars and mark the exact spot on a map.

With a small hand-held Wolf gave detailed instructions out of the subterranean space to Werner on the rock plateau above. Wolf had set up a small folding table in the middle between the four massive columns. A tiny neon lamp weakly lit up the interior of the frightening structure. But it gave enough light to make all the preparations. Wolf mounted to the table a large, rock crystal, shaped like a prism, on a rotating base. Then he gave Werner by radio the command to turn on the laser.

When the beam hit the crystal, all the room was flooded with diffuse green light. Despite the safety glasses everything around seemed to Wolf as if it had been enchanted. The entire vault was radiating as if veiled in emerald, and far to the other site of the valley, a distinct dot of light showed up at Mount Untersberg.

Linda marked its position on the map as well as she could. The next day the evaluation was examined. The spot at which the laser beam had impinged Mount Untersberg proved to be insignificant. It was located lay on the bank of a small mountain stream, which was surrounded by bushes. But on closer examination on the ground, a few days later, the three of them discovered the opening of a small cave.

Wolf went up again the next day to the spot by the stream and brought a shovel that helped him to enlarge the opening a bit.

The cave seemed to reach deeper into the mountain than he had anticipated.

Was that really the very cave in which legend assumed the Black Gem from the East to have been hidden by the crusader? And why had Hitler ordered to set up this mark of crystal to accurately show the way to there?

He would come back together with Linda and take there that Gem that they had brought from Egypt together. Would this provoke a temporal phenomenon?

Linda was a bit hesitant. What would happen if they should just disappear and re-emerge a few weeks or months later?

Or were these all the same just fairy tales?

In any case, she accompanied Wolf finally to that place on the mountain, near the stream, and she crawled with him through the opening. Inside, the cave became wider. They could walk upright even after a few metres.

Linda scanned the rock walls with her flash-light. On the ceiling she could clearly see traces of soot from torches. One obvious proof that people had been there, though quite a long time ago. Then suddenly Wolf bent down.

A small metal object on the ground had caught his attention. It was an old Wehrmacht's petrol lighter. He put it in his pocket, and they went on slowly. After fifty metres, the cave grew even wider and issued into a cavern like a hall, indeed it took the form of a temple. No, this was not a natural hollowing, this was clearly man-made, and it had served a ritual purpose without doubt. Symmetrically arranged torch-holders on the walls and finely carved stone plinths gave this room an ambience of sacredness.

In the middle there was a block of stone. And on it, as if offered upon an altar, there were two black, orbed, flattened Gems.

They lay side by side. These Gems looked the same as the one which Wolf and Linda had brought from Egypt. So then the story of the Knight Templar who had hidden the first Gem was true? And as well the rumour spread by the unknown visitor to the internet forum who had indirectly hinted at the way to the cave? But then the second stone was certainly that one which Hitler had ordered to be taken from Egypt. But why would the Führer deposit the Gem in this cave if he ascribed so much Dominion to it? What was again the mystery behind that?

Whatever, now the third Gem should also find its rest beside the others. Wolf arranged the stones in the shape of an equilateral triangle. They touched each others now no more but he left spaces of about thirty centimetres between them. An eerie feeling yet assailed them both as soon as their stone was set down with the other two: Would weeks have passed outside till they had left the cave and returned to the woods?

Nothing like that happened. When they got out, everything looked as usual. Wolf's car was still standing at the forest road where he had left it. So there was no time lag!

As they drove back on the small mountain road, they passed St. Mary's Pilgrimage Church, and there they had to pause and wait a little to allow for a procession. A small statue of Mary was carried by a priest, followed by a trail of believers. For a moment it seemed to Wolf as if Maria looked at him directly while smiling. Was she Isais of the legend, the Mesopotamian goddess by whose orders the first Black Gem had been brought to Mount Untersberg?

He quickly dismissed that. It was probably the hardships of the past few days that played such tricks to his mind.

But Linda had a similar feeling with regard to the statue. 'By accident', Wolf insisted, and they drove home.

There he pulled the old lighter from his pocket.

The object had to be more than seventy years old. At the bottom the Reich's Eagle carrying the swastika in its claws was imprinted.

Of radical changes Bard had spoken, the Egyptian artist from the oasis of Farafra, when several of these stones would be combined. So where were these changes now?

# Chapter XX

▲

## THE ENTRANCE

Wolf continued to search the internet more intensively during the following months, without finding any new evidence.

But then one day there was a fierce storm, a storm of giant magnitude. Large parts of the forest on Mount Untersberg broke, and fallen trees had to be removed. Thus new forest roads were cut up to the mountain. It was a chance to get more easy to previously inaccessible sites, Wolf thought.

Once again he sat in the little Cessna and flew a few laps of different altitude around the legendary mountain.

He had to obtain the approval of the tower at Salzburg Airport, for much of Mount Untersberg was within the area controlled by the airport. During his flight he only had to respect some helicopters which on the northern side of the mountain were employed to remove wood. The forest roads, just cut into the mountain, shone in bright red of marble. Guiding the aircraft control with one hand and keeping his camera in the right hand he relentlessly clicked the shutter. About two hundred pictures he shot on this flight within one hour.

He quickly found on these photos a new access that might comfortably take him near those places where he suspected the temporal phenomena to occur. Another glance on the satellite maps in the Internet: He was hardly surprised to find that this small area lay as well in the extension of Hitler's 'Y-line'. With regard to this, he no longer believed in accidents, anyway.

Wolf decided to reinvestigate the area in which his daughter had once been gone for two minutes of his time. More than fifteen years later and with more sophisticated technology this was probably much easier to be accomplished than back then when they only had their watches as a tool.

Werner's office provided all the useful information on the terrain up there at the mountain. The equipment was extended by electronic stop watches, VHF radios, GPS and a magnetic field meter. A few times they went up the paths to the mountain, crossed the ravine on the old suspended tracks and came to the abandoned quarry. From the first time on some spots revealed a deviation in the GPS by several hundred metres. The stop watches and other measuring instruments, though, did not yet indicate anything. It was noteworthy that the variations got stronger or weaker at certain times.

Wolf entered the measurements meticulously into the maps and so established a detailed record of the minuscule temporal lags detected. Slowly but surely, an accurate map was growing that narrowed down the region which was affected by temporal phenomena.

It took a few months, then it was time. The details given by the man from Munich and the various reports of the police and mountain rescuers, as well as their own test results, centred on a relatively small area at some rather inaccessible part of Mount Untersberg. Wolf wanted to conduct a first exploration alone, because if he should really disappear for a while, then at least it would be only him. Linda after all was a teacher, and her absence from school was not so easily to be explained.

Now finding the exact place should not be so difficult any longer. A small radio receiver tuned to the strongest local stations was sufficient. If due to any temporal anomaly the channel was no longer audible or would suddenly sound like a chipmunk on helium, then he was on the right track.

Wolf slowly climbed up the old way. He came to the ravine with the tracks, passed through the old quarry and went even higher into the rough terrain until he came to a large rock face. He did not notice that he now no longer heard the radio station. The steep rise demanded his full attention. The door in the rock face he did not see before he was standing half a metre in front of it.

Ordinary metal door, stonewalled into a crevice – Wolf tried to open it, and he succeeded without much trouble. Inside was a lighted corridor, laid with simple tiles. On the wall hung a kind of coat rack on which some clothes were hanging, looking like dark robes of monks.

Rapidly he shut the iron door and intended to withdraw. When leaving he looked one more time after him, and he saw no more door. Carefully, he went back at the wall. At the last moment the door popped out of nowhere into the rock face again. As if it was from a science-fiction motion picture, Wolf thought somewhat confused. Once again he stepped back, the door vanished. Closer again, and there it reappeared with a slight flicker.

Surely no one would believe that, thought Wolf and began the descent. He had set out for the mountain at about twelve o'clock, spending maybe forty minutes away, but now dusk had already set in.

So several hours seemed to have passed since he had shortly opened the door up at the rock face. In fact, the clock in his car at the forest road now showed eight o'clock in the evening.

How long would he stay away for good if he attempted to enter the hallway that led into the mountain? With these thoughts he went home. At least he now knew where the site was. As a precaution, he had with his camera made some photos of the location around the door so that he could any time rediscover the site of the entrance.

Linda could hardly believe it when Wolf told her the next day of his discovery. She was not sure if he did not just allow himself some joking. Wolf's story sounded too incredible.

Now it took a further few weeks until Wolf recovered the guts to pass the hidden entrance that might potentially lead into a different time. Again there was good weather when he went across the ravine and through the old quarry back to the spot at the rock face. This time he succeeded in very quickly finding the place again. At a distance of about half a metre, the metal door re-appeared, and Wolf went inside.

Light from the incandescent lamps on the walls illuminated the hallway sufficiently. Wolf saw that at the coat rack on the right side there were still hanging those dark brown monks' robes which he had seen during his first examination already. He halted to inspect the robes more profoundly. And suddenly he was startled by a voice.

'Where are you from, Sir?' A man of about forty years asked him that in good German.

The stranger was standing right behind Wolf. He was dressed a bit old-fashioned but neatly. Judging by his accent he was probably not from this area, but from Northern Germany.

'I am from Salzburg', Wolf replied, staggered.

The next question of the fellow was: 'What is the date today?'

Wolf told the other that it was the 27th of August.

'What year?' another question rang.

'2007.'

The man looked pensively. 'You need to get out of here quickly. You will be searched for, Sir, for you have already been in here for many hours."

'But I would like to ask you some questions …'

'Not here! Not now! Come along fast', the stranger replied and hurried before Wolf back through the hallway and to the front door. He grabbed Wolf's arm and shove him out the door into the open.

In the meantime, out at the edge of the forest dusk had already broken. The stranger had as well left with Wolf. After a few steps, the door was not visible any more. Wolf was just waiting that the fellow from the hallway would disappear as well. But it did not happen. The guy looked at Wolf piercingly.

'What are you looking for up here on the mountain at all? How did you find this door?'

It seemed to Wolf that this man posed no immediate threat for him. He told about his long search for the temporal phenomena, steeped in legend, and then asked the other who he really was and where he came from.

'I am a guardsman', replied the man from the mountain, 'my appointment is, among other things, to make sure that this entrance shall remain undetected. Only very few men have found the door within the last seventy years, and then only by pure chance, as you did now. A lot of them did not return home. We could not afford to be discovered. But now something has occurred that we were always afraid might happen: The temporal flow inside the mountain, or at least in our base, apparently will soon adapt to that of the outside world. Recently there is something going on that we cannot explain. You need not fear us, Sir. But perhaps you may assist us.'

Wolf did not understand a word of what the guardsman said. Was his opposite in fact from another time?

'As a token of our good will and that we really have need of you, take this, Sir' and he handed Wolf two gold coins, 'these are certainly of some worth in your time as well, and if you really decide to help us, we will be able to make you a rich man. There is very much of this in our base. Come back, and we will inform you what to do for us.' He turned silently and walked towards the rock face. Wolf stood transfixed, gazing after the fellow and having to witness how just before the face he immediately disappeared.

Meanwhile, it began to grow dark in the mountain wood and Wolf had to rush to get without peril back across the ravine on the tracks at the rock wall. After half an hour he reached his car, and only then he realised what he had just seen and heard.

When he arrived at home and examined the pieces of gold with his instruments he found the authenticity of the 24-carat gold coins confirmed.

Should he now tell Linda what had happened? Would she believe him or secretly doubting his mind?

On the one hand, she had already witnessed some things that would be hard to explain to any outsiders. Yet his encounter with the Guardsman was somewhat swashbuckling. He might show her the coins, but what would they prove? Coins could be bought, even gold coins. No, in order to demonstrate her he had to take her there, to the door in the rock face. Linda, however, was absolutely not free from giddiness. And in order to get her up to the old quarry they had to cross the ravine on the track and the slippery planks lying on it. Linda would never dare to go that way.

For the time being, Wolf told nothing to anyone.

In the following weeks he obtained from the municipal office of the small village at the foot of Mount Untersberg some old documents that were kept in the archive: maps that would show the location of the quarries, roads and old tracks.

Two lesser paths were marked, leading through a ditch to a developed well that was centuries old, and from there straight to the quarry, not far from the spot where Wolf had discovered the entrance in the rock face. This way Linda would certainly accompany him.

The way was probably longer and steeper, but not as dangerous as the walk on the tracks above the ravine.

In any case Wolf wanted to wait for a weekend when Linda would not have to teach in school the day after. For, since they would have to cross the threshold into the mountain, they would suffer an inevitable time lag. And Wolf had understood that this might mean even some days. It was the only way, though, to re-establish contact with the guardsman.

In fact, the following Saturday the weather was good enough to follow the old, steep path to the quarry without difficulty. It was pretty overgrown and there was no doubt that hardly anyone was using it now.

After half an hour they got to the old surge chamber. A muffled noise arose from the depths of the ancient building, and from its lower end water shot out like a torrent.

'Another twenty minutes, I guess, then we will be up at the rock face', Wolf said to Linda, and after a short rest they further followed the now increasingly steeper mule track. The old quarry was a novelty for Linda, seeing it for the first time. Wolf went on with her along the tracks, and the she was able to gaze from the other side into the ravine and on the suspension bridge over which she would not go. It was a marvellous sight, but also a bit scary. Deep down she could hear the rush of the mountain stream. They went back again, and a few hundred metres further Wolf pointed at the large rock face: 'Over there is the entrance.'

It took fifteen minutes through the steep forest, then they stood before the rock. 'Where is here supposed to be an entry?' Linda asked in surprise.

'You'll see.' Wolf stepped in front of the spot where the door should be, and Linda watched in horror as he disappeared from sight.

After about two minutes he suddenly returned. 'I have only made one step forward and immediately back', he told Linda who could not help but stare in amazement.

'But you were gone for minutes!' she replied.

'Well, that's the time lag', he tried to calm her down. 'I was not even behind the door yet. But come on, step here, and together we will make a step forward.' He took her by the hand and they approached the rock face. The next moment, Linda saw as well the metal door showing up out of nowhere. This time, Wolf opened it, and they could both see the lighted hallway. To the right there was the coat rack with the dark monk robes, and a uniform jacket was now hanging on the wall, too.

On Wolf's loud 'Hello!' the guardsman came from a rear door on the left, at the back end of the hallway. Wolf wanted to greet him and introduce Linda when the man, just like the first time, urged them for a rapid leave from the base.

'Get out, quickly! Into the meadows! Otherwise too much time will pass for you.'

They had barely spent a minute in the mountain. Yet outside dusk was again setting in already. And when Linda became aware of that, she realised that indeed a time lag had smacked them.

The guardsman was still with them, and with a laugh he said to Wolf: 'You were very quick to pay us another visit, Sir! After all, you have been here just two hours ago.'

Wolf shuddered when he heard these words. For him, it was three weeks ago that he had first opened the door. Also, Linda was a little upset, but she quickly composed herself again; and after introducing herself she asked the fellow where he came from.

'In Dortmund I was born. Then I spent a long time in the factory, Zement, in Ebensee, I do not know whether it is familiar to you. It was there that the long-range missiles were built by us. Either the Russians or the Americans will have taken them, I suppose. By the way, I am

Obersturmbannführer Weber – Joachim Weber, to be precise. I would have been glad to introduce you to the General. But currently he is asleep, for it is the middle of the night, and today I am on duty. Return in six hours from now, then he will be up and ready to talk.'

'What General?' Wolf asked in surprise.

'General Kammler', was the curt reply of the guardsman.

Linda was now totally confused. Before noon they had arrived on the mountain and at the rock face, now it was late afternoon and already growing dark. How could they return in six hours, at night, in the dark? Wolf calculated in his head and then told her that the Obersturmbannführer had suggested to return in two or three months.

'This we will do, see you soon', Wolf said and wanted to say goodbye with a handshake, as Weber suddenly pistoned a salute, lifting his right hand, and murmured rapidly: 'Heil Hitler!'

'This one has deceased a long time ago', was Linda's reply.

'Years of habit', the Obersturmbannführer said, and now he extended his hand to a farewell shake. 'I am aware that I will have to re-adjust myself. Be seeing you!' And after a few steps, he was disappeared before the rock face.

Linda and Wolf had to hurry down. It was better to get to their car down at the village before the gathering darkness overtook them. In the night, the mountain and its crevices were absolutely the most dangerous.

# Chapter XXI

### THE GENERAL

Weeks passed again. Werner, the police officer, had meanwhile gathered some accident reports on people who had been found dead on the mountain.

Strangely enough, in some cases the time of death, as determined by the medical examiner, had laid only a few hours before the time of finding the corpses. Said people, though, had mostly gone amiss several days before already.

It seemed therefore as if the victims first had vanished for some days and then lost their lives after re-emerging.

Maybe they entered a temporal shift for a few minutes without noticing, and then they randomly returned to standard time in the dead of night. The panic which must have struck these unprepared people was hard to imagine.

So in complete darkness and difficult terrain they tried to climb down. And fell to death on the steep faces of Mount Untersberg.

Late autumn arrived fast. Before the first snow would come Wolf and Linda had to return to the entrance, for much later doing so would not be possible any longer. In slippery grass and on icy roads the mountain was too perilous. So at last, time had come: At one of the very last beautiful weekends in October they went back, up to the rock face. This time they chose a different, slightly shorter path that took them through another quarry. They crossed a ditch on the ground of which a mountain stream was passing, and then came on the other side to the old surge chamber.

'I'm curious about the General', Wolf said to Linda, as they ascended the trail through steep mountain forest.

'For my turn, I have never spoken with a real General before, in particular not with one who was more than a hundred years old', Linda laughed.

When they arrived at the entrance, they opened the door and found the guardsman waiting for them in the hallway.

'Gentlepersons, you should prefer to wait outside while I will call the General. You will have more time to converse thus.'

Wolf and Linda retreated a few steps, and the metal door in front of them disappeared, as expected, with a light flicker. They waited some time before the rock face, then there was another flicker, and a middle-aged man with a striking face was standing before them. Immediately after, Obersturmbannführer Weber appeared behind him.

Wolf prepared to introduce himself and Linda, but the General interrupted: 'I know who you are, mister. Weber has already informed me. Call me Obergruppenführer Kammler, General of the *Waffen-SS*. How did you find a way to here?'

Wolf began to tell of the underground vault in Obersalzberg, of the legend of Isais and the Black Gem in Mount Untersberg, of the talks with Bard the artist about the White Desert. And of the four Germans who vanished on the mountain, and of his own experience with his daughter Sabine.

'Indeed I do remember that much, mister! About two weeks ago one of our guardsmen informed me that there had been one man, about forty years old, with a young girl, over there on the old slag heap of the quarry. Both of you had looked straight at the hooded man. It was pure coincidence that he was out just then. We have had several such encounters of our guardsmen with outside folk already. But that never posed a threat to us. For who would believe them, even if they claimed to have seen a man with a hood, a monk or a giant dwarf at Mount Untersberg?'

'Why in fact did he wear robe and hood?', Linda asked in-between.

'This tale is a long one, therefore I will cut it short', the General began, 'when in April 1945 we returned with our Train from Bohemia, saving the research documents, we made a detour to Garmisch-Partenkirchen first. Our destination was at the southern edge of the town, the Upper Bavarian Research Centre, code name: Cerrusit. This was one of the very latest underground factories that I had set up on behalf of our Führer. Down below, those modern jet-fighter aircraft were built, the Messerschmitt ME 262. Our Train carried everything required. The vehicles were loaded with rice, with flour, coffee, spirits and cigarettes, in short: with everything you need to live. We declared the baggage "strategic research material", so as to avoid displeasure by the Wehrmacht and the populace. Our plan had to be kept secret, absolutely.

'Within the next few days I gave order to retrieve something else important from the nearby town of Mittenwald. In the local Alpine Troops' school, a few tin boxes were now stored that a few days before had been brought there from Bohemia on my command. The *Oberst,* the colonel of the garrison, had meant too well and hidden the boxes in the wood already. Fast they had to be dug up again, because time was running short. The American forces had already advanced to within less than fifty kilometres from Garmisch-Partenkirchen.

We made another short detour to the nearby Benedictine monastery of Ettal. There, in the monastery, a big military hospital was housed from which we acquired medical supply for our Base here in Mount Untersberg. Some boxes of monastery liqueur, too. For safety, we then took a few robes of the monks with us. They rendered us good service later, as you have seen yourself, mister.'

He turned to Linda: 'I will hope that this shall answer your question about the monks' habits, lady.'

General Kammler went on to tell:

'In the morning of the 29th of April we arrived with our vehicles close to Salzburg, here below the mountain, where our men from Ebensee were already waiting for us. The report on the bombing of the Obersalzberg mountain a few days before, and the extensive destruction of almost all the buildings up there, concerned us very much, though we all already knew what was lying ahead of us. The last thing that I heard on short-wave radio was the Führer's Death Report, at the next day. For that reason, I then chose the abandoned, bombed Mount Obersalzberg as a hiding place for the second 'flight capital deposit', since I assumed no one left up there.

'Well, as I remember now, I still have a good draft in the station for you, my good people: there is some monastery liqueur from the Benedictines left. We took quite a couple of boxes from the local winery. You should taste it once, for it is really excellent. At your next visit you will get a bottle of it.

'And if you prefer, you may take a seat over there on that tree trunk, at the edge of the wood; I think this conversation will take longer yet', Kammler said, pointing to a tree that had been overturned by the wind and lying there for many years already, as it seemed. The bark had fallen off, and the smooth trunk provided a reasonably comfortable, dry place to sit on.

'Concerning those four Germans and the matter of your daughter, it ought to be said that there are many places on the mountain, and especially here, near the entrance to the Base, where such temporal phenomena sometimes do occur sporadically. For uninitiated hikers this is fatal. Perhaps they may find themselves suddenly in darkest night and then suffer some accident when attempting to descend in darkness. That way probably those tales and legends about the mountain developed. Years ago we have through many attempts created a map as well, which is quite accurately depicting where extreme slowdown of the temporal flow may occur. But because these fields are not always permanent and may fluctuate, we are always carrying a flash-light with us when outside the Base. For if one of us should unexpectedly hit on such a zone of temporal distortion, he should yet find back to here even in the dark. In the interest of your own safety I recommend you strongly to take my advise, gentlepersons!'

With a smile Linda pulled a little flash-light out of her backpack. 'I always carry one along with me', she told the bewildered General who at once examined the small LED more closely. 'Lady, will you share some of these lamps with us next time? We will pay well for them!' the General exclaimed.

'No problem', replied Wolf, who had several such items at home.

He returned to the issue of the mysterious Black Gems from the Egyptian desert, speaking of the stone under the pyramid, the Ka'aba in Mecca and the Gem of the Knights Templar, for if General Kammler could tell something about them it would certainly be interesting.

The General was obviously surprised to hear Wolf's information of the Gems. 'I deem that by chance, we may have found in you the right man to assist us, perhaps, mister! You seem to have thoroughly dealt with this somewhat extraordinary subject. Well, I consider it appropriate to tell you a little more then.' He sat down on a rock opposite the two of them and started again, telling:

'Last year we still did not know what was causing the temporal anomaly. Well, there was one theory among us, linking to the affinity of Black Matter to the Black Gems. This so-called Black Matter, or Dark Matter as it was first named, should really only exist in outer space, so it was thought. Until our experiments convinced us of the opposite. And the Black Gems are no meteorites, not at all, mister, they are rather claimed to be made of chert, that is, flint. Apparently it was liquefied by the heat of a meteorite impact when hurled into the air high, then again assuming an orbed shape by the atmospheric friction while dropping back to the ground.

'Intense gravitational forces that arose during the impact of this particular meteorite suggest that some Black Matter was accumulated there and attached itself to the extremely heavy Black Gems. Density and abrasiveness of flint are after all quite significant.

'We also have investigated into the obscure stories by Hitler and Himmler, ascribing "supernatural effects" to the Black Gems. But their suspicions were based on nothing but old tales and not on scientifically researched facts.

'Our experiments in Thuringia in the Final Years, applying an apparatus that we called Die Glocke or The Bell, revealed no more than that Black Matter really is. Because it shows up in low quantities only, it may influence gravity but very little. The flow of time, however, is affected like that of water in a sluice. In a region that is interspersed with Black Matter, time is much slowed down. So in a way the legends are right if they are going to promise eternal life to the owner of such a precious (some have called it the Philosopher's Stone as well). Even that you can make gold with its aid does not seem altogether far-fetched. A sufficient concentration of Black Matter, acting on a heavy metal over some period of time, might possibly change its atomic structure so that transmutation will occur, that is, a "transformation", into an even heavier metal, such as gold.

'At that time, 1943, two years ago, the Americans probably heard through the grapevine some details of our experiments with Die Glocke. But obviously they were not even aware what they were touching at. I suppose they wanted to develop some method of altering the magnetic field of their ships, so as to confuse the magnetic detonators of our new torpedoes. For our detonators were making use of the magnetic field that warps around any metal object on the earth. In case of a ship, the field is strongest below the keel. Once a torpedo shall explode there, it means the demise of the whole ship. And our torpedoes had a very high rate of success.'

Wolf interrupted the General, 'General, you're not talking now of the Philadelphia Experiment, are you? At that time in August 1943, the Americans were going to make a destroyer invisible ...'

'Yes, mister, that was indeed in the port of Philadelphia. The ship's name was *Eldridge*. Yet they did not only install a powerful magnetic field but also provoked this temporal effect that we were referring to as *Chronos - Chronos* and *Lantern Bearer*, those were our code words, because of the blue and green light phenomena inside the electric field during the experiments. To make it briefly, the destroyer simply disappeared in time. You are observing a small-scale version of the same phenomenon here, at the door in the rock face, as you both have witnessed, gentlepersons.'

Wolf was amazed that this wondrous tale should be resolved in such a simple way. He had already read books about this experiment and seen motion pictures.

'Did not the Americans try to achieve 'invisibility from enemy radar', was not this the aim of the experiments with the *Eldridge*?' he asked the General.

'Man, our radar was never a real threat to the Allied seacraft! No one could seriously have been afraid of that. No, their whole concern was, as I said, protection from the magnetic torpedoes!' The General breathed deeply and said:

'But we had developed weapons in 1944 already, far more effective ones, with which conventional technology in general was no longer to be compared. Both of you will probably be hardly able to imagine any such devices. Unfortunately, till the end of the War, none of them advanced to production stage. Maybe I will be able once to allow you a glimpse into the latest technology of our day. You will be amazed, that I can ascertain you.'

It sounded almost like a promise. But what could Kammler reasonably have in mind? The development of technology within the last seventy years had far surpassed his research without doubt. Or maybe it didn't?

He appeared very trim, smart. Was he really that very General Kammler who had been responsible for the underground buildings and the high-tech weapons of the Third Reich, more than seventy years ago? Wolf, who in recent weeks had extensively researched on Kammler in the Internet, asked him directly now whether he actually was the very same person. On this Kammler returned to the Base, after a while he came out again and handed to Wolf a small bag. In it there were, wrapped in cellophane, the golden cord of a general's sabre and just new, golden epaulettes of a general's uniform.

'That was part of my baggage', the General said, 'it is alright if you keep this, mister, now I will not need it any more for certain. I have never used these things anyway, as you may tell from the bag.' In fact, on the transparent, no longer used packaging there was printed the reichsadler with the swastika.

'Perhaps you may also deliver us a few items, that is, magazines and books. In the past we have sporadically consumed newspapers from the village downhill, anxious to be up to date. Moreover, you might be willing to exchange some of our money, for with our gold coins we will hardly be able to pay in any shop.'

'I will do that: stuff for reading, and a few of these LED lamps I will bring you next time as well', Wolf said and stowed the items of the General in his little backpack.

'Now our main concern is this, that since a few days ago, the flow of time has changed dramatically. We can measure this by leaving a watch out here and very briefly return behind the entrance in the rock – in the same way that you and your daughter detected the temporal distortion by way of your wristwatches. Typically, the ratio of the time delay in the core area of the Base is about 1:300. But now apparently our time inside the mountain will soon flow with the same speed as it does out here. It may not take much longer and the entrance might become visible for everyone.'

'Well, what if you just signed up with our authorities and would tell as much as that? You could get a new passport and ...'

Kammler interrupted Wolf:

'Man, as soon as we did that we were all handed over to psychiatry! If I submit my passport and they should read my day of birth to be the 26$^{th}$ of August in the year 1901, it would turn out that I was actually 106 years old. What do you think would happen then, mister? I do not think that you will handle such matters much differently from how we did in the Greater German Reich. And if your authorities really became convinced that the temporal anomaly was real, and after they had seized our gold reserves, we would find ourselves in front of a tribunal, like all the other commanders of the Reich did at the end of the War. Yes, we do have received some time ago information on the convictions of former SS-men who were eighty years old! Neither would we be spared from that, even though you do not execute the death penalty any more in Europe. But we would of course be charged with war crimes, if only the development and construction of the V-2 rockets.'

Wolf could hardly believe what the General was saying. After all, even during the Nuremberg trials Kammler's name had been briefly mentioned but once. To say nothing of an indictment or even a conviction *in absentia*. In his opinion, the General would not have to face any harm, but this did not deter Kammler's belief.

At any rate, they did not have to fear Kammler now, as it seemed, because if he had been determined to protect the Base from being discovered by eliminating Wolf and Linda, that would have been an easy task for the SS-men.

*Two Hikers Missing on Mount Untersberg, Fallen into Ravine, Recovered Dead, Foul Play Ruled Out,* such the newspapers would read.

But in a way the General was perhaps indeed in need of outside assistance. Just for that reason, they were now in no danger from him. Wolf, however, wanted at all circumstances to discover the origin of the temporal phenomenon, even if Kammler's absolutely unemotional way of thinking made him appear rather suspicious. But there was no way of avoiding him.

Wolf offered to the General to take him and Obersturmbannführer Weber on a day-trip to Mount Obersalzberg. Perhaps Wolf and Linda could thus obtain some useful information from them. They agreed on an appointment a few days later.

# Chapter XXII
▲

## Mount Obersalzberg

Back at home, Linda fetched an old copy of the 'Tabula Smaragdina' from the shelf. The Tabula Smaragdina, the Emerald Tablet, was an ancient text translated from the Arabic; alchemists of the Middle Ages had used it as their basis for acquiring the Philosopher's Stone. An old sketch that accompanied it showed the following words, inscribed in a ring:

VISITA INTERIORA TERRAE RECTIFICANDO
INVENIES OCCULTUM LAPIDEM

Which in modern language read: *Visit the interior of the earth; in rectifying discover the hidden stone.*

She placed the book in front of Wolf on the table and said: 'If you take these lines just literally, and if Herr Kammler is right about that meteorite theory, then what's written here might actually be a sort of code for using the Gems.'

'In other words, you think I've got a Philosopher's Stone in my glass cabinet?' Wolf said, laughing. 'Then go ahead making gold, you are allowed to take the Gem from the cabinet for that. I for my part would consider it more reasonable if we asked the General for a gold bar as a present.'

Linda pouted a little, she merely wanted Wolf to read the Tabula Smaragdina once more and more attentively. Anyway they consisted only of a few lines below the magnificent drawing from the Middle Ages.

Wolf began after all to read the ancient text of the Tabula Smaragdina:

1) *Tis true without lying, certain & most true.*
2) *That wch is below is like that wch is above & that wch is above is like yt wch is below to do ye miracles of one only thing.*
3) *And as all things have been & arose from one by ye mediation of one: so all things have their birth from this one thing by adaptation.*
4) *The Sun is its father, the moon its mother,*
5) *the wind hath carried it in its belly, the earth its nourse.*
6) *The father of all perfection in ye whole world is here.*
7) *Its force or power is entire if it be converted into earth.*
7a) *Seperate thou ye earth from ye fire, ye subtile from the gross sweetly wth great indoustry.*
8) *It ascends from ye earth to ye heaven & again it desends to ye earth and receives ye force of things superior & inferior.*
9) *By this means you shall have ye glory of ye whole world & thereby all obscurity shall fly from you.*
10) *Its force is above all force. ffor it vanquishes every subtile thing & penetrates every solid thing.* [1]

And if he interpreted that literally, it could mean this:

The one thing, or rather the Black Gems, were cast by a meteorite impact from the womb of the earth high up into the atmosphere. Their appearance, their shape, they received from the friction of the air, molding the hot liquid substance into the form of a flattened orb. Then not only was there released extreme heat, but on that unique occasion also enormous gravitational forc-

---

1 Translation by Sir Isaac Newton, c. 1680 [Translator's Note]

es, which caused an attraction, or accumulation, of the so-called Black Matter to the heavy Black Gems.

A Black Gem, however, might only truly unfold its Dominion if it went back into the 'earth'. That might mean it would really begin to act in power only inside a cave or a pyramid, where it was surrounded by huge masses of substance.

'Maybe we can use it to do something', Wolf said meaningful and looked at Linda thoughtfully.

Suddenly he had an idea. When he together with Linda had been months before in that small cave on the other side of Mount Untersberg, adding the third Black Gem to the other two, what had then actually happened, exactly? Wolf remembered how he had set the Gems apart and rearranged them with the third one into a triangle. Could this have somehow caused the alteration to the speed of time which the General had spoken of?

When they had been in the White Desert two years ago, in the Oasis of Farafra, hadn't Bard the artist mentioned some ancient Bedouin traditions according to which the Dominion of the Black Gems was mightiest when several of them were brought close together? And the Gems now were no longer close together.

'What if we took back that Gem that we brought uphill, and rearranged the other two again the way we found them? This might set back the temporal delay factor down in the Base of the SS men.'

'It might be worth a try', Linda admitted, 'let us go again tomorrow already, the weather is said to be fair, anyway.'

The next day, early in the morning, they made their way to the town of Ettenberg, got the stream up to the small cave and entered for the third time the old temple-like space inside the mountain. Linda removed the Gem which they had placed there on the rock months ago, and set up the two others again, touching each other, as they had been before.

Wolf took back his Gem from Egypt. Then they went out of the cave and through the woods back down to the road. Morning was still cold, and Wolf turned on the heating in the car as they drove to the other side of the mountain. At the lower quarry, they left their vehicle and went in the morning dew of the mountain forest up to the rock face. Kammler and Weber were already waiting outside on the steep slope. They were now dressed like two tourists. Following Linda and Wolf to the car, the two men were amazed when they perceived the interiors. Those many modern instruments, such as air conditioning, navigation system and built-in car phone, the radio which was integrated in the dashboard screen, all this distracted the two visitors from the past.

For their first time they were taking place in such a modern vehicle that was offering every comfort to them. Wolf explained the functions of each device, causing doubtful glances by the SS-men. The following drive was very quiet, as the two of them still tried to digest everything seen. At last Wolf said:

'Is it possible that the time delay factor in your Base is now back to its normal value?'

Kammler and Weber looked at each other questioningly, this statement from Wolf they could not handle.

'What do you have in mind, mister?' the General asked.

'Just tell me if it should turn out to be.' Wolf left it at that. He travelled with them halfway around the mountain and straight up on the Obersalzberg, to Hitler's former Berghof, or rather to what was left of it. They got out of the car and followed the short walk to the ruins of Hitler's previous retreat. Kammler was deeply impressed by the changes that this region had suffered within the last seventy years. Only remnants of the Berghof's retaining walls were still to be seen in the forest. And when they received their tickets to the bunker tour at the hotel *Zum Türken*, once having been the seat of the Reichssicherheitsdienst, the Reich's Security Service, and passed through the turnstile at the entrance, the lady at the cash told them:

'Be careful when going down, it is very steep there.'

Smartly, skilfully *zackig* as had been the standard of his age, issuing a loud and sonorous '*Jawohl!*', Weber marched past her.

The woman looked puzzled for the Obersturmbannführer whose stalwart pace and almost military response made quite an impression on her. Like that she might have imagined an SS member – not guessing how right she was, evidently.

The four visitors stepped down over steep stairs, past machine-gun stands, deep into the bunker system. The guests from the Third Reich marvelled, silenced, at the subterranean passages and rooms. They had been advised to speak as little as possible, for their somewhat outdated military jargon might have attracted unnecessary attention. And in no way they must raise an outstretched right arm for the Nazi salute! That could mean fierce trouble for all of them. When after half an hour they came up to light again, Weber and Kammler looked outright unsettled. No guards, everything accessible – such a thing had after all been almost unthinkable for them.

Then they drove further up the Obersalzberg. And where the barracks of the SS and their garage hall had been, Kammler looked, startled, just at a vast, empty space. On the hill where Reichsfeldmarschall Göring had had his country house, the two SS-men could now enjoy the magnificent construction of the Interconti Hotel.

Wolf wanted to introduce them to the interior of the building, too, and so they left the car in the parking lot outside the hotel. Kammler and Weber were visibly surprised about its modern architecture. They went to the bar and sat down at a table. Wolf ordered four glasses of whiskey on the rocks while the General propped his arms on the table, resting his head on his hands as if he did no longer comprehend anything. At the next table sat two well-dressed fellows, and they interrupted their conversation as they noticed General Kammler's helpless attitude.

'May I help you, are you not feeling well?' one of them asked. 'I'm a doctor, do you have any trouble?'

'Thank you, mister, but I am recovering', Kammler refused, 'it is just a headache.'

'Then swallow this', the fellow at the other table said, 'and you will feel better.' He handed Kammler an aspirin and asked the waiter to bring a glass of water for the General. 'Are you from northern Germany? I am asking that because of your pronunciation. Is the air at this height causing you problems, maybe?'

'Yes, it does – actually it does not, but be that as it may, I am already feeling better – I am Herr Kammler, thank you very much, mister', the General introduced himself.

'Pleased to meet you. My name is Ariel Eichenblau, from northern Germany; my grandfather, Arthur Eichenblau, once had a house here on Mount Obersalzberg, a bit further down, right adjacent to Hitler's Berghof. He was the inventor of aspirin, by the way, which I've just given you, and he has survived the concentration camp in which this sinister SS folk had locked him up.'

At which the General's intestines seemed to reach boiling temperature. So a Jew was sitting right at the other table, and he had just swallowed a Jewish tablet of aspirin! His world was trembling along the seams.

Linda and Wolf silently exchanged a meaningful look. Then Wolf said, afraid the situation might get out of hand, 'We should leave now, for we still have big plans for today', He motioned to the waiter that he wanted to pay now.

'Outrageous! Jews! In our Führer's Restricted Area!' Kammler was still beside himself with rage as he was re-entering Wolf's car at the parking lot. From his perspective, this encounter was absolutely blasphemous.

Next it was scheduled to introduce the guests from the past to the Documentation Centre of Mount Obersalzberg. Kammler and Weber shuddered as they entered this newly constructed building. Too much they recognised from the many photographs and documents. The General had to pull himself together clearly not to loudly scold about this version of the events in the Third Reich that according to him was absolutely wrong.

'It is not my purpose to deny that there had been these death-camps in the Reich. Of course there were! Few have known about them. But we were not the only ones to have these camps; the enemy, too, eliminated entities that were deemed useless. Nothing is said here of the hundreds of thousands of Poles whom Stalin purged during the cleansing of 1940!

'Men of the Waffen-SS were present when two years ago – of course I mean in 1943 – our Wehrmacht found mass graves in Katyn Forest and opened them. There were a total of more than fifteen thousand people, all killed by the Russians and hastily buried there. This was in Poland, too, as well as Auschwitz, Treblinka and Sobibor.

'Out there at the entrance it says Documentation Centre. But this is rather a trial centre. Why is no such thing documented here?'

'Perhaps because these victims were Polish people, and because it was not the Germans who had been responsible but the Soviets', Wolf said.

'Are there again many of those Jews in the Reich today?'

Linda said, noticing that Kammler again turned red from anger, 'There's no Reich left, Herr General, and you won't hear much from the Jews, either. We're now confronting others: the radical Islamists who have already nestled in large numbers in Europe. These guys account for terrorist attacks that caused the deaths of many',

The General took a hard breath and replied, 'I have always been a great admirer of Prince Eugene and of Lord Skanderbeg of Albania. These two men have saved us from the Islamists centuries ago already. How, for heaven's sake, is it that today, as you say, such people are numerous on the territory of the Reich?'

'As I said just before, there's no Reich any more, there's now a united Europe, the European Union, and in the various member states there are very liberal immigration laws prevailing. We must hope that we won't witness how such radical elements will imperil our occidental civilization. The destruction of the World Trade Center towers in New York, with thousands of victims, is on the account of the radical Islamists. And in Europe as well, in Madrid, a few years ago almost two hundred people were killed in a terrible terrorist attack. Individual governments are trying to prevent such attacks through targeted surveillance, but no one may feel safe any longer.'

'lady, the more I am listening to you the more I must assume that of the German order and discipline there is not much left!'

'Well, we just have exchanged either against a liberty that in your time was not available for everyone. People today are readily used to it and cannot think of things being different any more. But probably we even have too much of liberty, and that may not turn out too good in the long run', Wolf said.

Meanwhile, they had arrived at the toll station of the panoramic road, and Wolf saw in the rear mirror that in the face of the closed barrier their two guests got nervous. In their memory, a bar was likely always staffed with a guard, checking thoroughly anyone who wanted to pass. And certainly here, in the Führer's Restricted Area.

Wolf tried to keep them calm when he noticed that Weber's hand was already touching a pistol gun hidden under his jacket. He stopped the car at the toll booth. Linda passed a Euro bill through the window, and the woman at the cash returned a receipt and a brochure of the road. The bar lifted. They drove on. Visibly relieved, the General asked where their road would take them.

'We'll visit now Hitler's secret underground vault of which I've already told you at the rock face', Wolf said, and he turned right into the woods and onto the closed forest road. After a few hundred metres they reached a small wooden hut, and there they left the car. First they walked down Hitler's old, unpaved road, before they turned into the young wood. Soon they were already standing before the ruined entrance to the underground structure.

'Here was once a beautiful meadow', Kammler said', and a large beehive, I remember it well.'

'Shall we go down into the vault, Herr General?' Wolf asked. 'We have enough light for everyone, and also it is not completely dark down there, because of the half overgrown light wells.'

'No way, mister', said the General, 'by command of the Führer, any of his secret buildings, if they were not destroyed, had to be equipped with vials of yperite. Do you know anything about yperite gas? It is one of the worst inventions of the War. This weapon penetrates through clothing and causes extensive burns of the lower skin, which in most cases leads to agonizing death.'

'But that was over seventy years ago. If such a weapon really had been hidden there, it would long ago have become ineffective', Wolf said.

'Save that 'if', man! Soldiers of the Waffen-SS always accomplished everything most thoroughly. And as I said already, this was an order by the Führer and must be executed under any circumstances, including throwing one's own life into the bin. Therefore you can assume with certainty that before the end of the War, some warfare agent was placed into this vault. So if I was in your place, I was less damn sure that the yperite really has become ineffective after seventy years. The poisoned bunkers of the First World War cost the lives of many of my men, because they also believed then that the agent had gone after so many years.'

As it became obvious that the SS-men would not set their feet into the underground structure, Wolf had no other choice but to return for the car.

'I've to tell you something concerning the yperite', Wolf turned to the General. 'About four months ago, when we were for the third time in Hitler's subterranean vault, for more than an hour I carried out measurements of various kind. And when I went down on the crumbling stairs I scratched my right foot, near the ankle, at a branch that was lying there on the ground; it was only a slightly bleeding scratch, nothing worse than that. But sometime after I had touched various things down there with my fingers, I ran a hand over the small wound on my foot and wiped off the blood that had already dried. In the evening at home, the right leg felt very warm; and then I got a sudden high fever – more than 41 degrees. My heart rate increased within an hour to one hundred and eighty, while the blood pressure dropped to an incredibly low level. At first I thought it was a sunstroke, as that day we had also been strolling around on some sunny slopes of the Obersalzberg, and I had been wearing no head covering. The foot began to turn red at the same time, and only now I thought again of that scratch. The small wound was now caked. Maybe an infection, erysipelas? But there was absolutely no pain, and in case of erysipelas the affected spot is said to hurt like hell. I had no idea what that could be. Then late night I took an antibiotic, for safety, as I always have some available on my desert trips in Egypt. Next morning the fever was still the same, and the lower leg was full of blisters that were filled with a yellowish liquid. A few hours later they had almost reached up to the knee. The country doctor, a friend of mine whom I consulted at once, then diagnosed an atypical erysipelas. He gave me very strong antibiotics and told me to go to the hospital, which I refused. After four days the fever suddenly fell to 38 degrees and stayed eight days on that level, then normalised to body temperature again. The blisters also began to slowly regress, however, the foot remained bright red. After two weeks I consulted a skin clinic. The chief medic also diagnosed a recessing erysipelas and gave me antibiotics again, of which I had to that date already taken one hundred and fifty, of 1000 milligrams each. The redness, though, persisted. After another month, I again consulted the chief medic of this skin clinic, and he wondered that the leg was still reddened, but he prescribed merely a skin-care cream.'

At saying that, Wolf pulled up the right leg of his trousers a bit and showed the General his foot. 'Almost exactly four months ago that happened to me, and the redness is still there.'

'That just looks like a healing burn from a warfare agent, mister', Kammler opined. 'You were probably very lucky, for that might have caused your demise. Yperite, or, in other terms, LOST, evaporates with time in the air, but in a cool environment, as it is here on the top of the mountain and even more so in the subterranean vaults, it may happen that a part of it will crystallise.

'With your hands you probably have transferred residues of such a crystalline warfare agent into the open wound. At the Base I will give you a book later where this is exactly described, and as well you may read what you can do now. But I presume that in six months the reddening will be gone, too. You have really been lucky, mister, the shock alone might have killed you. So you see: I had not been not wrong when warning you against yperite at the vault!' They sat down again in Wolf's car.

'Now I will show you something else if you drive a little further along this road, into the wood!'

So they drove along the same road until they arrived at a passing place. Once, the General said, from there they had had a very nice view over the valley and the town of Berchtesgaden below. Now, however, there were trees everywhere and almost nothing could be seen of the landscape behind. Into this thicket the General wanted to lead them, however. They left the car, and he pointed to a path on which after a while they reached a small pond in the middle of the wood.

'This overgrown path that we just tread has once been easy to manage by heavy vehicles, weighing ten tons. As I told you at the mountain, there was a contingency plan in case that for some reason we might no longer be able to enter the Base. For this we needed flight capital, or, more precisely, *gold*.

'On the day of our arrival in Salzburg, when no one had been left in command on Mount Obersalzberg, I gave order that several boxes of gold bars from the Reichsbank should be brought up here in haste, and a safe hiding place be found for them. In the woods on the Obersalzberg there was still an American Navy radio squad around, sending some reports overseas. These radio men briefly saw our vans passing by, two half-tracks of the SS-division Hohenstaufen. But the day before, surprisingly, snow had fallen, and so there was no question any longer of digging in the tin boxes. Their sites would have remained visible for days. I decided then to let the gold drown in water.

'This had the additional benefit of avoiding to produce a complicated treasure map that only would have challenged confidentiality. A pond there was, and this was the only one up here.

'The boxes were opened right on the vehicles, beside the pond, and the bars simply thrown into the water. The bottom of the pool was already very muddy then, and the heavy bars sank in immediately. No one could later read from the tracks that the cars had stopped here. After a long drive through the woods, the soldiers spent the night in Bormann's alpine hut, having in mind to descend with the half-tracks across the so-called Eckersattel pass into an opposite valley next morning and so continue to Austria. If someone would have followed their tracks, he could not possibly have said whether anywhere on the long road anything had been deposited. – Alas, the six members suffered an accident on the narrow icy mountain trail, fell down with their cars, and all of them were killed.

'So, no one but me and the two of you now know of this hiding place, mister. You can take the gold, I think all in all approximately 1,200 kilograms, or about one hundred bars. On return to our Base I will give you one such gold bar, so that you will know what to look for.'

Kammler was leaning his chin on his hand. He looked at Wolf and then said: 'In return I expect from you to do us a favour, mister. What that will mean to you I shall tell later.'

'Very well, if it is within my power', Wolf said, though he had to swallow quite a lot. More than one thousand kilograms of gold, of which no one knew anything – that surpassed his imagination by far. When driving down into the valley he wondered what Kammler was up to when speaking of 'do us a favour'.

They took the two SS-officers for dinner in a big restaurant that was right at the foot of Mount Untersberg. Significantly, under the gable of the building there was a wall painting which was displaying the so-called Wine Waggoner of Mount Untersberg. For a legend was told how a long time ago some wine waggoner had been asked by dwarfs at the foot of Mount Untersberg to unload his freight at their dwelling inside the mountain. They would reward him lavishly for that. The waggoner agreed, and they led him to an entrance into the mountain where they unloaded the wine, and then they gave the man a large amount of gold. But when he returned to the daylight, many years had passed. Kammler and Weber were visibly amused when Wolf took them in front of the inn and detailed to them the meaning of the picture. Back in the lounge, the General sat down at the table and suggested:

'That sounds almost the way it really is inside our Base. You would not suffer anything else than this waggoner! If you spent even one day with us inside the mountain, more than a year would have passed here, outside', the General said, 'and, besides, there is enough gold in the Base, too.'

In Linda's eyes flashed again a dollar sign as soon as she heard the word *gold* from the General. 'Couldn't you use your gold bars to take care yourself of everything you need? Such a bar of twelve kilograms will after all be worth over two hundred thousand euros, and you have so very many of them.'

'At a first glance, that would seem plausible, lady. But you cannot sell such a lot of gold, whether in Austria or in Germany, just like that. You would be questioned about its origin, and taking it outside of Europe is a pretty hard thing to do, either. Even if chopped in pieces, any metal detector would indicate those gold bars at the airports. And to carry such amounts in the luggage is as well quite impossible.'

After a short interruption Kammler went on, 'But if you could retrieve something from Spain for us, mister, it would be of great help. That is what I wanted to tell you up at the mountain top before.'

'What do you mean, Herr General? Why from Spain? And what shall we bring you?' Wolf asked.

The General nodded. 'I see that I have to explain to you first.

'In recent years, we installed an underground research facility, a kind of laboratory, on the Spanish island of Fuerteventura. I cannot now specify to you what was behind this, mister. But there were most important projects conducted by us. The last radio message from Fuerteventura informed me of the first successful test run. The key element to it were crystals that we should as well have required for our experiments with Die Glocke in Germany. But at that time it was no longer possible to launch a retrieval. Allied forces were already all over. The technicians in Fuerteventura encased those parts that we need in soldered cylinders of lead and deposited them in a kind of safe, to be retrieved at a later date. No one might have guessed that it would take so long, though. Now the items that we want you two to retrieve for us are these two small cylinders of lead. They are about 25 centimetres long and 5 centimetres wide. I am not in the position to specify to you what exactly is their content, but under no circumstances you must open the cylinders, read that! I will deal out to you a precise map of where and how you may find the containers. In no case will you release any information about us or the investigation into the cylinders to third parties. We rely entirely on you, mister.'

The SS-men thought the food at the inn very tasty, after having eaten nothing but canned food and durables for months. Linda took from her little backpack a fifty-piece pack of pens and some LED flash-lights which she previously had acquired for Kammler, and she handed them to Weber. The Obersturmbannführer investigated these novelties – for him – with interest into things he had not yet seen.

After the meal, they returned with Wolf and Linda back to the old quarry and appointed another meeting when the map with the hiding place of the lead cylinders should be handed over. In the end Weber was ordered by Kammler to retrieve the book on warfare agents from the Base. After some time he came out again and put it into Wolf's hand:

'Herein you may read what these warfare agents are able to and what more you can do personally to achieve more rapid healing of your injury, mister.' But Weber had brought another thing, for the right side of his jacket was hanging down low from some weight. He took a gold bar from the inside pocket, and Wolf could tell from his movements what weight this rather small piece of gold seemed to have.

'I promised you that previously, mister; these are 12.5 kg of fine gold from the Reich. I hope you shall turn it into money quickly, so that you will have covered the expenses of an air-travel', Kammler said.

And to Linda, Weber gave a small box, looking like it was new, filled with ten pencils, and a flash-light. Both were marked with the reichsadler and swastika and with the stamp of the Waffen-SS. Kammler said: 'This you will take in exchange for your lamps and pens, lady, as souvenirs from us.'

Wolf, however, just stared at the gold bar in his hands and could not yet fully comprehend what he had received. The value of this bar actually had to be about two hundred thousand euros.

On the way home, Linda asked Wolf quite incredulously, 'So is that for real, we've really been on the road with the General, Kammler, and this Obersturmbannführer Weber? And they pushed a bar of gold into your hand? And before that, they've taken us to a place where allegedly a hundred of such bars are lying?'

Wolf replied tersely: 'It's the same thing as with the dwarfs of Mount Untersberg. They also wear a hood, and the dwarfs from the fairy-tales have always had a lot of gold, too. The SS folk are just a little taller and smarter, but otherwise it's quite the same old story. Anyway, in a few hundred years, everything that we have just witnessed will be yet another decent legend, no doubt. – And so we're now under command by General

Kammler to retrieve two lead cylinders from the Canary Islands?' Wolf looked inquiringly at Linda.

'Consider that these people are unpredictable. Their mode of thought is completely different from ours. Do you really want to do such guys a favour? God knows what they're really up to! The way I perceive Herr Kammler, he has told us even less than half the story. As soon as they got what they wanted, they will no longer need us, and then ...'

Wolf interrupted Linda: 'You're quite right, but then, they could do well without us, as indeed they have during the last sixty-two years. While we can't do anything at all about it. Or do you want to go to the police and tell them that since the end of the War there is a General of the SS dwelling in the mountain on a hoard of gold? I can well imagine what would happen then, and you know it as well, I guess. See you in the padded room then, but I will bring you a cake, of course.'

'Well, I think there must be a way to gain distance from these fellows – a temporal one. Now look! If you take this Black Gem that you found in that chamber under the Great Pyramid and add it to the other three in the cave, I mean, all four of them tight together, then, if Bard was right, the Dominion would much increase. This might mean that the time distortion inside the Base will be enormous. This way, we could remove General Kammler and his fellows into a very distant future!'

'It sounds possible, but before I want to understand what's behind this temporal phenomenon at any rate. And now let's see that we start looking for the bars in the pond', Wolf interfered, 'once at last we should think of ourselves. At the very next opportunity we'll be up in the woods again and try to fetch a bar of gold from the pond.'

'One bar? I'd take more than that', Linda said.

'Do you have any idea how much one item of that is weighing? More than twelve kilograms again. And two of them make already for twenty-five kilograms. Try to carry that downhill to the car.'

'Well, leave it at one then', Linda, delicately shaped, sheepishly returned.

'I will tomorrow cut a few finger-thick slices of that first bar and melt them into a lump with the welding torch. Then the reichsadler will be gone, and if anyone should ask questions, I will have melted some old family jewels, coins, and remains of dental gold. Next week I will try to sell two slices in the gold refining establishment.'

In the evening, Wolf looked into Kammler's book on warfare agents, and he was amazed and appalled at the same time about what was there to be read on the agent mustard, or yperite, as Kammler called it. This book, dated 1941, as well contained pictures, even coloured ones, and they showed exactly those same blisters on injured body parts that Wolf had had on his leg. The typical fever curve was just the same as his. Probably he had not even needed antibiotics. Reassuringly, however, he found that the symptoms should in his case disappear within a year.

The cutting of the golden bar next day was easier than he thought. With a normal hacksaw it took less than five minutes, and soon a beautiful plate of gold was lying in front of him. Even the melting in a tin can took just minutes of applying the welding torch. Cutting the can off the re-solidified gold was then a bit more tedious, but no big problem for him, either.

Even the sale of gold in the refining establishment went smoothly. There were 2,354 grams of gold with a purity of 99.87 percent, and after showing his passport and stating his personal data, Wolf received the convenient sum of 38,560 € cash.

First of all he was going to a buy an off-road vehicle. This would allow them to access the mountain pond much closer, and transporting the gold bars would be easier with such a vehicle as well. But it had to be a used one. Otherwise, people would wonder where Wolf might suddenly have so much money from to buy an actually useless, new, expensive off-road car.

# Chapter XXIII
▲

## In the Lion's Den

A few days later, Wolf received an email from Franz, the hotel manager. The text read: 'Hi, Wolf, I got some interesting news for you. If you can spare some time, come along to Egypt, I will introduce you to some people who are probably quite interesting. Take a rental car again. A nice suite I have already kept free for you. Greetings, Franz.'

Wolf had no idea why the hotel manager might have sent him that. What news did Franz want to tell him, and who did he want to introduce Wolf to? Was that supposed to be a surprise?

Well, why shouldn't he fly to the land of the Nile now, in October, where at this time there were bearable temperatures?

But it seemed he was expected alone, without Linda. That would indeed be less entertaining, but for the sake of curiosity that already had Wolf firmly in Dominion he would come. A flight was quickly reserved, and Wolf gave Franz the arrival time by phone.

'However, you can only three nights stay in here in the hotel with us, then you will have to continue to Quseir, there I have reserved a room for you in the Mövenpick Hotel, where you'll spend the remaining four days', Franz told him on the phone. This made Wolf completely confused. Why could Franz, now in October, provide a room for three days only? What game was being played there? Was Franz also involved in the subject of the stone from the old passageway?

The arrival at the airport in Hurghada was the same as ever. Wolf expected Aladin to take him the rental car straight to the airport. Instead, though, in the arrivals hall he was already approached by an Egyptian who held a large sheet of paper in hands, reading in English: 'Mr. Wolf'. The odd thing was that this fellow was walking directly toward Wolf as if he knew him, and the sign with the name he straight held out at him. Wolf nodded, and wordlessly the Egyptian handed him a little sheet with a phone number. Quickly, he disappeared in the crowd of tourists without having said a word.

Incredulous, Wolf looked at the piece of paper. It read out an Egyptian mobile phone number, and nothing else.

After he had taken his luggage from the conveyor, passed customs and went outside, he could already see Aladdin from the rental, who immediately welcomed him warmly. But Aladdin had brought him a different car. Wolf had wanted an automatic sedan, but this time he received a vehicle that was only in a limited way suitable for off-road driving. And the tank was full, which absolutely was not common. Neither did Aladdin request a security deposit as would otherwise have been required. Which was meaning that the drive to the hotel could begin at once. It was already dark when Wolf sat down behind the wheel. When he briefly turned on the interior light, he saw a note lying on the front passenger seat, and there was written the very same phone number which he had received from the Egyptian in the airport building. Should he call this number? Wolf drove the car through the checkpoint of the airport and was already on the pretty highway, when suddenly his phone rang.

'Mr. Wolf', a voice called in proper English from the device','stay a short while before the large police checkpoint at the end of the town of Hurghada, and wait a little there', and then the caller hung up.

What was that supposed to be again? Well, wait and see. Shortly before reaching the checkpoint, he remained on the roadside and had waited barely a minute when a dark, heavy sedan stopped next to him. The door opened, a well-dressed Arab got out and came to Wolf's car. He opened the passenger door, entered the car and pulled a piece of paper from his jacket. This he shove into Wolf's hand and said in good English: 'If you show this letter, you can pass everywhere. Keep it well. You will be have need for it.'

Without a word, the stranger got out again, and the sedan quickly drove off with the man at a fast pace.

The document was written in Arabic and wore an official-looking stamp that also contained only Arabic characters.

Wolf started his own car and drove as usual, without being controlled, through the checkpoint. He did now no longer worry about the events and reached just after fifty minutes the noble Sheraton hotel at Soma Bay.

Unhindered, he passed the inspection for the hotel entrance. He simply showed the smart card serving as a room key which Franz the manager had given him years ago as a souvenir.

Once in the hotel, the welcome was warm as ever, and Franz received again a nice piece of smoked bacon, for which he was happy every time because pork was simply not available in Egypt. Franz sat down with Wolf at the table and told him of a certain Professor Coock from the University of Liverpool. This scientist was currently directing the excavations at the nearby town of Quseir. The professor had dwelt in Franz' hotel until the day before yesterday, because as well here, in the mountains of Safaga, some ancient sites had been visited. Franz had casually told him about Wolf's exploratory trips through the mountain desert. This aroused the interest of the English, and so Franz suggested to him to arrange for an acquaintance with Wolf. Now, however, the professor had already left for Quseir, and therefore Wolf should follow him to the the hotel Mövenpick.

After dinner, Wolf went to bed, he was tired. Still, he could not sleep at once for he was too much concerned about this peculiar trip, which had begun very different from usual. The next day he planned to meet Raghab the fisherman, in any case. But things turned out different.

At breakfast on the terrace, where Wolf was sitting a table of its own, he got, seemingly casually, into conversation with an Egyptian.

The man turned the issue discreetly but firmly to the Pharaonic Port of Myos Hormos near Quseir, about ninety kilometres off. There were currently excavations going on, he said. Under the guidance of a professor from the University of Liverpool there were some remains of the old buildings getting exposed. Wolf had often in recent years looked around in this ruined town; he knew exactly what the stranger was talking about. He let the Arab in the dark, though, thanked for the information and told him that he would during the next week anyway be in this area and might have a look at the excavations.

After a long bath in the beautiful hotel pool Wolf strolled all alone for the first time through the sprawling facility, when he met Gamil.

Gamil was a technician, responsible for the pool, and he warmly welcomed Wolf. They had known each other for many years already. And when they were talking, Wolf learned from him that Said Hamam, the Egyptian State Archaeologist, had dwelt in the hotel until the day before. So what was this about again? Another coincidence?

When in the early afternoon Wolf was sitting at the pool bar, there was suddenly that Egyptian again whom he had met at breakfast.

'I heard you were here in February, and then you and your companion drove up into the mountains?'

'We did; but you know that tourists like us are only allowed to travel on certain routes here in Egypt, allegedly because of the danger of terrorism. For this reason, we drove only a small distance on an old road to a mining village', said Wolf.

'You had been that February in Luxor, too?' Now the whole thing seemed to assume the character of an interrogation already. What did the stranger want of him, and what did he know? Wolf tried to keep in check his thoughts, probably the Egyptians had learned some things from Franz and was just as curious as all the Arabs.

'There had been last February a terrible thunderstorm in the mountains. At least seven people were killed. All of them were drowned in rushing water of a wadi. Did you hear that time of the storm in the mountains, too?'

'Indeed', Wolf lied complacently, 'we heard of that, but thanks be to Allah, we were far enough away from it. At the coast we even saw the water from the wadis gush into the sea.'

'You were then registered at the Quseir checkpoint, but you did not come from Luxor, as you had indicated at that time.'

With this statement, the stranger had now revealed that he did know almost everything and therefore had to belong to some state organisation. But which one?

Wolf reacted quickly. 'We did come from Luxor, but in Luxor we chose the bridge across the Nile to the west bank and continued at the Nile along the small road to Qena. We wanted to visit a Coptic monastery and then the Temple of Hathor Temple at Dendera.'

'Then you would have taken the Convoy Road directly to Safaga, yet in Quseir you came out of the mountain desert. I don't quite figure that out?'

The man was obviously very intelligent and his reasoning was perfectly logical. But even here, Wolf could once again quickly pit himself against the other. 'You're right, it would certainly have been the shorter way. But my had planned to show my companion the rock inscriptions and drawings in the valley of Bir Umm Fawakhir. For that, we drove thirty kilometres back from Qena, to the town of Qift, and from there straight into the hieroglyphics valley. In this way, we did not pass any police control until we finally got to the checkpoint behind Quseir. On this route we did not have to pass the Luxor checkpoint and could therefore not be registered there.'

The Egyptian seemed to boil with rage inside. Wolf's data were irrefutable, although he was clearly convinced that Wolf told the untruth, or at least was concealing something important.

To Wolf it was thus obvious that it really only was about the Gem. The Egyptians would have never bothered so much just to find out where he had been travelling.

So there was a great interest in this little Gem, but what was the true reason?

He thought of the 'permit', written in Arabic, which that man on the highway had given him the night before. Was this stranger also one of Hamam's men? What then should the permit serve for?

The Egyptian apologised, got up, took his mobile phone, and left for a call.

Shortly after he came back and stepped at the bar, next to Wolf.

'You're probably familiar with Dr. Hamam. He has instructed me to contact you. We know that you've been driving around in the mountains desert quite often and meanwhile know your way rather well there. We are looking for hidden mine tunnels from the Pharaonic period. Did you struck at anything like it during your driving? Have you seen any such entrances into the mountains already? Can you help us in this respect?'

So that's how the land was lying! Dr. Hamam was obviously really looking for the Black Gem. The Egyptian, however, referred to that with not a single word.

'In the hieroglyphics valley there are many of these tunnels, partially collapsed, but some are still well preserved. It is certainly dangerous to go in there. The rock is very fragile.' Wolf spoke on purpose of the ancient gold and emerald mines, the existence of which must be known to any archaeologist, and especially to Dr. Hamam. But he would take care not to mention the porch, at which he had been in February with Linda and Raghab.

'These mine tunnels are already known to us', replied the stranger, 'somewhere else you have not seen yet such entrances?'

'Alas, I am afraid I cannot help you here.'

From his glance Wolf could tell that the Egyptian did not believe anything of what he had said. He simply took his leave politely with a few phrases, just as it was customary for the Arabs.

Wolf was still standing for some time at the bar, drinking his mango juice slowly, wondering whether he should visit Raghab at all now. Being a local, Raghab also hat not been registered at the checkpoint back then. His name appeared nowhere. But if Hamam's men ever got Raghab into their hands, the tale of how the Black Gem was discovered would no longer be a secret.

So Wolf decided not to visit the fisherman for the time being, for presumably, he would be secretly followed.

Nevertheless, he went on the same afternoon in the nearby town of Safaga to visit Yussef who was running a small gift shop there.

His guess was correct. Shortly after he had entered the shop at the only road in Safaga, he saw a dark car stopping on the side of the road. Both the car and the two Arabs who exited, seemingly interested in watching the window displays, just did not fit into the ambient of this sleepy eastern town. No Egyptians would place himself before a window of a souvenir shop. In addition, the vehicle had a car-plate from Cairo. Wolf knew now that he was shadowed.

After he had drunk a tea, talking extensively with Yussef, he got back into the car and returned to the hotel. He intended to discuss this subject with Franz, who was after all a compatriot of Wolf, but he had the same day left for Cairo went on and would not back before the day after the next. Then, however, Wolf would already dwell ninety kilometres away, in the Mövenpick Hotel in Quseir.

The next day passed without incident. The day after the next, Wolf packed his suitcase and in the evening went on to Quseir. Driving by night in Egypt has always had its own charm. In the dark, most drivers would travel just with dim limiting lights, and when they noticed oncoming traffic, they would just turn on the main beam. Thus the opposite got always blinded. Sometimes people were driving even completely without lighting, and that brought forth a dangerous situation for Wolf. There was a rather slow moving pick-up truck, completely without light, which unexpectedly popped up in his spotlight, and only with a quick evasive manoeuvre Wolf avoided ramming into the car. Otherwise, the drive was quiet.

The Mövenpick Hotel, at the outskirts of Quseir, also belonged to the exalted five-star category, and Wolf was expected already. A very nice bungalow has been assigned to him, and as a sign of welcome, a bottle of red wine and a fruit bowl had been arranged on the table.

Wolf wanted to call Linda on his mobile and tell her all about the last few days. Yet – why would the Egyptians not also eavesdrop to the cell-phone? The satellite phone – that they would hardly reckon with! It was stowed in the luggage bag. The battery was fully charged, and Wolf had to take it outside. The phone needed unhindered access to the sky, but that provided, it was operable all over the world.

Linda answered with a somewhat sleepy voice, because there at home it was nearly midnight and one o'clock already in Quseir. She was surprised that Dr. Hamam invested so much effort into the Gem. Did he also know more about it? Ibrahim had after all told them back then in Cairo that some years ago how Hamam had found in Khufu's pyramid and nearby, below the Sphinx, ancient records telling of the secret tools of Dominion that the Pharaohs had possessed.

'Take care of yourself, and above all, avoid unnecessary risks', she said before hanging up, knowing at the same moment that those words had no meaning for Wolf. Nothing or no one would prevent him from trying to unravel the mystery of the Black Gems.

Since he was already here in Quseir now, he intended the next day to make a quick excursion to Bir Umm Fawakhir, the valley with the hieroglyphics, about a hundred kilometres away. It had been during his last involuntary visit there that the helpful Egyptians with his pick-up had left them the much needed fuel for driving home.

At the checkpoint, the guards at first did not want to allow Wolf to pass through. After all, it was forbidden for foreigners to travel through this area. But after a minute his acquaintance, officer Mahmoud, came out of the concrete building. Again it was their standard greeting, and Wolf told him that now anyway he did not want to travel as far as the Nile, but only up to the petroglyphs in the mountains. In no later than four hours he would be back from there.

After the voyage, that without Linda's manifold comments became already monotonous, Wolf had a tea at the only village in the mountains. There was nothing else, anyway. He then drove the last ten kilometres to the constriction in the mountains, parked the car there and began with his new camera to photograph the most beautiful rock paintings, when suddenly another car stopped at the road.

It was a new, dark sedan. Four people got out. Two of them were well-dressed Arabs, the others, a man and a woman. Tourists, was Wolf's thought. So he was not the only one who was allowed to drive here. The man, in mature age, showed his companion some rock inscriptions. Wolf noticed by the language that they were probably from England. When they came up a bit closer, Wolf addressed the fellow, showed him particularly beautiful reliefs and telling him a little of the Pharaohs' base with their gold and emerald mines.

He also mentioned the ruins of the ancient port of Myos Hormos. The fellow asked, 'Are you an acquaintance of Professor Coock from the University of Liverpool? He is the chief of the excavations at that place you are talking about, and I'm the one who pays for them.'

Wolf was taken aback. So that was why this couple could drive the way into this valley just like that.

'How have you been able to come here by the way, sir? How did you pass the checkpoint?' That was the next question to Wolf.

'I know the on-duty officer', was Wolf's succinct answer, but the English settled with that.

Leaving this short conversation, Wolf went on the final five kilometres to the well with the spiral staircase. He drove the car for some distance off the asphalt road on the path to the well. The car with the four other guys followed, and they all visited the interesting, deep shaft from the Pharaonic period. When Wolf finally said farewell and wanted to leave, his car dug into the sand. All the other four were needed to get the vehicle moving again fifteen minutes later.

Wolf was glad when after another hour he was back at the checkpoint.

The next morning after breakfast he set out to the excavations at Myos Hormos, the largest ancient port town at the Red Sea. It was just a short distance walking, nearby the hotel, across the coastal road and towards the mountains. From afar, he could already see the tents which offered the excavation members shelter from the sun.

Like a curious tourist he strolled through the ruins of the ancient city, occasionally lifting the camera to his eye as if he was taking images. But before Wolf could reach the tent of the excavation team, suddenly a dark blue pick-up drove toward him, stopped in front of him and two police officers indicated in broken English that Wolf must not stay there.

Right – the permit, that sheet that the Arab at the highway of Hurghada had given him, yes, there it was in his pocket. Wolf quickly pulled out the piece of paper and showed it to one of the constables. He took it to his comrade, and both of them investigated it, transfixed. They apologized to Wolf, muttering something of a misunderstanding and asking whether they should take him by car to the excavation chief. He politely declined, rather determined to walk between the already excavated ruins.

Half way to the tents he was met by a man. Like Wolf he was wearing an Australian Akubra hat. These head-covers were completely made of rabbit fur, light and extremely insensitive. Mainly because of the brim they granted adequate protection from the sun. These hats had somehow become a trademark of excavation chiefs. Even Said Hamam was almost always seen with one of them.

The fellow, obviously English, turned out to be Professor Coock from the University of Liverpool. 'I have been observing by binoculars how the constables were controlling you; but as you were left alone by them, I have to assume that you are one of us and connected to archaeology?'

'Yes, in some way I am', said Wolf. 'Has Dr. Hamam been with you some time during the last few days?'

'You are acquainted with the Doc? Yes, he was here indeed, but I prefer to believe it was just a routine visit, for he is obviously looking for something else, something he believes to be up in the mountains. I cannot guess what he is really looking for there.'

'Never mind. I'm in Egypt to do some research about the life and work of Queen Hatshepsut; that's kind of a hobby of mine', Wolf replied, leaving the professor in the dark about his true purpose.

'In that case you have found the right person and place', he said, 'for Hatshepsut it was who more than 3,500 years ago built this town for her expeditions. She was sort of the founder of this port, in Pharaonic times known as *Thagho*. The Ptolemies later called it then *Leukos*, and only in the Roman era it received the name, *Myos Hormos*.'

Wolf kept the professor talking. Evidently, Cook was happy to talk about the results of his years of research to someone who was interested. When the English finally was finished with his explanations, Wolf told him of his chance meeting the previous day with the financier of the excavation. 'So you have met Peter Vandenberg? Indeed, yesterday he left for Luxor. Actually he is a Swedish banker and industrialist.'

'In any case, he is a very likeable and helpful man. Without him probably I would not have got out of the desert so quickly. Tell him my greetings, please!' Then Wolf returned to the topic of Hamam, asking the professor what the state archaeologist had been talking about.

'He seemed somehow aroused, and if any of us should find a round black gem in the size and shape of an orange, it was to be reported to him immediately. Sanctions he threatened, such as prohibition of further excavation up to the expulsion from Egypt and even imprisonment, if his instructions were not followed. Hamam is now also obsessed with returning all those cultural treasures to Egypt that have a long time ago been brought abroad. As I remember, just before my departure from England there was a burglary in the British Museum of London. An attempt was made to break a glass display case on the first floor. And what do you think was kept in it? A gem, black, and the size of a flattened orange. This stone was found in 1872, in the Great Pyramid, in a shaft of the Queen's Chamber that was opened at that time. Since that time it has remained in the museum in London.'

Wolf now understood quite clearly. Was it wise now to tell the professor everything? Of Mount Untersberg, of Bard's tales of the Black Gems, the temporal phenomena likely connected to them? For the time being he would rather wait, although the professor was certainly no friend of Hamam.

Professor Coock continued: 'I am having my dwelling over there at the Mövenpick Hotel, maybe we can meet there for dinner today, in the evening, I would like to talk to you further. But now I have now my men directions for tomorrow, for I am going to Bir umm Fawakhir and Luxor where I will meet Peter Vandenberg.'

'With pleasure. I am also dwelling in the Mövenpick; see you then in the evening', with these words Wolf departed and walked slowly back through the ruins and to the hotel.

So for dinner, he met with the professor, who was waiting for him already at a table near the end of the terrace. 'I am pleased that you have come', he was hailing Wolf, 'there are some more things I have to tell you.'

'This is based on reciprocity', said Wolf, taking a seat. The waiter brought a bottle of red wine. 'And I do have one question, since you were telling me this morning about the Gem that was found in the Pyramid of Khufu by one of your fellow countrymen a hundred years ago. What do you think was this Gem for? What was its function?'

The professor looked searchingly at Wolf, as if he still was not quite sure whether to trust him. Finally he started, however:

'You know very likely that years ago, a German engineer – what-was-his-name? – examined the southern shaft in the Queen's chamber of Khufu's pyramid with a remotely controlled tracked vehicle. Also on the north side of the chamber there is just one such shaft. They both have a square profile and are very narrow, only 20 by 20 centimetres wide but nearly sixty metres long. The footage of the video camera integrated into the robot was extraordinary! When the engineer discovered a locking door at the upper end of the shaft and wanted to continue research, Dr. Hamam abruptly stopped him. This is apparently very common here in Egypt. Think of Howard Carter, the discoverer of the tomb of Tut-Ankh- Amen. He as well was stopped by the authorities who were anxious to reap glory for their own kin.

'Well, our good Dr. Hamam is still a trace more ambitious than his colleagues of old. When it became apparent that in the pyramid there still were undiscovered corridors, he let all musings be depicted as mere gossip. Even the head of the German research institute he has made spreading such nonsense. He himself, however, ordered the opening of a corridor above the Great Gallery from where it was on the shortest way possible to access the chamber which the German engineer suspected to be there.'

'Yes', said Wolf, 'I have heard of that; but very likely it didn't get him anywhere.'

'That's what you think! Dr. Hamam has very obviously found something. For that reason, he even had a surveillance camera installed at the opening in the ceiling of the Great Gallery. Shortly thereafter we already heard through the grapevine the rumours of a hitherto undiscovered maze in the pyramid. Officially, there was nothing about it. As well nothing on why access to the pyramid was prohibited. Just renovation works were mentioned. Last year, for the Bayram festival which is the end of Ramadan when all Muslims celebrate, some of my colleagues investigated this shaft built by Hamam. The procedure was not at all that difficult. However, before they had to set the camera out of service. First, they screwed out the fuse of the little power distributor before the pyramid, laying a piece of paper in-between before they screwed it in again. Then they waited until all the guards were at the sunset banquet. Everything else was easy.

'They climbed the ladder, which was standing at the end of the Great Gallery, and crawled about twenty metres through the newly made break, when suddenly they found themselves a beautifully carved, ancient, but unknown corridor. They did not need to go far until they found themselves already behind the locking door that the robotic vehicle of the German engineer had filmed from the other side. They pushed the small stone slab, which had a bronze handle, to the side. There was, however, a second locking stone, half a metre deeper inside. This, too, they opened and looked down. At the wall in the corridor, directly underneath the little exit of the shaft, there were several hooks of bronze.

'I guess that Gem which is now in the British Museum had been fastened at a long rope and was swung down with force, so that it came to rest near the wall of the Queen's Chamber. This might well explain the broken floor on the first three meters of the shaft. There, of course, the heavy Gem must have impacted each time, and thus damaging the floor. By means of the hooks of bronze at the wall, the Gem could then be pulled back a little bit with the rope, then the rope was fixed at them, and thus the black stone could be arranged in a position to the Queens Chamber that was defined to the inch precise.

'My colleagues went on and came to the opposite inner side of the pyramid. There they found also, just as on the south side, two locking stone plates with handles. and they looked down into the northern shaft. As well those bronze hooks at the wall, under the shaft opening, and they were the same as on the other side. The orbed stones were presumably lowered down into the south and north shafts at the same time.

'In that corridor, my colleagues went around the whole pyramid inside and saw on this occasion several branching hallways and stairways, of which no one had ever heard yet.

'Alas, they had no time to examine all of that more closely. They had to be out again before the first guards would return. Then they switched the power for the cameras back on and no one noticed anything.

'But don't ask me for what purpose these Black Gems had been lowered down from above at long ropes. In any case we must confirm that this was a tremendous constructive work, two built these two shafts in the pyramid that precisely.'

Now it was Wolf's turn after all. And being told such a controversial discovery by the professor, he had no other choice but to tell himself all that he heard so far about the Black Gems and what he had seen, too. He tried to be as concise as possible, yet it took more than two hours until anything of importance had been told.

Professor Coock was clearly surprised. For the first time he now heard of temporal phenomena in connexion with the Black Gems. But then, he dealt with purely archaeological things. Wolf's links with this unfamiliar subject made him very deeply thoughtful. Long ago all other guests of the restaurant had already left the terrace, just Professor Coock and Wolf were still remaining seated at the corner table.

'You are in a dangerous situation', Coock set in after a long pause, 'Hamam sure knows a lot, maybe even everything about the Black Gems and what they can be used for. He will not leave you alone until he has certainty whether you are in possession of a Gem. Be on guard, Hamam is not to be underestimated, he has a lot of power here in Egypt.'

'Yes, here in Egypt. But three of such stones are hidden deep in a cave in the massif of Mount Untersberg, and as wide as that even the arm of Said Hamam will not grow.'

'Right here you are in the lions' den! Don't forget that. It may be that you will soon be visited again.'

'Tell Mr. Vandenberg my thanks again, when you meet him tomorrow, and my sincere greetings', said Wolf. They both stood up from the table, it was already after midnight.

It was too late to phone-call Linda, Wolf thought, and went to his bungalow.

So he had at last confirmation of his suspicions about the Black Gems. The unveiling of the interior of Khufu's pyramid, however, he would have to keep for himself, in order not to put the professor into danger.

Wolf decided to follow the advice of the English, and it seemed advisable to leave Egypt quickly. If he would leave via Hurghada, though, waiting for him at the airport was easy game for those who knew so much about what he was doing in Egypt.

Wolf called Linda via satellite next morning, and she reserved for him a ticket for a scheduled flight from Sharm el Sheikh to Munich.

He paid his bill at the hotel and explained his premature departure by saying that he still wanted to stay two days in the Sheraton Hotel in Safaga. If anyone was asking him, he was available there.

Instead, he drove the same afternoon without a break to Hurghada. He felt sorry that he could not pay a visit to

Raghab the fisherman this time. But in this situation, it was simply too dangerous. He often looked into the rear-view mirror, but no one followed him. At the parking lot outside the office of the rental car company in Hurghada, he left the car and threw the car keys unobtrusively into the mailbox. A taxi took him to the ferry port. With the fast catamaran ferry that took off at 18:00 o'clock in Hurghada he planned to go on to the Sinai Peninsula.

But at the ticket office he learned that the ferry was already booked out.

He remembered the sheet of the Arab on the highway, and without a word he showed it to the man at the counter.

He left with it for a moment outside, came back again after a few minutes and said with a wry smile, 'All right, sir, here is your ticket.' And when Wolf took out his wallet and asked for the price, the fellow said that nothing was to be paid, it would be just all right.

During the ninety-minute voyage to Sharm el Sheikh Wolf wondered for a long time what office might have issued this strange permit that opened all doors to him.

Another taxi took him to the airport. At 21:15, his plane was supposed to take off, heading for home. In just over five hours, he would be back in Europe. Linda would be there in the night, to pick him up from Munich Airport. Good thing that the next day was a Sunday and she would be able to sleep long enough. The ticket was, as agreed by telephone, waiting at the check-in.

Yet an eerie admonition struck Wolf as he went through the passport control.

But he could pass unmolested. He wonderer whether to call home, but no, he better wouldn't. At this point, any risk was to be avoided. His cell phone he had already switched off in the hotel in Quseir, so he could not be pinpointed any more, either. Also, the boarding was completed without incident, and on time the plane departed from Sharm el Sheikh.

On the return flight Wolf had enough time to think about the new information by the professor.

At Munich airport Linda was waiting for him, in fact already somewhat stressed. 'Now look at what you are doing! Once you forget the drinking water for the journey into the desert. And now I have to go for hundreds of kilometres, on the road, in the night, just because you ought to pick-up this black pebble back in February.' Yet she was smiling again, knowing full well that Wolf would likely have to report many things this time. Previously, at the satellite phone, she had got only some vague hints from him.

On the drive back that took them about two hours, Wolf told her the remarkable tale of Professor Voock. Linda was stunned. 'I had already thought that the ancient Pharaohs might have constructed Khufu's pyramid as a kind of Stargate.'

'We will research into that more precisely', said Wolf, 'after all, we have a total of four Black Gems available in the cave.'

Linda already guessed what Wolf had in mind. It sounded as if there was another adventure to come, as she could judge from the undertone in Wolf's voice.

# Chapter XXIV

▲

## The Hot Plate

The end of October was drawing near. Snow was already lying on the mountains around Salzburg. Nevertheless, Wolf desired to drive once more to the underground vault at the Obersalzberg, before the onset of winter.

It was a kind of inspiration that led him look around up there in this cold and rainy season. Linda did not want to come along at first, eventually her curiosity won over, even though she had no idea what Wolf wanted on the mountain at this time.

After the short drive, they had to leave the car at the beginning of the forest path because the snow was lying about twenty centimetres high. So they trudged fifteen minutes through the winter forest to the spot where the vault was located. It was not easy at all to locate the entrance now. In the deep snow everything looked indeed somehow different.

Linda suddenly exclaimed, 'I can see the concrete slab, now we're almost there.'

Wolf was taken aback. What concrete slab? Did Linda refer to that one which Werner had uncovered back then with the small spade?

But there was snow all over! The slab ought to be covered by it, as was the surrounding forest ground.

Yet it was hard to believe what he saw. This small, exposed spot of concrete, barely half a metre wide, was free of snow, and what was the most amazing, it was absolutely dry. All around, the snow was lying twenty, maybe thirty centimetres high. Just not on the slab. That could not be some geothermal heat, for then, there in the woods, where the ceiling of the vault was underneath, there should as well not have been any snow. Here was something wrong.

'We will come up again next week, with devices that can measure the temperature', Wolf gasped.

But then a sudden fall of temperature spoiled all plans. Snow fell even down in the dales. Without snow chains, it was no longer possible to drive uphill to the forest path. So it took a few more days until the road was passable again.

Tightly wrapped in warm winter clothes, they were trudging a week later once more through the woods. This time it was a bit more tedious, because there was lying almost half a metre of snow by now. Arriving at the vault, Wolf could hardly trust his eyes. The piece of concrete slab, exposed in May, was still completely free of snow, and dry.

The thermometer indicated at the surface of the concrete a temperature of seven degrees above the freezing point, while the trees around were cooled down to two degrees. The air temperature in the wood was below freezing.

Now, Wolf tried its magnetic field meter. As well it read values at the slab which obviously deviated from those of the environment. But the biggest surprise was when Wolf put the Geiger counter in position. The measured radiation value at the concrete exceeded the normal values several times and was almost at a dangerous level for human beings.

'Shall we ask the General if he can comment on that? Perhaps he knows?' Linda was by now seriously stirred from this matter. 'He is asleep now', said Wolf, 'we won't get him sooner than in three months from now, and anyway I don't think that he has much of an idea on the purpose of the vault.'

'You mean he keeps hibernating, like a bear in his cave?' Linda laughed heartily about her joke.

'Not in fact. But as the time in the Untersberg Base passes three hundred times slower than outside, eight hours of sleep inside correspond to about 2,400 of our hours, being one hundred days or, in other words, three months.'

'Yes, I see as much as that; yet the term "hibernation" sounds somehow preferable to your exalted maths', Linda teased back.

Wolf made use of the cold season to commit further research on the General. He procured a few books and searched the internet for days, looking for information on Hans Kammler. The few photos that showed his face looked like him to a hair precise. Especially in the final year of the War, the General had indeed been one of the most powerful men in the Third Reich. His powers had been far beyond those of other Generals. So why had Kammler's name been hardly mentioned at the war crimes tribunal in Nuremberg? Remarkably, he also had not been indicted and sentenced in absentia, as were many others. Why had no one looked for him seriously? Probably, Wolf concluded, each of the Allies believed that he was hiding with the opposite side, exchanging knowledge against his freedom. In that case any kind of search would have been in vain. Kammler obviously had carefully planned his exit, as he had always done.

Could he be charged with anything? The most plausible demonstration that it was not like that was stated by the Nuremberg Tribunal itself: no indictment, no conviction and no search.

'So are we facing a most clever war criminal or a brilliant organiser and planner?' Questioning, he looked at Linda.

She replied: 'In his own view, nothing he has done was connected to atrocity and even less to crime. As a dutiful SS General he did everything in his power to serve the People, the Reich and the Führer. I do not think that he actually shared in Hitler's and especially Himmler's shrewd ideologies. With everything that he has said till now he does not make me feel he was a criminal. I would prefer to call him a sober, very intelligent man.'

'What was going on in the Third Reich he observed from the perspective of his time. Today we are perceiving that otherwise, of course.'

'Every great commander, no matter what nation, anyone who has taken decisions in time of war, is in hindsight a criminal. The Pharaohs who were not at all squeamish in dealing with prisoners – the Roman emperors whose mass executions by gladiators in the arena today entertain us in our motion pictures – any of them felt right about what they were doing, even while humanity was stomped under their boots. But hindsight lets people quickly forget what happened back then.'

'Somehow, Kammler had a point about stating on the atrocities of Katyn and in Poland in General. Stalin has sent for killing several hundred thousands of people there. "Cleansing", that was how the Russians called it. But have you ever heard that Stalin was named a war criminal? As far as I recall, Boris Yeltsin was the first one to officially admit in the 90's that the Soviets had been responsible for the Katyn massacre. And what do you think, did the Russians ever pay reparations to the Poles for these atrocities?'

'Hardly so, as unlikely as the Americans are paying reparations to the descendants of the eradicated indigenous tribes.'

'While in Nagasaki and Hiroshima they quickly testes their atomic weapons at the end of the War, when Japan was already ready to capitulate. A few hundred thousand casualties, yet their was no acknowledgement of guilt in this mass murder of civilians, and no reparation. But today they are pretending to be a global cop and wage war against the various Axis of Evil.'

'Do you remember, our stay in India, on the Andaman Islands? This Cellular Jail in Port Blair, the huge prison camp, the star-shaped plant of the English? Where many thousands of Indian freedom fighters were cruelly tortured until after the War, tied at cannons and thrown to the sharks? From the skin of the slain, lampshades were made. Do you remember how much this was shocking you ten years ago? Experiments on human prisoners were carried out there. Has anyone claimed that this cigar-smoking Churchill, former British Prime Minister, was a war criminal? Also reparations have never been mentioned.'

'While we are already in mass murder, then what about the elimination of more than a million Armenians by the Turks, in 1915? Is there today in this country a documentation centre in which the Turks are confessing their guilt? Is there a reparation for the Armenians?'

'That is absolutely correct. Nevertheless we should not overlook that here in our part of the world, in the time of Kammler's activities, tremendous crimes against humanity had been committed, even though double standards are applied today. Like that it is, after all, history being written by the victorious.'

Wolf shrugged his shoulders. 'It was wise to lay the past to rest n peace. We at least acknowledge what injustice has been committed here, the other nations that you mention may not claim this for themselves and prefer to remain in egomaniac ignorance.'

Yet Wolf still wanted to discover the mystery of the temporal phenomenon. He would check whether the General could give more information on that.

Another thing that kept himself and Linda occupied was Haman's research in the pyramid of Khufu that the English professor had told of. Undoubtedly, the Black

Gems were involved. Whatever they might have been effectuating. Perhaps the pyramid builders had back then erected a kind of timegate? In this case, research on the web was to no avail. For there was nothing else beyond Professor Coock's statement.

And the Egyptian archaeologist, Dr. Hamam, would never allow anything go public. It was also strange that Said Hamam just now had started a campaign to get Pharaonic artefacts from all over the world back to Egypt. Was he after one of the Gems? He even had considered to obtain a copyright on pyramid building, valid for all countries in the world, but that had earned him only a compassionate smile of the professional world.

Now it was obvious for Wolf: Hamam had by his secret openings in the pyramid of Khufu acquired such hot information about the technology of the Pharaohs and its originators that he needed even more authority for further advancements.

Haman had to convince the highest governmental circles that any his projects were going to succeed just fine. This then would make quite a lot of money come back to him. And money was, especially in Egypt, able to do everything.

# Chapter XXV

▲

## THE RAM'S HEAD

This winter was lasting a long time already. Wolf thought of Bard's stories about the talking head in the Tunisian mountain oases. Was there something to it or was that once again the famous Arab imagination? After all, it was said to consist of the same material as that of the Black Gems, and the Knights Templar had been mentioned in this context. If he should pursue the matter, then now in winter. Yes, he would use the cold season and book a one-person flight to Tunisia. And at the same instance he ordered a Renault Mégane to be adopted right at the airport in Monastir.

The car cost more for one week than the flight from Munich and back. Linda, who at that time had no holidays and had to teach in school, could not accompany him this time. But this journey would hardly mean a problem. Just that Wolf had to take care of his water supply himself for once. Linda also did not worry much about Wolf, she was already accustomed to the notion that for him everything always turned out reasonably well. He had the satellite phone, GPS, and the maps, after all. Wolf was probably well prepared for this journey, so much she knew from her previous voyages with him.

At the morning of departure, at breakfast, Linda said:

'If I won't receive a message from you within a few days, then I will suppose you will have been kidnapped.'

She was referring to some tragic cases in neighbouring Algeria the year before.

'No one will kidnap me, not even Al Qaeda', said Wolf.

'That I might well believe. They would be entirely unable to provide as much food as you are consuming every day!' she confirmed shrewdly.

Wolf pretended to be offended: 'All right, I'll just take a taxi into the desert. That's safer than the car, but it will cost much more and I won't be able to bring you a present.'

'Wasn't meant that way, but just take care, listen to me!'

It was a bright day when Wolf arrived at the airport of Monastir. The procedure to get the rental car was a bit more complicated than in other countries. But the main thing was that he had his own vehicle. Petrol was much cheaper than in Europe. Wolf set off for the city of Kairouan as soon as he had adopted the car. His goal was, Kairouan. The drive from the airport there would take only one hour.

To his surprise, there was little traffic on the quite beautiful roads. He had the traffic routes in Tunisia quite different in mind. But much had obviously changed since he had been there last time, twenty-five years ago. He was amazed that people here in Tunisia well understood his Egyptian Arabic, too.

Early in the afternoon he reached the holy city of Kairouan. A hotel was quickly found. And the next morning a burning curiosity seized Wolf. Was he able to find the Imam whom Bard had mentioned in Farafra? After breakfast he went for a look.

On the way he asked a salesman for the great mosque. He went through the nearly deserted streets. At that early hour, there were no foreigners yet to the bazaar in the city. Even from afar, the multi-storey tower of the massive structure guided him to the Sidi Oqba mosque. Then a thought came to Wolf. If he would get an Arab cloak, everything might be easier, for perhaps the mosque was at that time still closed to tourists. From a Tunisian trader he bought the man's personal djellaba and put it on. And soon he was facing the mosque, rather impressed by its three-storey tower and the dome.

He walked across the yard with the sundial and with mixed feelings entered the interior of the grand Islamic place of worship. Was the Imam present at all? He asked in Arabic a pilgrim who showed him to the entry of the prayer room: There he might find Sheik Mohammad Abdul Yussef.

In the semi-darkness and with his cloak on, the guard let him pass without hesitation. Wolf knew the inside only from Bard's narration. But with instinctive certainty, he immediately found the prayer chair with the twelve steps. An elderly man with a dark blue cape sat there on a bench below. When Wolf asked him for the Imam, the man looked at him and said in plain English: 'May I help you, sir?'

Wolf was taken aback. So this was the Imam of Bard's narration?

'I was asked to send you greetings from Bard', replied Wolf.

The Imam looked up in surprise:

'From Bard, my friend in Farafra? How's he doing? May Allah bless you for bringing me message from him!' The Imam spoke these words of joy in Arabic, but Wolf could understand them to some extent.

Wolf told him about his visit to the artist in the Farafra oasis and tried to explain to the holy man his purpose in Tunisia. He also spoke of his search for the Gems in Egypt and of what Bard had told him.

'You've courage and determination, sir. So maybe I can indeed help you. I'll specify for you the way to Picture Hill.'

'What hill?' asked Wolf in amazement.

'There's a mountain that we call Picture Hill in the region near the border with Algeria. Sometimes stones are found there on which graphic images are wrought, like a relief. And they're made of very hard flint. According to tradition, there'd been a long time ago a highly advanced civilization which was lost with the emergence of the Sahara. These remarkable stones are said to derive from that epoch. It's the same area where the Talking Head was found.'

'Yes, Bard has already told me, and I've also read something about it', said Wolf.

'Most people don't know much about these things any more, and you won't be able to ask anybody on your way to there. But you're going to find the way to there. I'll tell you.

'If you approach from the Chott el Cherid, the salt lake, you'll have to cross Lake Silence first. That's not a real lake, but just a very quiet plain where absolute silence reigns. A short distance later you'll reach Temptation Road that is paved with glittering crystals. We call it that because almost everyone who's passing there will have a stop and bend for the calcite crystals which are lying there everywhere on the floor. Don't stop, though, and don't waste your time, however sparkling the ground. The track then goes on towards the north. If you crossed without delay, you'll get to Picture Hill at the right time of day, in the late afternoon, and if it's Allah's will, also to the Talking Heads.'

Wolf interrupted the Imam, 'And what has this got to do with the time of day?'

'Now that's quite easy to explain, sir: Because right now, in springtime, these picture stones are best seen in afternoon. That's because of the low angle of the setting sun. Those raised, relief-like pictures then are casting slight shadows, and because of that you'll see them much better.

Verily, these stones and images up in the hills are evidence of a bygone civilization, and powerful Dominion is going forth from them. May Allah safe you, sir. That's all I can tell about it.'

Wolf thanked the imam, said goodbye and went back through the narrow streets to the hotel. He was so much lost in thoughts of the graven images, he was not even aware that he was still wearing the djellaba.

The Arab at the hotel front desk, though, was very much aware. And he even made a remark of appreciation when he saw Wolf enter in the national dress.

The next day he left early in the morning, and as early as mid-day he reached the great salt lake. Wolf had no eye for the landscape, now he wanted to arrive in the mountains latest in the the afternoon. Lake Silence was traversed quickly with the car. But when he came to the calcite crystals, he slowed down the car abruptly. For there was a bike lying beside the road.

An accident, Wolf thought, and halted.

But no, it was no accident. A young woman stepped up the road embankment. She was about twenty-five years, had dark hair and was like a tourist dressed in jeans and sweatshirt. Some of these sparkling crystals she hold in the hand. When she saw Wolf, she greeted him in English.

Her name was Dana; she was an IT student and came from Serbia-and-Montenegro. All alone she went with her bicycle through half of Tunisia. Two weeks she was already on her way. She even had brought a tent. Wolf offered her to take her along; she accepted the invitation gladly. Her bike, which she had brought from home on the plane, was easily dismantled. It was quickly stowed away in the spacious trunk of the car.

Wolf asked: 'Are you not afraid, as a woman biking through this Arab country all alone?'

'Not really', she replied, 'all the people here are very friendly and helpful, I was already invited to eat with

Berber families. And to sleep, if necessary, I have after all my little tent', with that she pointed at her big backpack and saddle bags which were now lying on the rear seat.

Wolf thought it was pure folly, but this girl with her twenty-five years there was just very carefree. In a few days she wanted to return to the island of Djerba from where her flight back to Belgrade would depart.

'I'm going to the mountains at the Algerian border, near the mountain oasis Tamerza', said Wolf, 'but today I must still return to the city of Douz, beyond the great salt lake. I have a room reserved in the El Mouradi Hotel. If you like, then, I'll get you one, too, on my expenses. Tomorrow I will go back to the coast, then you may come along if you like to.'

Dana was happy about the offer, for the last ten days she had hardly been able to talk to anyone.

'What is your business in the south of Tunisia?' asked she.

He, however, had no intention to tell her the whole story, and he said only that he was looking for stones, something that Dana readily settled with. An hour later they came to the edge of the mountains. Wolf allowed himself to be guided by the directions of the imam and his own intuition. He turned from the paved road to the right onto a bumpy gravel track. After a few kilometres, they reached a valley where even a few giant palm trees were growing.

There, they stopped. Wolf wanted to walk a little around and have a look while Dana agreed to unwrap her alcohol stove, starting to make coffee. According to her original plans, she would have ridden by bicycle to the three well-known mountain oases. But a free night in a hotel and a cab for the long journey to the sea she could not really refuse. In that case, the oases, which at any rate were crowded with tourists, were no longer that important.

'I will climb the hills somewhat and be back in an hour. Keep guard of the car meanwhile. When I come back, we'll drink coffee.' And Wolf vanished among the palm-trees, looking for a path up the mountain.

Half an hour later he arrived on a flat plateau on the hillside. Next to it was a scree slope on which he found rocks as large as his palm, and there were strange images on them.

Yes, indeed they looked like vivid images of stone. Now he knew why the imam in Kairouan had called this Picture Hill. The material was clearly flint. But how had this immensely hard stone be carved such vividly?

While Wolf was pondering, his eyes fell on something odd. Among the stones there was a fist-sized thing that looked like a ram's head.

He took it in hand. The small ram's head was definitely not of natural origin. But how on earth could something like this have been made in the distant past? What tools were used to shape such a thing out of solid flint? But the most important question really was, by whom?

Within a mere hour, Wolf had found everything he had set out to find on this voyage. As so often, his intuition had once again led him to the right place. Loads of stones he seized in his backpack. Only the ram's head he kept in his trousers' pocket. Then he went back to the descent. When he came down at last, Dana had already her second cup of coffee. But there was still something left for Wolf.

He presented his findings, and she was amazed about the things which Wolf had brought. She, being a sober student, had absolutely no idea how Wolf managed to know where to look.

Then they went back to Douz. During the two-hour drive they exchanged what they knew about the desert, and decided to detour from the road to the coast next day to the oasis of Ksar Ghilane, deep in the Sahara.

This oasis had indeed been on Dana's wish list, but such a trip of more than eighty kilometres, right out into the desert and in part across sand-blown tracks, was not to deal with on a bicycle.

At dinner in the beautiful El Mouradi hotel on the edge of the desert, Dana said, 'I don't think that with this car we may just drive to the oasis. In my guidebook it says that you need an all-terrain vehicle for doing so.'

'We will try that after eating', said Wolf, 'up the large dune before the hotel.'

'What? You're not really going to drive a mere standard car into the desert sand?' Dana exclaimed almost appalled at Wolf's prospect.

Yet, after they had drunk their hibiscus tea, they sat in the car and Wolf drove indeed straight into the desert. After a wide sweep in the flat land, he steered the Renault Mégane up the dune on its less steep side, more than twenty metres above the ground. The sand was firm enough. Even on the steeper descent at the front, the car stayed well under control and did not stuck.

'Ksar Ghilane, here we come!' Wolf let the car roll out in the sand and then placed it back on the parking lot.

For Dana he had reserved a nice room for her own in the hotel, and now it was time to sleep. But before, Wolf went outside to talk to Linda about his findings via satellite phone.

'I'm curious about this ram. Who knows what properties it might have? Is it a talking head? Has it been chatting with you lately?' Linda laughed and wished him all the best for the return trip.

The breakfast next morning was the best thing that Dana had had on her travel. She quite marvelled at the beautiful hotel, here at the immediate edge of the Sahara.

After Wolf had refilled the car with petrol, they drove the seventy kilometres to the divergency that was leading to the oasis of Ksar Ghilane.

Contrary to the description in Dana's travel guide even this road was easily manageable, and just one hour later, they enjoyed the sight of this fairy-tale beautiful green oasis amidst endless sand dunes. A bath in well, forty degrees hot and crystal clear, was then the culmination of that journey.

After two more hours of driving through deserts and mountains, they reached the town of Gabès at the coast. This was Dana's final stop. From here, she wanted to ferry with her bicycle to Djerba and get the return flight to Belgrade.

'Thank you for everything, maybe we'll meet again in Serbia, then I will invite you to a meal', she said to Wolf. They exchanged their e-mail addresses, so as to send each other their photos. For a while he still looked after her, admiring the courage of this girl. Then he turned back to the road. There were still several hundred kilometres to go, and it would soon be dark.

For him as well the journey was over the next day. The Renault Mégane was returned, a little snack at the airport in Monastir was followed by a quick phone call to Linda, and then departure to home was already imminent.

In the plane, Wolf took the ram's head from his pocket, examined it closely and wondered what this head might have been made for.

He would tell Bard about that, after all, thanks to him he had made this finding. Without Bard and the Imam in Kairouan, Wolf would never have found his way to these mountains.

Linda marvelled when she saw the picture stones. But when she held the ram's head in her hands, she thought that something stirred her. But Wolf suggested it might be pure imagination.

'We will set that head to the Black Gem from Khufu's Pyramid, then we'll see whether there is any effect', said Linda.

'What do you think was bound to happen then? I have carried it around in my pocket for three days. In any case, this is a very peculiar thing, and its material is obviously related to that of the Black Gems', said Wolf. 'Likely then that the legendary Talking Head of the Templars was also made of flint. After all, it was as well found at Picture Hill.'

'We could ask the General if he has heard of the Templars' head. And if so what he thought about it', said Linda.

'Well, I for my part don't expect Kammler, this dry technocrat, to comment on that; we'll see.' Wolf places the ram's head next to the Black Gem from Khufu's pyramid, in front of the little statue of Osiris, and closed the glass display case.

# Chapter XXVI
▲

## THE LEAD CYLINDERS

At last spring woke in the Alps as well, the snow was largely disappearing from the slopes of Mount Untersberg, and the three months had passed, after which another meeting with the SS men in the mountain was scheduled.

Linda and Wolf took the Jeep, as far as the road permitted, up the Untersberg, and after they had arrived at the rock face with the door, a short call was sufficient to bring out the Obersturmbannführer, Weber. He hailed them, 'Good morning! The General will arrive soon!'

'Well said, your good morning', said Wolf, 'for three months we haven't been here again.'

When the General left the Base, he had already the promised maps available. 'Indeed the temporal deceleration in the Base is back to normal. How did you know this, mister? It is just as you told us last time when we drove to Mount Obersalzberg.'

Wolf merely shrugged his shoulders and said, 'So everything hunky-dory with you, mate?'

'It is my impression that you might know more about this than you tell us', mused Kammler.

'Herr General, I believe that's right back at you.' Wolf returned a smile.

Kammler pondered yet a moment and then said, 'As you have already told me that you are a pilot, it will be the best option, mister, if you will guide yourself a minor plane to the Canary Islands. This way you also will not have to face the usual controls as if you were travelling like an ordinary tourist. The access to the cave is found in the south of Fuerteventura. A mansion in the countryside is hiding it. On the maps which you will receive from me, you will find everything precisely marked. Once you have arrived inside the house, you advance from the ground floor to the basement. There is a heavy iron door, behind which follows a corridor leading to a spiral staircase. This you step down. The staircase exits into a very large, natural lava cave. Right at the end of the stairs there is a bricked passageway, leading deep into the mountain. Follow it to a wall on which there are boards mounted displaying different symbols. Firmly press that one which is featuring the sign of the Egyptian goddess, Sekhmet, then it should allow to open and release a small bay. Find the two lead cylinders inside. By no means press any of the other boards! That would have disastrous consequences and might cause your death!

'I hope you will find everything as it was installed a year ago – I beg your pardon, sixty-five years ago. There is a second access to the lava cave, which is lower by about sixty metres, at the edge of an artificially raised mound. Through there, the machinery and equipment for the subterranean experimental facility was transported inside. Up to there there should be a paved access road. All I know is that there is at least this second access, there may even be some more emergency exits. But about this I cannot tell you anything else, mister.'

Saying so, he handed to Wolf the maps, showing all detail drawn up. There were four of them. The first one was a navigation map for aircraft; being pilot, Wolf could easily recognise that. The south of Spain was depicted and Gibraltar, the North African coast, Cape Juby and the Canary Islands. A course line for aircraft with the necessary degree information was marked out. At the southern end of the island of Fuerteventura, just at the

Atlantic coast, the second map had an airfield. The third map displayed the Jandia peninsula with the arid landscape of dunes, desert-like, as the northern link to the rest of the island. There was a marked route from the airfield over a steep pass down on the mountainside. There was a building, the mansion in the countryside, and the fourth map was a detailed plan of it. Wolf took the maps, looked at the General somewhat distrustful and said:

'I'll prepare what's necessary, and then I'll send word to you another time before we take off. Here I got something for you.' He handed Kammler a cell phone, including operating instructions, spare battery and a charger.

'That's a prepaid one, so you can always reach us. I have uploaded a credit of several hundred hours of talk time. It works anonymously. You have to leave the Base, though. Up from the Untersberg woods you will anywhere find perfect uplinks. Our phone numbers are already stored. But if you use it, get some distance away from the Base entrance. Otherwise, in theory, you could be tracked and targeted.'

Kammler looked suspiciously on the small mobile phone and turned again to Wolf, saying, 'Another thing I have to tell you, mister: Once when you have recovered the lead cylinders, you will be best advised to take them to the airfield at the southern tip of the island. Hide them well there and pick up the items again on your flight back with your little plane from there. Else the cylinders might be discovered during a control on the large airport.'

The General was right about the check, and pilots of private aircraft had to pass a metal detector on all the major airports, too. But how was he supposed to land on the old runway in the South without permission? General Kammler had no idea about these things; in earlier times it might have worked out like that, but today?

Wolf would find out what could be done.

Kammler yet thanked for the phone, then departed, and Wolf and Linda turned to the descent.

'Do you think that they can use the phone?' asked Linda.

'Why not? German instructions are supplied, and regular electricity to recharge the battery they also have in their Base', said Wolf as they followed the trail in the steep mountain forest down again. Before they went home, they visited the great inn at the foot of Mount Untersberg. Linda sat down at her favourite table, being the one next to the green tiled stove, and said:

'Do you trust that you can fly to Fuerteventura yourself? Don't you think this is too far away? All the way you will have to guide the plane yourself.'

'We've already often flown long distances', said Wolf, calculating in his mind, 'this time it will be about two thousand nautical miles, that makes for, say, twenty hours of flight time one-way. Three days should be enough.'

Linda's glance did not bode well: 'Three days out and three days back. Do you think I want to spend my Easter vacation in a narrow Cessna?'

'If you want to speed up we should charter a jet plane. But I will compensate you with a very nice hotel in Fuerteventura.'

The first thing that occurred to Wolf back home was to send a mail to Franz the hotel manager, asking whether for this voyage to Fuerteventura he could arrange for a suite in the local Sheraton hotel for an affordable price .

Then he began to prepare for the flight to the Canary Island. Indeed he had often carried out some long-distance flights with the small Cessna; but this time, alone with Linda, and, so to speak, on a Mission Impossible, it would certainly be a good deal harder.

# Chapter XXVII

## MOROCCO

Wolf had many times been to the Canaries. Even with private aircraft departing from Gran Canaria he had visited each of the other six islands.

But a three thousand kilometres far journey to Fuerteventura, straight from Salzburg, was but a little more challenging. This time he would take a four-seat Cessna. The blue and white plane had the mark OE-KFW. With this reliable, robust engine Wolf had already made some long-distance flights.

Before, though, he was about to meet again with Kammler. This time, Wolf could drive by his new Jeep much further up the mountain than as usual by car. It was not long until he arrived at the rock face with the door. Obersturmbannführer Weber called again the General.

'This is a key that I will give you.' The General handed over to Wolf tubular thing with three little plates at one end, spreading apart like a star. On the other side the tube had a handle. 'If the Sekhmet board should have a hole, just put the key into it, mister. Twist it slightly and pull the handle firmly, then you can pull out the board if it should be stuck. But under any circumstances, do not try to open any other case! With this key, besides, you can as well open the iron door in the basement of the mansion, if you should find it locked.

'You will already have studied the maps. I hope you will still find find things more or less how they were originally built. And I will say it another time: If you find the cylinders, do not open them under any circumstances! I wish you and your companion the best of luck, mister.' With that the General left. Wolf went down to the car and drove back, foreboding already that they would need a lot of luck during the upcoming voyage.

Linda's job as a teacher left her only the Austrian school holidays for free time, so Wolf had the schedule the ten-day journey absolutely on the time of Easter. Then, Linda would have eleven free days in a row.

The flight plan, the equipment, maps and personal baggage, everything was arranged and acquired quickly. Wolf was hoping for good flying weather. Linda had never before been flying this far in a small plane, so once again slight anxiousness gripped her when early in the morning they took off, heading for southern France. It was glorious weather, and soon they had crossed the Alps. The route led over the Main Chain to Milan, Italy, on to Genoa, Monaco and Marseille. Linda enjoyed the sight of the Côte d'Azur, which on her side slowly passed by. In Aix-en-Provence, the first stop was scheduled. The second day made them arrive in Málaga after a refuel in Valencia. It was a long flight day, but Wolf did hardly need to care about the navigation, since they almost all the time were flying along the Spanish coastline. Still, that day took him more than seven hours at the control stick.

Next morning in Málaga, the take-off proceeded normally, only that this time the flight would take them into a different continent. After an hour they reached the southern end of Europe.

The Strait of Gibraltar was below them. They passed the Rock at the left, and Africa was within reach, as if they crossed a mere lake. Wolf called Tanger Control on radio contact, and they were guided over the mainland toward Casablanca. One hour later the white houses of the great Moroccan city came in sight. The landing clearance was issued in an English that was interspersed with Arab words. A worn-out Super-Constellation stood alone on a lot of the airport. The customs formalities were relatively simple by African standards. A snack on the first floor of a canteen near the runway, and off they were again toward Agadir. Even from over a hundred kilometres away the lighthouse of the city was clearly visible from the air. On to the south their course took them, several hundred kilometres along the endless beaches of the Atlantic coast. Sometimes the dunes of the Sahara reached up to the sea.

A final refilling stop was scheduled on an airfield in Tan-Tan, a small town at the edge of the Sahara. With what little gasoline was left in the tanks, trying to reach Fuerteventura airport would have been a too daring undertaking.

It was already late afternoon, and the evening breeze from the desert had been fully set in. The small Cessna was dancing like a leaf in the wind while approaching the runway of the military airport of Tan-Tan. The touchdown was then actually not as difficult as initially thought, since over the runway the turbulence were less powerful. However, what disappointment when the officer in charge informed them firmly that there was only kerosene, available, in other words: petrol for jet aircraft, and as fuel for the Cessna, they could at most fetch cans of automotive gasoline from the desert town, ten kilometres off. A ladder and a funnel to fill the wing tanks he would gladly like to borrow them. But with what petrol was left in the tanks, they would 'probably' reach Fuerteventura, anyway. They should simply try.

Wolf gratefully declined. Automotive gasoline was really not the right fuel for the small aircraft. But an attempt to access the Canary Islands with the last drop of petrol, and in headwind, that wasn't either what Wolf wanted to engage in.

On the flight map he saw that the next city was El Aaiún at the Moroccan state road toward Dakar; it was within reach, and also in that direction there was a tailwind. A phone call to the airport in El Aaiún revealed to Wolf that there really was aircraft petrol available, at least in barrels.

They called a cab to take them to the city of Tan-Tan, and in the only hotel a decent night was guaranteed. But before, they had in the restaurant a good oriental dinner, and finally the mandatory peppermint tea.

'What do you think? Will we find anything when we are guided by Kammler's maps?' Linda took a long sip of mint tea.

'In any case, thanks to Franz we will have a beautiful dwelling place on the island, a suite in the local Sheraton hotel, as intended', said Wolf, laughing, and as well annoyed that in this small desert town there was not even a beer available, not to mention wine.

'What is it possibly that Kammler needs so urgently?' Linda chewed thoughtfully on a date which tasted much better here than at home.

'Some technical device perhaps, or radioactive material, who knows?' Wolf pointed to his flight case. 'In there is the micro bracelet Geiger counter, that will help us to check on it.'

Wolf was entering the coordinates of key locations on the island in his GPS. From the air already he was about to get an overview of where they had to go by Jeep later.

The next day was the most risky one. After departing in the morning into a clear, quiet air, they flew at low altitude just over the only road to the south. An hour later the indicators for both tanks were almost to zero. And of El Aaiún there was yet nothing to be seen. Some anxiousness crept into Linda.

'Are you really sure that the airport will come up soon?'

Wolf tried to appease: 'If we run out of petrol, we may try to land on the road, if necessary, and just wait for a car from which we could get some gasoline.'

'But the lorries are running on diesel, and I have not seen a single passenger car', said Linda. 'And where has the road gone, by the way?'

Wolf yawed starboard and was forced to realize that without noticing it they had left the road.

Should he climb now? From a greater height it was of course easier to re-locate the streak of asphalt in the desert. But climbing meant a greater petrol consumption. And just now, with almost empty tanks, they could not afford that.

'We will assume a GPS-guided direct course to El Aaiún. Three hundred feet above the sand dunes. El Aaiún is only forty-one nautical miles away', said Wolf after a glance at the instruments.

'Are you sure we really have a height of a hundred metres?'

Linda knew that the instruments had last time been adjusted in Agadir. If the air pressure had changed by now, it was well possible that they were flying much lower than the altimeter indicated. They had in the desert no evidence for estimating the height. The dunes might have been two metres high or even twenty.

'I would like to avoid an emergency landing here as well. But in a few minutes we will be in El Aaiún', he tried to calm her. 'Can you give me something to drink?' By now the sweat-soaked shirt stuck on Wolf's back.

'This time I have to disappoint you', said Linda, 'we have five litres of engine oil, life jackets and the big automatic life raft, but this time there is no water on board.'

'I would not want to imagine how we would fare after an emergency landing in this desert without water!' Wolf responded – and at the same moment he saw the first houses of El Aaiún appearing, flickering under the sun.

'I just hope that's not a mirage', said Linda and looked in passing on the two petrol gauges. They were now completely at zero.

Shortly after Wolf had reported at the tower of the airport, there came the saving answer: 'OE-KFW, cleared to land runway 27, wind 240 degrees, 24 knots.' They only had to pass over another part of this city. And despite the strong wind, Wolf gently touched down with the small plane on the giant runway.

A military pilot of a large transport aircraft whom they met at the airport wanted to invite them to the Russian UN headquarters for a welcome drink, but Wolf refused politely. They wanted after all to get to Fuerteventura the same day. An Arab pumped by hand a barrel of aircraft petrol into the tanks, while the formalities were completed. On Wolf's question whether they could stop over he the former Cape Juby, now called Tarfaya, at the narrowest point between Africa and Fuerteventura, he learned that it was no problem. There was neither radio nor control tower, but a landing on their own responsibility was quite possible without further notice.

When the Cessna was again in the air at last, Linda said:

'Are you serious? You're not really going to land on this small sandy square before the houses of Tarfaya?!"

'Why not? Antoine de Saint-Exupéry had in Cap Juby for a time a job as a postmaster; and he was landing there all the time, and with much larger aircraft.'

'But you're not Saint-Exupéry, even if you have come to resemble him in shape ever more in recent years', Linda snapped with sardonic regard at Wolf's obesity.

With a slightly sinister glance, Wolf retorted: 'Go teaching schoolchildren reading and writing, and stop telling me how to fly.'

Already they had arrived over the Cape of Tarfaya at the Atlantic coast, and Wolf descended slowly. From there, it was the shortest distance by sea, only about one hundred kilometres, between the African continent and Fuerteventura. Wolf extracted the landing flaps, and the little plane noticeably slowed down. The airfield below was only a simple track of dirt. It could hardly be difficult to land here.

Since there was no radio contact and the landing had to be at his sole discretion, Wolf decided to check on the good condition of the track first. At low speed he flew in thirty feet above the runway toward the small settlement. Only now he realised that about the middle of the track, a sand dune of about one metre height had piled up across the entire width.

'So much for landing', said Wolf, in one smooth motion pushing the throttle again so that the engine roared, and pulling the plane straight up. They flew across the small harbour of Tarfaya out to the open sea beyond, and instead of sand dunes they had now only foam-crested waves underneath. 'Now there's only about a hundred kilometres of Atlantic left till the southern tip of Fuerteventura. There we will just investigate a bit from up in the air. Most interested I am in the old runway on the coast that General Kammler mentioned.'

Linda looked down with mixed feelings. They had a life raft on board, but was an emergency landing, in the event of an engine failure, at all possible in this turbulent sea? The engine, however, had no reason to fail, not knowing that there was water under it.

After half an hour they were already above the peninsula of Jandia, a part of Fuerteventura. Wolf could clearly descry the remains of the old airfield. The landing strip was, just like the Y-shaped wall on Mount Obersalzberg, oriented at the cardinal directions. Right at the sea, aligned exactly north-south, and exactly one thousand meters long. That looked like German thoroughness. Only now Wolf knew where to go with the off-road vehicle

At the west coast they flew over the small town of Cofete which in fact consisted only of a few small houses or huts looking like barracks. From the air they could see a windmill, which was probably used to generate electricity. Shortly after came the old mansion in sight that the General had also told of. Like a small fortress with a round tower it was visible at the foot of a hill rising steeply behind. Very well discernible from the air were also some large tailings dumps near the building which from the ground probably were no longer recognisable as such.

'Have they been mining something here at that time? What natural resources are there on Fuerteventura?' Linda looked at Wolf inquiringly.

'I don't know, maybe at that time they planned to build some base', replied he and flew a tight circle around the building.

Wolf's camera clicked incessantly, he photographed everything that later might be interesting, and was preparing for the landing in Puerto del Rosario. Just before they flew starboard over the mountains, they perceived a huge wreck in front of the sandy beach, lying in the waves. Half a ship of enormous size was there in the roaring surf.

'This is the "American Star", explained Wolf. 'It was to be towed to Thailand. In a storm, when the hawser of the towboat tore, she ran up and broke into two parts. That was in the early Nineties. Linda gazed down with mixed feelings on the half of a ship below.

Then came the town of Puerto del Rosario already in sight, and a little bit further south there was the runway of the airport. At that season busy air traffic prevailed. All the time the big holiday planes landed or departed, and the small Cessna got the landing clearance between two approaching Airbusses. After parking the aircraft and the relatively simple customs control for the passengers of private aircraft, they went to the rental counter. From Austria already, Wolf had reserved the vehicle: a Land Rover Defender of a kind that the British and Israeli military used. They could take it over right at the airport and drive no more than seven kilometres south to the newly built Sheraton Hotel. Linda, though, was horrified when she looked at the almost expedition-grade, Spartan, heavy Land Rover.

'A normal car wouldn't have been enough, eh? Next time you will probably reserve a tank?'

'Not a bad idea', said Wolf, 'but I am afraid they would not allow us to park it at the Sheraton Hotel.'

Shortly after they reached the hotel. Franz, the manager of the Sheraton in Safaga, had not promised too much, this house certainly deserved its five stars. But would they be able to make use of the luxury of this facility at all?

Thanks to Franz, at the front desk they were received by a German lady named Ramona like VIPs, with champagne, and they were given a beautiful suite on the second floor, from which they had magnificent views of the pool and the sea beyond.

'Why can't we make for once a holiday like other people, too?' said Linda, clearly fed up with Wolf's adventure tours once again.

'We aren't really here on holiday. This time it's, so to speak, a business trip. We want to earn something, don't we?'

But on Linda's somewhat sad look back he was quick to add: 'Look, the evenings we will spend in this hotel, anyway, and maybe we can even lie on or two days at the pool or beach in the sun. For swimming you will surely have an opportunity, I promise.'

Linda knew Wolf only too well, being aware that he would hardly keep this promise. 'I'll remember that!'

# Chapter XXVIII
▲

## FUERTEVENTURA/VILLA WINTER

Next morning after breakfast, they drove with the Land Rover to the south. On the well-built road through the mountains, past extinct volcanoes, they reached after some fifty kilometres the beautiful desert country of Costa Calma that had attracted Linda's eyes from the air already. After another half hour past swanky resorts they came to Morro Jable. Here the road ended, to be replaced by a bumpy track with grooves like a washboard, that trailed along the coast in endless curves. Another half hour, and they arrived at the south-western tip of the island, there where the old, disused runway lay at seaside. In the middle, next to the taxiway, a building might have been. There were traces of foundation walls visible in the gravel. Probably the petrol tanks had been positioned there once.

'Now you'll see why this time we need an off-road vehicle.' Wolf took a sharp right bend off the road. The Land Rover bounced across a field strewn with head-sized boulders to the runway. There Wolf accelerated, and with more than a hundred kilometres per hour he speeded on across the quite clean gravel track.

'Will you take off?' asked Linda, feigning coolness.

'I'd like to, but the elevator jams!' Wolf laughed heartily. At the end of the runway, he stopped and drove slowly the entire length of the airfield back, as if searching for something.

'That much for what we need to know here', said Wolf, 'and now for the mansion!'

They had to drive the same way back into the mountains until at a small turn-off there was a sign for Cofete. After a few more kilometres of winding mountain roads they climbed a pass, from which a magnificent view of the west coast of the island opened up to them. Sandy beaches where no man walked, and towering hills behind.

'Doesn't it look like the island of Robinson Crusoe?' said Linda dreamily, with windswept hair, as Wolf abruptly pulled her out of her mind, addressing the subject of Kammler.

'Where did the General get these exact maps from? All the details depicted on this old plan are absolutely identical with what is here even today, seventy years later. Incidentally, the mansion is mapped as "Chalet Cofete" here.'

'That's because hardly any people are living here. There are only a few huts down there in front of the hill. And power lines I haven't seen anywhere till now.' Linda photographed and nodded phlegmatically, but this might have been due to a certain feeling of hunger the teacher might have felt. After all, they had not eaten since breakfast at the hotel.

'In Cofete there should it be a pub. We will try to get something to eat there', muttered Wolf and directed the Land Rover down the curves of the slope.

'Watch out! There's a car approaching!' Linda gazed with anxious glances down the steep precipice.

At least now, when Wolf wanted to escape into a small siding, the bad lock of the steering was irritatingly felt. He had to set back somewhat in order to squeeze into the tiny gap at the rock face. The small car which was coming towards them now had enough space and drove by, honking. Of course, with such a tiny vehicle it was much easier on the narrow road than with the voluminous Land Rover.

Except for a few day-trippers, most of which were travelling with all-wheel-drive Suzuki cars because of the bumpy track, there were no people seen near Cofete. Only in the bar was a waiter who served the two of them not only a beer but also a goat roast with potatoes. Linda looked suspiciously on the goat meat, poking around in it with her fork. 'Next time you could at least ask me before you just order me something exotic like that.'

'What do you mean by exotic?' Wolf looked at her in surprise. 'Except for a toast from the microwave, the goat roast is the only thing to eat here.'

The goat was good and she liked it eventually. The food was not like in the Sheraton, but her hunger did compensate a bit. Also, they never got to eat goat meat anywhere else.

Somewhere outside growled a diesel generator, apparently providing power to the electric devices in the kitchen. On Wolf's question whether it was possible to enter the old house on the hillside the waiter said that this was known as the Villa Winter. This property had been built by a wealthy German to whom before the War the entire peninsula of Jandia had belonged. Also the airfield in the south was his work. Up in the mansion now was now living a poor old Spanish lady and her two brothers. She would certainly be glad for a visit and the associated tip. But much there was certainly not to be seen. Ever and again tourists came along to view this relic of the Nazi era. By now it had become quite an attraction for tourists who came with organised Jeep-safaris into this area. Also, mysterious rumours were told about the villa. But these were stories, nothing else.

Wolf paid the bill; the waiter cleaned the table and the two went outside. A strong gust of wind whirled dust across the square in front of the bar. Wolf looked around another time while getting into the car: 'The wind wheel up the hill behind the bar serves indeed to power the cabins here. But not that huge mansion on the hill over there – where did those people get their electricity, in this remote area?'

He turned the Land Rover around and drove the narrow dirt road toward the old mansion. It was about one and a half kilometres, Kammler's map said. The rather bumpy road even worsened closer to the property and turned steeper. Wolf switched back to first gear.

The mansion, the Villa Winter, looked really impressive. But the large round tower on the left side of the building displayed, however, the traces of time. In some places the white plaster had already fallen off. After all, this house was about seventy years old already.

They left the car in front of the entrance gate and saw from afar the old Spaniard whom the waiter in Cofete's bar had mentioned. Rosa she was called, though that wasn't her real name, he had said. With a tip of ten Euros, admission including guided tour should be guaranteed, thought Wolf and gave the old lady a bill in hand. The lady, visibly pleased, was then very talkative, but only in Spanish, so that Wolf and Linda did not understand anything of her ramblings. Anyway she was quite friendly and guided them all over the house.

On the ground floor of the tower, Wolf noticed a huge old electrical panel with fuses. But then, where would the power have come from for that? Presumably, somewhere around a diesel generator must have been installed, meanwhile removed. The heavy iron door in the basement that Kammler had told of they also discovered soon, but Rosa indicated that she had no key for it.

Wolf had some experience with locks and asked if he might try to unlock the door. As Rosa seemed to have nothing against it and even left them alone in the basement corridor, Wolf tried to break the old key-lock with a ratchet brace which he always kept in his flight case.

Linda was surprised when indeed a few minutes later he had opened the door. He illuminated what was behind with his little torch.

'There is a wall of bricks inside. The entrance is paved over with concrete', Wolf said, visibly disappointed.

They climbed back out and hit on Miguel, the older brother of Rosa. 'I will try if I can learn from him whether there is some other way to get inside the mountain', said Wolf, and went with Miguel to a small square uphill of the villa. An awesome watchdog barked, furiously baring his teeth, but when it saw Miguel, it calmed down quickly. The Spaniard went into a kind of hut and waved at Wolf to enter. In the dim light he could be recognize a rusted manhole cover on the ground. Miguel pointed with his hand down. The lid opened easily, Wolf lifted it and looked down on a ladder.

'I think I have now found an entry', he said to Linda, after he had returned to the Land Rover.

Of course they could not now just enter, though, first they had to distract the old Spanish lady and her brother. They went back to the mansion, found Rosa sitting in the courtyard under a banana tree and knitting, and asked her whether she would like to be taken to Cofete. The old lady happily nodded and called her brother. Miguel also wanted to come along, and they all got into the car. Back at the pub, Wolf and Linda allowed both to exit, told them they would drive on down to the *playa*, the seaside, and took their leave.

Wolf drove really the way to the beach. 'We will leave the car down here and walk back that kilometre or so. This way nobody will notice when we will have a little bit of a look down the manhole.'

At a small cemetery, fenced with a wall, that was just near the sandy beach, they parked the Land Rover. Linda took a sausage along which she had bought at the petrol station for a snack. 'This is for the dog, that it will leave us alone!'

Wolf took his pilot's case, and before long they were back behind the Villa Winter, at the square with the hut.

The dog barked at first, but when Linda threw the sausage at it, it became quiet and let them pass. Now the two stood in front of the manhole cover.

'First you climb down as I cover the flap behind us again, then the old lady and her brother won't know at all that we have entered here when they come back. They will believe us to be down on the beach, anyway.'

# Chapter XXIX

▲

## THE LAVA CAVE

The ground was just a few metres below. Once at the bottom they took their headlights from the flight case. With mixed feelings Linda followed Wolf into the darkness.

A short passage led several metres inside the mountain, ending in a kind of smoothly paved hall, where stood a large diesel generator. The grey-painted engine was visually in an amazingly good condition. Hard to believe that this generator should have been there for about seventy years already. Even oil was still in the sight glasses at the top of the generator.

At the end of the space and to the right there was a passageway like a cave, and on many grid steps the way led ever deeper down. Once a lighting system must have illuminated this subterranean structure, as was demonstrated by orderly arranged power lines, scattered lights and switches on the walls. In the pale light of their lamps, they finally arrived at a spiral staircase which led down into a large pit, the lower end of which even Wolf's powerful hand lamp could not illuminate. Much more than a hundred steps this spiral staircase led down, until the pit suddenly widened into a vast lava cave. At last down at the bottom, they saw on the left side some locked doors in concrete tunnel entrances. Wolf's wristband radiometer beeped, signalling a marked increase in radioactivity. To the right was an open brick tunnel, just as Kammler had described it.

'Well, what do you say now? Everything as the General said!'

After about twenty metres the passageway led into a large space in which those very protruding doors, shaped into boards, set like locker boxes at the left side.

'Let's then look for the cat-goddess' mailbox', said Wolf.

'It's not a cat. Sekhmet she is, the lion-headed Goddess of War, She who Bringeth the Kiss of Death', Linda said, almost imploringly, and as hushed as if no one should be allowed hear her, 'she is not a joking matter for you.' She turned around, flashing her lamp at the right side of the room.

'Look, there!' She screamed and stumbled back against the wall of boards.

Wolf whirled around, and in glow of his lamp he saw two human skeletons lying. Their not yet decayed uniforms revealed them as soldiers.

In sheer fright, Linda smashed with her backpack against one of the protruding boards, and it fell down, and shattered. From the opening revealed a small, orbed object rolled out, dropped right before Linda's feet.

'Down on the floor fast!' Wolf stooped at once, and with full force flung the hand grenade back into the passageway. Then he threw himself flat on the ground.

The blast in the cavern was terrible. All around, boulders and pieces of concrete tumbled down. A rapidly expanding cloud of dust darkened the room. Hard turned their breathing. A deafening, metallic creaking and clanking suffused the cave. Then there was dead silence.

When the dust finally lowered, Linda got up on her feet. She was trembling all over.

'That could have turned out very badly', Wolf said, 'remember, Kammler had explicitly warned us against opening any other case. By all likelihood these two fellows', and he pointed to the skeletons, 'were caught the same way by a hand grenade. Quite an effective way to protect something. If we hadn't had the General's warning, we might be dead by now.'

Linda was in terror to the bone when Wolf again turned to the wall of boards. Yet she was the first one to discovered the board which showed the cartouche and seal of the Egyptian goddess, Sekhmet. It was rather inconspicuous and small. But it was clearly to be identified, if one knew what had to be sought. Even the small hole in the middle of the board was there.

Wolf hesitated, but then pushed Kammler's key into the opening of the board and twisted it.

A short firm pressure on the door, then a forceful push at the handle of the key. Readily the case gave way. Wolf set Sekhmet's board carefully on the floor and flashed his lamp into the small shaft behind.

Inside were the two lead cylinders Kammler had spoken of. Yes, they were still there. After more than seventy years. Wide as bottles of beer and about twenty-five centimetres long.

They were not particularly heavy, so probably the lead tubes could not have a considerable wall thickness. The Geiger counter showed absolutely no increase of the radiation level near the tubes. If there as something radioactive inside, the sensitive device would in any case have indicated it.

'Each of us will take one cylinder', said Wolf, giving to Linda one lead tube which she tucked in her backpack, opining, 'now I am looking forward again to when we will be out of here, for today I have indeed seen enough.'

'Me, too. Let's say, half an hour to up the spiral staircase, and then for a toast and a beer in the Cofete pub', said Wolf.

They went through the concrete passageway back to the lava cave. And when they arrived at the spiral staircase, both of them froze with fear.

The supporting bar around which the climbing steps were writhing had been torn off right at the base by the explosion of the hand grenade at and bent. Apparently the grenade had detonated right at the bar, and a three-metre-high segment of the stairs had collapsed down. No way to get up there any longer.

'We're down here! Caught! Imprisoned! And those two Spaniards don't even know we're here! Not a soul will look for us! And if ever anyone should wonder about the Land Rover at the seaside cemetery wall, they will just think we went for a walk or swim!' Linda stammered in a strike of claustrophobia. 'And how long will our torches operate? Do we have backup batteries?'

'Really, I am not happy, either, that I've blown up the stairs. But the General has said something of a second entry, hasn't he? We should look for this one! Batteries I still have. However, from now on we will use only one of the torches. For who knows how long it takes us until we have found this other exit?'

All the doors on the left wall of the lava cave were locked. And it did not look as if there were exits beyond. They seemed more like storage rooms, and one peculiar door featuring some indefinable symbols resembled most closely a laboratory access. Branching off to the right was a rough-hewn passage, leading straight into the dark without a slope. Here too, power lines and lights were mounted on the walls.

'I have a guess. Unless my orientation deceives me, this tunnel will lead towards Cofete. Gone down deep enough we were already, a few hundred metres more, and we should be near the pub.'

In silence they walked down the absolutely straight passageway. A quarter of an hour later the light cone of Wolf's lamp fell on a wall of solid masonry.

But this was not a concrete wall as before in the big lava cave. No, these were modern concrete bricks, from more recent times. Wolf and Linda thus were really just at the pub of Cofete. Yet, obviously, the second entrance to the maze had been bricked up after the War.

'We shall perish miserably here!', Linda screamed. 'I wish I never had consented to fly to this darn island with you!'

'Look, if they built such a costly base here before the end of the War, then, I am sure, they had several exits. We will just go on. See that? Over there, we shall turn right.' He pointed to one, in the cone of the torch barely visible, diversion. They had to follow it only for a few metres to stand once again in front of a spiral staircase, like the one above, near the Villa Winter.

'Not a step I'm going to walk any more!' Linda ascertained. 'Who knows where we still might get to down there? I would rather knock on the concrete brick wall, maybe someone will hear us.'

'In my opinion that was a waste of force. What do you want to knock with at all – your hands? Believe me, there is certainly another exit.'

Linda had now switched on her torch again. Wolf approached the spiral staircase, and this time as well he was not able to see the lower end in the shine of his strong light. Reluctantly, Linda followed him. Once again there were more than a hundred steps until, when they reached the bottom level, there opened a large natural cave. But even here it looked similar to the lava cave upstairs, with many doors. Followed the only path, from a distance they heard a faint noise, or a splashing.

'The sea, that is the sea!' cried Wolf. 'Deep enough we'd have gone down in the meantime, about a hundred metres in height.'

The noise grew louder, and Linda felt increasingly prepared to smell the sea water. A small passage branched off to the right. Wolf, however, went straight on, pursuing the sound of water.

After a minute the tunnel issued into a kind of giant lava cave, with a quay wall like a subterranean small harbour. In the dim light of their lamps, they could perceive to the right at the concrete wall an old submarine. Thick steel cables attached it to the wall. Between the boat and the concrete were strong planks, or at least the remains thereof. The submarine was still afloat, and this, after seventy-five years.

'This is one of the exits', said Wolf, 'the boat has got in here somehow, so there must also be a way out.'

'Indeed. But in case you haven't noticed, this is a U-boat. U-boats can move under water. We on the other hand will not dive that far, even if the exit was still intact. And anyway, the underwater channel leading into this cave is probably silted in. Else we would see a glimmer of light, wouldn't we?'

'I guess we would. The water is much too calm, that's why the boat is still afloat – look, Linda! Over there, switch off your lamp!'

Wolf pointed to a small beam of light which at the end of the U-boat fell on the water.

'Where is that coming from?' Linda drew some hope again.

'Do you see the iron ladder at the wall over there? It disappears further up into an opening in the cave ceiling above the water. This could be a kind of emergency exit. From there the light enters. So I think we are right below the beach area.'

'I see. But the lower levels of the iron ladder have been destroyed by the salt water. Only farther above it looks as if they were in order.'

'You're right. Then we try from the boat. It rises high enough.'

'How are we to get from the boat to the ladder? There are at least two metres between.'

'We'll take the board there', Wolf pointed at the crossing to the submarine which was lying at the wall. They moved it over on the boat, climbed across and then carried their little bridge to the U-boat's stern. Luckily it was not heavy, and Wolf was able to prop it with much force on an intact bar of the ladder. 'Now I will keep that thing in position while you get across and climb up the ladder at once.'

To Linda this construction looked rather suspicious, and she felt a little timid as she crawled the slanted board upward toward the ladder. At this moment, the heavy submarine moved back a few centimetres. The bridge swayed, Linda staggered and slipped backwards on the smooth wood. She shortly screamed, and then she plunged three metres down into the pitch-black water.

Wolf had to grip the board tight, so that it would not fall into the water and hit Linda who by now had emerged again.

In the pale shine of Wolf's light she swam along the dark hull of the submarine, back to the quay wall. There, a staircase led out of the water and up to the wall. Wolf received her amidships, she was bedraggled as he helped her back on board.

The second attempt to cross their bridge to the ladder was finally successful. Wolf had to tighten his flight case to the belt of his trousers, so that he had both hands free. Then he crawled as well over the wooden bridge. They climbed up the clamps which led ten metres vertically up, as in a manhole.

There was a tiny crack through which daylight fell inside. The ladder ended on a concrete platform. A small, very low room was at the top of the manhole. At the ceiling was a concrete slab which could be opened from the inside only. An iron rod served as a pivot bolt. Although it was rusty, due to its length of about one metre Wolf could turn it without much effort, and open.

The plate itself had a considerable weight, yet he could push it somewhat aside. at least so far that he could lift up Linda and help her to climb out.

'Wait a bit. I'll scratch away sand and stones up here, then you can more easily shift the lid from below, else you won't get out of here.' Even in this situation she had to tease Wolf for his girth. Painstakingly he drew himself through the opening and to the outside.

'Come on, look where we are. We are celebrate resurrection, so to speak!' Linda pointed to the graves all around. Right in the little cemetery they had left through a tomb, shifting away its plate. And the Land Rover was most conveniently placed just before the cemetery wall.

Linda of course was all wet from her plunge into the water, and with her soaked jeans she could not sit in the car now. Without further ado, she put on her bathing suit, which was still lying dry in the Land Rover, and threw a beach towel over her body: 'So the cylinders we got, now we can go back.'

Wolf replied, 'I am just thinking of the fact that we will be hardly able to get the lead cylinders through the metal detector at the airport. Kammler was quite right, it will be better if we take them to the airstrip.' He started the car. Again he drove over the pass, back to the old airfield in the south of the island. Near a prominent plate of stone at the end of the runway he stopped, took out the two cylinders and hid the lead tubes under some boulders.

'In the next few days no one will find them here, I assume. Moreover, no people are coming here, anyway. This old airport is not that interesting and hardly noticeable at passing. We will then retrieve the lead cylinders during the return flight.'

'I don't understand. Do you want to land the Cessna on this dirt field? Without permission?'

'Look, if we keep low enough at the southern end of the island, Canaria Control won't get us on the radar. We're going to land here, retrieve the cylinders and take off at once again. The whole action will take us only a few minutes, then we will get on the radio as if nothing had happened. Half an hour later, we'll be already about Africa in the Moroccan air space.' Wolf turned his Land Rover and drove off the runway, back on the road.

'I'm dying to know what's inside the two containers', said Linda.

'To know where to get good fish and cold beer, that's more important to me right now', Wolf said, driving back again.

Just before a lighthouse, close to the romantic yet hazardous rocky coastline, in a tiny town, there were three pubs. Linda could sit on the terrace even in her bathing suit, enjoying an exquisitely prepared parrot fish. Soon the sun would set behind the sea.

'Why is General Kammler so much interested in these cylinders? Why did he order to hide these things, and above all, what might be in them?' Linda asked during the return trip.

'Many questions at once, but I am not able now to deal with them as I might. I will have to set up the flight plan tonight. The Moroccans, you know, want to have the plan 24 hours before departure. And the day after tomorrow we will go home again.'

The next day, while Wolf submitted the flight plan and scheduled filling stops by fax to the Moroccan authorities, Linda had at last a chance to recover at the pool a bit. During dinner in the hotel, Wolf then returned to the subject of the Black Gems.

'The General has discovered something that is connected to the Gems and the slowdown of time. Then they built some kind of technological device, but according to his own admission it does not really work properly. Now he sends us to Fuerteventura to get something for him. Presumably his men are still working on this design. Here, on the island, in the underground spaces, experiments were carried out then which may be possible only in this off-side, remote area.'

'Quite possible', said Linda, sipping her glass of Spanish red wine, 'but what has the whole subject got to do with the Black Gems?'

'Remember the cartouche of Sekhmet on the board in the cave? Why did the SS-men use an Egyptian symbol down there? Would not a Teutonic rune have fitted them better?'

'Agreed, Egypt somehow comes into the story, but still I see no link to the Black Gems.'

'I once heard that Himmler, in the last year of the War, set up a network named "Sekhmet", but, besides this bit of info, I don't know anything about it.'

'Quite sufficient that this name appears yet anywhere else than on this board; so there is likely a connection. And think of the passageway from which we've taken the last Gem, together with Raghab, there was also an image of Sekhmet carved into the rock. Perhaps all of this has really got to do something with this mysterious network?'

'But wait! There are even these old lore of Atlantis which Hitler and Himmler also subscribed to to some extent. As I recall, it was about crystals which were used for the transfer and production of energy. Kammler, too, spoke of crystals before we left, of crystals used for experiments. With this, the old film by Leni Riefenstahl, "The blue light", will assume a whole new meaning. And finally, Hitler supposedly marked the hiding place of the Gem in Mount Untersberg with a crystal.'

'Now the whole thing makes sense at last! Probably Hitler did not at all want to mark the cave with the crystal. Wasn't it possible that he directed the light, focused by the crystal, into the cave and straight on the two Gems? And if it should have been that way, they would have required at least one more mirror, for deflecting the beam into the cave.'

'And what was the point to the beam of light on the Black Gems?'

'Best to ask the General when we're back again. Maybe he can tell us something more.'

'That reminds me of another bit. Do you remember the day we visited the pilgrimage church of Ettenberg? That church which is exactly aligned with Hitler's Berghof, the vault and the ypsilon of stone up on the high ridge? There in the church, up at the ceiling, there's a big mural showing how a beam of light, emanating from a Madonna clad in blue, is reflected by a mirror. This beam falls on a blue gem on the head of a woman. Probably another coincidence? And just in this church, at the foot of Mount Untersberg?'

'Yes, you're right, that's strange, maybe it's symbolic?'

# Chapter xxx

## The Sandstorm

After the arrival at the airport in Puerto del Rosario, it was just as Wolf had said. They had to pass through a metal detector, and his flight case with his equipment, too, was x-rayed.

'It was good that we have hidden these things, now we only have to pick them up', said Wolf. The launch went smoothly, and already after fifteen minutes they reached the south of the island. Wolf retreated the throttle, allowing the plane to descend to three hundred feet, and turned in a long sweep to the port side out to the sea, leaving the flaps extend fully. 'I want to touch down on this gravel track with minimum speed. A flat tire we can't afford, after all we're landing without permission.'

While the speed warning was angrily beeping, the aircraft touched down gently on the gravel field, and Wolf rolled cautiously to the end of the runway, where the two lead cylinders were hidden under the boulders. Linda opened the door, climbed from the machine when the propeller was still running and fetched the container while Wolf turned the small plane with howling engine back to starting position. Linda was barely back inside and had locked the door when Wolf pushed the throttle and departed again. After half a minute they were again over the open sea and calling Canaria Control. But this time, the answer was not a routine message.

It was a weather warning. A sandstorm was closing in from Africa, it was suggested that they should turn back. Wolf thought only a moment, then he asked Canaria Control to review the flight plan. He had decided to approach the island of Gran Canaria, further south of them. He knew it from before, and there, on the south coast, was a private airport for small aircraft. Controls there weren't, either. To there they would escape.

Meanwhile, however, the dust storm was already on them. Visibility worsened noticeably. It was like flying through a lutescent fog. Barely two minutes it took until all about them was submerged in diffuse yellow.

Wolf asked the Spanish air traffic control for a higher altitude which was immediately approved, but even at nine thousand feet, the visibility was down to absolutely zero.

His concern against soon approaching the holding patterns of the great charter planes too closely caused him to change height another time. This time he descended to minimum altitude until he had sight of the sea. From a height of only three hundred feet they now saw the white-caps of the Atlantic waves below. And after twenty minutes flying low, they reached the small airfield of El Berriel, on Gran Canaria.

Wolf knew the leader of the local flight school. After an hour they sat with the old Spaniard, Fernandez, on the terrace of the airfield restaurant, drinking sangria. Fernandez changed the flight plan for them the non-bureaucratic way and got them a place for the night.

The next day, the sand storm had passed. It was wonderful flying weather. They started early in the morning and reached after a good hour's flying time the African coast in Morocco. A stopover in Agadir to refuel was followed by spending a night in Marrakesh. But before, Wolf showed to Linda an attraction of this oriental city: the performers' square, Djemaa el Fna, which was to be translated as 'Assembly of the Beheaded'. There until late night snake charmers, storytellers and water sellers were cavorting. For Linda the change was welcome; it made her forget the hardships of the last days a bit.

Next morning at the airport it was again time for a refill, and before, the weather report was obtained. They choose the same flight track as before when outbound. On all the way to France, the weather was fairly good, and on Easter Monday they landed in Aix-en-Provence. The weather forecast for the next and last flight day, taking them over the Alps, was not encouraging, however. South barrage clouds advanced low over northern Italy, and the only possible flight path through the valleys was passing by Venice to Trieste and then north through the Val Canale, up to the Austrian border. Wolf had flown this route many times, and usually, it was not very demanding for a pilot. Only this time, when they were passed on from Treviso Control to Padova Military, they were instructed by radio not to surpass an altitude of two thousand feet. Military activities, whatever that might mean, were to be expected. Wolf received this message only at the entrance of the valley. An answer was no longer possible, because of the low altitude and high mountains all around. The radio contact was disrupted.

The final order of the air traffic control was to be followed in each case, however, which resulted in the Cessna flying after a short while in low height above the motorway. The valley floor rose steadily, and the height above ground was now significantly less than one hundred metres. To make matters even worse, the concrete strip of the motorway below them which they had followed to orient themselves suddenly disappeared into a tunnel.

Linda had fallen silent. She was just looking anxiously at the trees rushing past, which she saw less than fifty metres from the aeroplane. Then came a dissection into another valley. Turn right or go straight? From this perspective, Wolf had also never seen this territory.

He had to act quickly, for if he flew into the wrong valley, at this extremely low height the closeness between the mountains would prevent turning back. There was hardly any time to think of the consequences of such a fault.

Right was right. Somehow the geography was present in his mind, and though the houses on the hillside drew dangerously close already, yet they were on the right course.

Linda saw a car on the road below, she could even descry the face of the driver. She thought of her children at home, and latest at the second rectangular junction of another valley into which Wolf dived with a sixty-degree bank turn she had trusted her soul to the Grace of Heaven. Their air speed was at least 160 kilometres per hour.

Luke Skywalker's flight through the canyons of the Death Star went through her mind. If ever she should survive that unharmed, she would tell Wolf this comparison later.

He meanwhile did not notice anything of Linda's expecting Doomsday. He was too busy flying the zigzag course through this narrow valley. On the left side of the mountain slope a few houses stood, and with some of them indeed, if only for a split second, he could look into the windows.

'Look out for any power-line posts on the slope! Such a cable spanning the valley at our altitude would likely be fatal for us.'

Another strong banking of the Cessna, this time in a left turn, staying calm, and out they were.

'A bit of entertainment does not hurt', said Wolf to Linda who looked rather desperate and did not say a word, 'since the first part of the return flight was so quiet, except for the dust storm, that it had been almost boring.' He wanted to encourage Linda to a response, but he did not get any. She just sat quietly in the cockpit, as if she would yet have to realise that life still went on for her.

At the end of the valley, which was now quite broad, they crossed the border to Austria. Here no Italian military aircraft were to be expect any more, and Wolf ascended. He called the Austrian air traffic control, requested an altitude above the clouds, and after half an hour they had finally passed the Alpine Main Chain.

When during their landing approach at Salzburg they drew rather close to Mount Untersberg, Wolf said: 'If the General in his mountain knew what we went through, just because of these two lead cylinders!'

'I would still be interested, rather, in what's inside', said Linda, calmed down again now, looking forward to the final landing of this journey. Since they were now coming from France, an EU country, no customs inspection was provided, and they could guide the plane straight to the hangar and unload their baggage.

Back home, Wolf at last wanted to inspect the lead cylinders. If he drilled one tiny hole at the end of the cylinder, then he could insert a micro camera which he had for his experiments at home, and see at the computer what was in the container. The drill-hole he could then again carefully seal with lead, and no one would notice anything. The drill was a simple matter, and when he put the little camera inside and watched the monitor, he almost stopped breathing. In the lead cylinder was, embedded in cotton wool, an elongated crystal in a beautiful blue colour.

Wolf, being most familiar with precious stones, could not tell from the images at the computer what kind of stone this was. A sapphire certainly not. Topaz was also out of the question. The crystal had a very deep, almost dark blue colour. An iolith, maybe? Wolf would have preferred to cut open the cylinder and examine the crystal with a refractometer. This was suitable for determining almost any precious stone. But if he had to bring both lead containers to the General, then they should remain unharmed. He had to show that to Linda.

She was also fascinated by the crystal. He saved a few images and then, intending to re-seal the drill-hole, lifted the cylinder briefly. Then, two small pieces looking like glass fell out of the hole. Linda bent down.

'These are ground stones, and clear ones.' She turned the pea-sized pebbles in her fingers. 'They sparkle like diamonds', she said.

'Whenever something shines, you women have but gold and gem in mind. But give me one of these stones, then I will tell you all the same what they are.' When he saw the precious stone, he guessed already that on his palm he held a flawless diamond of excellent quality and at least three carats. The diamond tester confirmed to Wolf that it was like that. Almost reverently, he placed the jewel on the microscope stage, in order to verify the purity of the gem.

He checked on the gem several times, not believing what he saw. Then he determined the weight even with the carat scale. 'Do you know what a diamond is worth? This stone has an excellent brilliant cut with wonderful proportions, absolutely no inclusions, colour: E or even D, and weighing 3.77 carats. If you ask me for a conservative estimate, I believe that this in any case is worth forty to fifty thousand Euros.'

'Forty thousand for such a small diamond? And the second stone is in a similar size and quality?' Linda took the cylinder, shook it slightly, and at once further diamonds fell out of the hole, which Wolf then immediately also examined.

'All of them are flawless diamonds. These seven small items have the same value as one of those twelve-kilo gold bars. Only that they are easier to sell than the gold.'

They shook both cylinders, and according to the noise inside, it was to be assumed that there was a lot of these diamonds inside. 'The seven stones we keep. That is now our reward for the hazardous journey. The General certainly will not notice that some stones are missing there. Now I will close the hole with a plug of lead, and in a few days we'll take the cylinders to Kammler.'

'Will you make me a pendant or a ring from one of these diamonds?' Linda asked, looking dreamily on the sparkling gems.

'Why not?' Wolf said with a sly smile. 'No one will believe anyway that you will have a real diamond of this size there, anyone will take the stone for a cubic zirconium.'

Linda's mind perceived herself already with a beautiful gold pendant, in the centre a resplendent stone of three carats.

But Wolf did not want to lose sight of his objective, the mystery of the Black Gems and their connection with time slowing down. Even gold bars and diamonds could not detract him from that. He wondered whether the General would tell them what the blue crystals were needed for, or was Kammler only after the diamonds in the cylinders? It would be much easier to turn them into money than the heavy gold. So was Kammler in need of cash, or did all of this concern the completion of some technical apparatus in the Base?

# Chapter XXXI

## Marble Stone

Chance would have it that just at this time a large international company promised half a million Euros for the creation of a database on ancient marble quarries, being a sponsorship amount to the local university. Out of interest where the marble blocks of the various shrines and temples of the ancient world were probably coming from, it was said, at least in the news on the web.

Wolf thought of the old quarries on Mount Untersberg were marble had been obtained in Roman times already. They were close to the sites of the temporal slowdowns. Were there other people on the track of the time phenomena?

In order to obtain more information, Wolf then visited an old friend, Christian, a professional geologist, who also dealt with archaeology. And when he told him about the Gems, Christian replied, 'Yes, there's indeed a connection between your tales of the Black Gems and marble. At Mount Untersberg marble is broken, the whole mountain is indeed mostly of limestone, and inside the mountain, according to tradition, the Black Gems were deposited. The Great Pyramid in Cairo is made of limestone, too. This links to the first Black Gem, that from the shaft to the Queen's Chamber which is now in the British Museum in London. The other black orb, the one that you brought from the underground chamber of the Pyramid, was virtually covered by millions of tons of limestone. And in the Eastern Desert of Egypt, in the area of Bir Umm Fawakhir, there are also quarries – that's where you got the third Black Gem from, the one in the cave of Osiris, during that mountain storm. These quarries have existed sine the Pharaonic era. The marble there is, by the way, green. The rocks in the White Desert, where Bard the artist met the fox, are also made of limestone. Presumably the Ka'aba of Mecca is also from this stone.

'Well, whether marble or limestone, these are only forms of calcium carbonate. So in each of these cases you listed, the Black Gems were deeply embedded in limestone.

'Of course now it would be interesting to know whether and why there should occur an interaction between the black flint stones and calcium carbonate. I really can't imagine that. But it's quite noteworthy that in all your stories in connection with the Black Gems always this limestone shows up. This trust, incidentally, which is paying so much for a list of such ancient quarries, may actually pursue other interests, who knows?

Someone should experiment with these Black Gems in an environment in which absolutely no lime is present, as in a lava cave.'

So that was it! The Germans had, before the War ended, probably relocated their experiments to the lava caves on Fuerteventura because they were free of lime.

Wolf asked his friend then also for the blue crystal in the lead cylinders, showing him some pictures of the endoscope camera. 'Christian, what kind of stone is there to make such beautiful blue colour?' He described the crystal in the lead cylinder as well as he could.

'It's conceivable that that was a hauyne, this is a very rare gem and usually found only in the shape very small crystals. A piece of such a size as you describe it I have never heard of.

'It could potentially also be a blue quartz crystal. That would then be a rock crystal, but a blue one. Such gems are very rare, but they exist.'

Wolf had to think again of Riefenstahl's motion picture. This film concerned a crystal grotto in the Dolomites, high on a mountain named Monte Cristallo. In nights of full moon, from this grotto reflected a blue light which one could see far down in the valley yet. Was this film produced in agreement with Hitler, perhaps? From its flights over the Alps Wolf knew that in the Dolomites there was a real Monte Cristallo. At least there was again a reference point to reality.

The ceiling fresco in the church of Ettenberg, where the beam of light was directed to a blue gem, also returned to Wolf's mind. But then, his imagination was running too wild?

'Do you think that there are connections?' he asked Linda in the evening, after telling of his visit to the geologist friend.

'Calcium carbonate, that's the building block of all life', she said, 'the geologist's right, we haven't even noticed that the Black Gems were always deposited in limestone. But on the subject of reflection in the crystals, this reminds me of something.

'Just think back to the Valley of the Kings. There the ancient Egyptian architects directed light by means of mirrors deep into the graves in the rock. And remember Abu Simbel, where Ramses II was to build a system which twice a year made the rising sun shine for a short period of time exactly on his statue.'

'Now that you are saying that, I remember again.'

'Well, Black Gems from Egypt, light reflections deep into underground tombs and temples, the sign of Sekhmet, the Egyptian goddess of war, all of this may have inspired Hitler, but what he actually wanted to achieve we don't know yet.'

Two weeks later, Wolf received an e-mail by Professor Coock from the University of Liverpool. 'Believe it or not, Dr. Hamam is now performing experiments in the Cheops pyramid. The Queen's Chamber is now rather often for a few days closed to visitors. At the same time, up in the secret passage, adjacent to the shaft opening, experiments with crystals took place. There was a leak in his staff, but a reliable informant who himself was present at the experiments. They illuminated the tiny shaft by means of a laser beamer, sending light through various crystals. A thin steel cable which led into the opening was also visible. Whether a Black Gem was attached to it I cannot say. At least the whole matter seems to be very important for Said Hamam, for at present there is almost nothing of him heard or seen.

'The crystals used there are not very large, about ten centimetres in length. What is examined, I cannot say, either. I do know that in the Queen's Chamber at this time measuring instruments were placed. I hope that this information is interesting for you.'

'It looks as if our friend, Hamam, had found at last a Black Gem', Wolf said to Linda.

'But obviously he also knows something about the corresponding crystals. Perhaps he found a not on that in the ancient records he discovered the other year?'

'Maybe, but why does he then experiment with different crystals?'

'We could give him a hint to try blue quartz.'

'The peacocky Egyptian shall figure that out himself, he always has to know everything better, anyway.'

'You're right, and we will Kammler pay our visit soon. By the way, the General seems to have felt an a fondness for crystals, doesn't he? Some of his underground facilities bore such names as *Bergkristall*, *Cerrusit* and *Quarz*. In a month we will go up to the Base when he should be up again.'

A few days after that, Werner came along with an important message. He had found that some notes concerning persons gone amiss at the mountain, were all of a sudden gone from the files. Even in the computer there was nothing left of them. These entries had apparently been purposefully deleted.

Even officials of the Verfassungsschutz, that was the secret service, were involved in this subject, so much he could tell. So who else did know of the phenomena at Mount Untersberg?

Werner pointed out that the four Germans who had disappeared years before from the mountain and then such a weird story had not suffered any penalty. They did not even have to pay the cost of the extensive search, either. Usually, it was common that people who through carelessness or as a joke triggered rescue operations on the mountain had to face a trial and then were asked to pay up. But in this case, not so.

'Too bad I didn't ask Manfred when I was in Munich what the police had actually told him when he retrieved his car from Salzburg after their return', said Wolf. 'I was just way too excited when I was listening to his story.'

'I think we can figure out, because I know some people quite well', said Werner.

'I doubt it', said Wolf, 'if even the Verfassungsschutz is pricking on it, nothing will be heard of course any more about it.'

Werner also told then that a few years after the incident with the Germans, blasts had been set in the area of the old quarry near the time holes. Officially it was said that they wanted to prevent homeless people from settling in the ancient ruins who might possible ignite a wood-fire. But few landloupers would wind up there, anyway, moreover, near the quarry was no wood at all that could be set aflame. With far less effort it would have been possible to remove a few metres of the old tracks across the ravine, and no one would ever have got there again.

There were just a lot of inconsistencies, which might have been consistent after all.

The phenomenon had eventually occurred often enough. And every time the authorities had been the first points of contact, getting well informed about the details.

Werner was asked to discreetly investigate whether in such cases the same officials, physicians or specialists had been called on. Outside helpers of the search teams had always been told that there was no such thing as a temporal phenomenon, for otherwise hikers would all the time disappear from the mountain. However, the fact was hushed up about that the phenomena occurred only in a very limited territory of Mount Untersberg and almost exclusively whenever people stayed at one place, for example during a rest.

But very likely no one knew of the SS-men's Base in the rock face.

During a late afternoon, Wolf drove his Jeep to the mountain, intending to explore the newly constructed forest roads. Though any of them was marked with no-driving signs and barriers were installed, Wolf's all-terrain vehicle coped with such obstacles like nothing. He just drove cross-country through the woods next to the barrier and returned to the road fifty metres behind it. A little further up the road forked, and he took the left one to get into the vicinity of the rock face where the Base was located.

The road suddenly stopped. At its end there was a building container, serving most likely for accommodating the working tools. Wolf stopped the Jeep. He took his binoculars and got out. As he was standing at the steep escarpment of the unfinished road stood, gazing at the wall, he absolutely could not see anything unusual. Between him and the entrance to the Base there was now only a deep trench with a mountain stream down below. About three hundred metres separated him from the rock face. But he was sure that the access to the door was still much shorter from up here than the one he had chosen together with Linda till now.

As he was walking back, he noticed several openings to the front of the building container that was facing the rock face, and in them, four items were hidden that looked like camera lenses. They were turned into different directions, but all four of them focused on the other side of the ravine. The container had no windows but only a door that was secured with a cylinder lock, so that Wolf could not open it.

Later that evening, when he told Linda of the little excursion, he said, 'Who knows what may well be in there?'

'Measuring devices or cameras probably that track any movement at the rock face.'

'So when we'll go up there in two weeks from now and the container should still be there, I'll cover its front side with a tarpaulin. Wouldn't want us to be recorded on video as we turn invisible near the door, would we?'

'Then there'll be new tales and legends', laughed Linda.

'I rather think not. But in any case we would then reveal the location of the entrance to the Base. No one would have such a great interest in the mountain that he set up cameras for nothing.'

'You're having the calcium carbonate company in mind?'

'That would certainly be possible. But maybe there are still others sniffing around.'

'I suggest that we fetch the gold bars from the pond as soon as possible. I wouldn't want anyone to outrun us in that. After that, you may devote all your time to your temporal phenomenon.'

'I know you can't resist gold. If we find it, you'll just quit your job and spend a vacation on Hawaii while I'm crawling around in caves and tunnels.'

In the following week the rainless spring weather continued. And so they drove the off-road vehicle up to the pond on the Obersalzberg. Before, Wolf had refitted a telescopic rod that he used to clean the pool with. Instead of the scoop he had attached a kind of rake to its end, consisting of two thin, resilient steel forks which would easily penetrate the muddy bottom of the pond. If they hit on a gold bar, the soft metal would leave visible traces on the solid spring steel .

The Jeep took to the forest road, actually its fragmentary remains, like a duck to water. Wolf switched to the slow four-wheel drive with differential locks. Like on an off-road circuit with swampy spots, tree roots and rocks and sometimes diving into the mud that it would rise to the doors, the powerful car ploughed roaring forward. Linda was once again close to a nervous breakdown. 'If we get stuck here, no one will get us out, then we need a helicopter!'

'This is an off-roader. It is designed for things like that. Here, it feels just like home', replied Wolf, concealing that he was also assailed by a queasy feeling. In such a terrain he had never driven a car yet.

Arriving at the pond, Wolf extended the six-metre telescope rod and tried to gently pry the bottom of the water body. Nothing, absolutely nothing could be detected. Then Linda tried another place. 'Look, I got something!' she cried at Wolf who stood on the opposite side, and lifted the long pole from the water like a fishing rod.

'Take care, keep the rod calm. Now lower it slowly, very slowly, do you hear that?'

Baffled, Linda obeyed the command. The next moment he had arrived himself at the end of the bar and carefully removed from the fork a round object, shaped like an egg, the size of an orange. 'A hand grenade you've been fishing for – worse, right on the trigger ring.'

Linda was startled and dropped the telescopic rod.

'Seems you emanate an attracting power to those explosive thingies. Think of the grenade in the lava cave that almost would have become our doom.' Carefully, he left the rusty hand grenade slide back to the bottom of the pool, where it immediately sank again into the soil.

Wolf then took some time to rake through the mud, without finding any trace of the gold bars. There was nothing of what the General had told them. Perhaps the bars had been discovered and recovered years before already, or were they just lying much deeper in the mud?

'Are you disappointed now?' he asked Linda.

'Actually, I never fully believed that there should lie more than a thousand kilos of gold in the water. But we have eventually the seven diamonds, and almost ten kilos of gold, too.'

'The most important thing for me is still the time phenomenon', said Wolf, 'we will certainly learn more about it when we next meet General Kammler.'

Werner called and had amazing news to report.

'In the course of an investigation into two girls missing on Mount Untersberg, I talked to a colleague who's a helicopter pilot. All helicopters of the Interior Ministry are equipped with thermal imaging cameras to search for persons, you know. Now the pilot told me that, when flying over the area above the quarry and also at another side of the mountain, again and again small, dark spots would emerge on the screen. This means that these places had to be substantially cooler than the surrounding air. In winter, when snow and ice cover the ground, this is not unusual. In the summer, though, these could only be an ice-cold mountain stream or small springs. There was, however, in this specific case, neither stream nor spring. The search teams are trained to localize heat-radiating objects that are shown on the monitor red and bright yellow. Nobody has hitherto paid attention to the dark, blue and black spots. So, if near the alleged temporal sinks the temperature should be lower than around, that would be a new approach to the exploration of this phenomenon.'

As a result of his job as a police officer, Werner had a good sense of context. He had noticed that the special area of Mount Untersberg in which a large part of the old legends was located, as well as many of the mysterious incidents in more recent times, was not accessible to everyone. First, a huge territory at the foot of the mountain was fenced as a drinking water protection area, and access bans were imposed. Just adjacent followed a military shooting range of as large proportions where also no one might enter. Furthermore, no walks were installed in this area. The inhabitants of the neighbouring towns had grown used to that over time, and so, no one wondered that along several kilometres the foot of the mountain was not accessible to them.

The time had come to take the lead cylinders to Kammler's Base. For safety, Wolf drove up the new forest road the day before already to check whether the container and the hidden cameras were still in place. But this time, everything seemed deserted and empty. Nothing unusual was present.

'We absolutely have to talk to Kammler about the Black Gems, what Sekhmet got to do with them and whether he knows anything about the ceiling fresco in the church of Ettenberg', said Wolf.

'I hope it will be answers that we get! Who knows – once he has received the cylinders, and thus everything he wanted, we will no longer be of use for him?'

'Probably we will', Wolf said, 'in the end, the cylinders prove to him that he can trust us, and ultimately we already know a lot about the temporal phenomenon.'

'Which might just pose a certain danger for us. In what way did he refer to the workers at the Base? "It was regular to rid oneself of accomplices", that's not very encouraging for us.'

'Yet I believe that he won't do us harm. Shall I go up alone tomorrow?'

'No, I will come along. I am ready to come with you. Now we have so much gone through together in this matter. Then it will turn out well this time, too.'

'Thank you. I will ask him for an extra gold bar for you.'

The next day was cloudy and the weather not rather fair. But ideal if you wanted to encounter no one on the mountain. They drove the Jeep up the new road and then climbed down the ditch. The meadow was somewhat slippery, a result of the rain of recent days. The climb to the mountain wood and the rock face behind was therefore a little difficult. Linda had the two cylinders in her backpack. Arrived at the wall, they passed the temporal discontinuity, and as before the iron door appeared in front of them with a light flicker. Wolf opened the door and called for Weber. Then they waited for a while, but nobody came. Again, Wolf opened the door and meant to call again, but then Linda discovered a paper on the floor behind the threshold. She picked it up quickly, and they retreated.

'If you provided the two lead cylinders, please put them on the floor in the hallway. We will contact you within several hours', the sheet read.

'Well, then we put leave them there and return in a few hours', said Linda.

'No good. I think they mean one to two months again. They always reckon in their local time', said Wolf, and he opened the sheet metal door a third time, whereupon Linda took the two cylinders from her backpack and placed them on the concrete floor.

When after a while they returned to the Jeep, they found that just behind there stood a new and modern off-road vehicle. Two guys got out, and one of them addressed Wolf: 'I'm sure you know that it is strictly forbidden to tread on these paths, not to mention to drive on them. What are you up to here?'

Linda was already saying that they were looking for mushrooms, but now in spring that was hardly credible, and also Wolf cut off her words, replying, 'I could ask you that as well. You don't just look like hunters, and I hardly believe that you are employed by the forest owner.' Wolf could tell from the registration plates that these men were coming from abroad.

'If you would kindly remove your car from here?' the guy responded, but now in calmer voice.

'It's okay, if you clear the way before.' Wolf just wanted to enter as the other fellow asked, 'What are you really doing up here?'

'Looking for time sinks!' This was meant to be a provocative answer, but it made the two guys wince as if by an electric shock.

'And for men in brown robes and hoods, dwelling in the mountain and sitting on a hoard of gold, who are said to be here.' Linda looked sideways and had to restrain herself from laughing. 'By the way, did the recordings from last week turn out well? Have you seen what you wanted to see? I'm talking about the cameras in the building container.'

Again, the guys exchanged glances. 'What do you know about the container? You have been more often up here, obviously?'

'Mind yourself first. For whom do you work?' asked Wolf.

'We are employees of an international company for geological research, performing measurements up here on the mountain.'

Ah, the calcium carbonate company then, Wolf thought. But what did they want, and, above all, how much did they really know? Wolf concealed his musings and answered, 'Indeed, we often are on the mountain, it's kind of a hobby for us both, and on this occasion we have just noticed the container with the lenses, you know, that's why we wish you a nice day now', said Wolf, got into the car and left the startled men behind.

'You have quite confused these fellows. Now they won't know how to classify us', Linda said, as they drove past the guys' vehicle.

'In two months we'll be back. But then we take the old way by the surge tank, for there, we will surely meet no one.'

Wolf got an interesting email from Apollo who wrote of blue crystals. According to him, these we used at the and of the War in Die Glocke.

'Die Glocke, that was Kammler's and his men's apparatus to alter gravity and time?' Linda remembered.

'You are referring to Chronos and Laternenträger?'

'That was certainly something similar, if not the same thing.'

'True, maybe all that Kammler needs are the blue crystals in order to set the apparatus in motion.'

'What you are making out of that sounds rather fanciful to me.' Linda raised the brow, incredulously.

'In any case I'm curious as to how the General would like to contact us.'

'Calling us by that cell phone which you have given him before our flight to Fuerteventura, I presume.'

In fact, General Kammler contacted Wolf a few weeks later by phone. It was two o'clock in the night, and he had set his cell phone to mute. The General simply spoke on the mailbox: We thank you for the procurement of the two lead cylinders, mister. Our equipment will now soon be operational. But we are now forced to make the entrance to the Base unrecognisable. New forest roads have been installed very close to the temporal discontinuity, and there is a danger that one of our people leaving the Base would be discovered. We cannot take any risk. Something looking like an avalanche will happen. We will resume contact to you soon.'

So what did the General have in mind? How did he want to conceal the entrance, which was hidden, anyway?

# Chapter XXXII

▲

## The Avalanche

One week later, radio and newspapers reported on a massive rock-slide at Mount Untersberg. Even the local TV station broadcast a message. Kammler had thus spoken the truth.

Certainly for a long time now, no one would be found venturing into this territory. According to reports, the risk of further avalanches was very high. Wolf, however, knew that Kammler would not blow up anything else, so they could if they wanted enter the area of the time sinks.

This they did, and went to the mountain to investigate the site of the rock face.

'I'm curious to know what really happened up there, the TV featured only images from a helicopter', said Linda.

When they left the wood, Wolf couldn't believe it. The rock face looked completely different. Large blocks of stone and boulders were piled high as a house just outside the entrance to the Base. Even some of the big old trees of the high forest were bent.

'What has happened here, where do all these stones come from?' Linda cried frantically.

'Probably from above', he pointed to the rock wall above them, well over a hundred metres high.

'No idea how Kammler has achieved that, but I suspect that in a divide high up they placed a powerful explosive charge. Then a huge rock has been split off and fell directly in front of the entrance', said Wolf. The door in the rock face was now buried deep, excavating unimaginable. Even with heavy equipment – with could not be taken up here because of the steepness of the terrain – the rocks were not to be removed.

Wolf looked at Linda somewhat disappointed.

'So much then for a second gold bar.' Linda looked back, crestfallen, and then asked, "Whether something has happened to the General and his men?'

'Probably not, they are safe in their Base deep in the mountain. I wonder whether they have yet another exit', said Wolf.

'They way I observe Kammler, he, being such perfectionist, has certainly thought of installing a kind of emergency exit when the Base was constructed. They left nothing to chance really. But I don't believe we will find that exit.'

'Do you think the men from the calcium carbonate company already discovered something about the time phenomenon? Little doubt that that's what they were looking for, considering the reaction of those guys when you mentioned "time sinks".'

'We'll see whether we will hear news from the General.'

'Very well, but do you believe in all seriousness that he will simply call us by phone now, through tons of rock?'

'Not through the rock, but as I said, if I conceive correctly of such an emergency exit by which he might leave the mountain for calling, we may just wait and see for a few hours.'

'A few weeks and months, you mean by all likelihood.'

'Maybe', said Wolf, bending down to a pick up a distorted metal item protruding from the big scree slope before the rock face. It was the handle of the iron door to the Base.

Suddenly his mobile phone rang. The number of Kammler's phone was shown on the display.

'This is Obersturmbannführer Weber speaking! The General has sent to inform you that everything with us is looking good. Thanks to your valuable help, our equipment will be operational now within a few hours. For a demonstration of its capabilities you will be invited. In addition, we can just see you, you are standing directly on the site of the avalanche. You will hear from us again.' The phone fell silent.

'Well, what did I tell you', said Linda, looking up high to the cliffs of the mountain, 'all they needed was some parts to complete their apparatus.'

'Yes, you were right, and these were certainly the blue crystals. But I'm curious to know what kind of a device that will be which they want to show us. A technology, he says, which completely differs from ours, as the General once told me?' said Wolf, as they went back down to the car.

Once more they visited the great restaurant at the foot of Mount Untersberg. Once more they sat at the same table as before with Kammler and Weber. The menu invited for lamb shanks. It was nearly Easter. They had to wait, for in a few hours, and that was the earliest in summer, the General was going to report back.

# The author

Stan Wolf was born in Passau in 1950. He spent the first years of his life at a farm in Germany. The author passed school and the education in steel construction in Salzburg, at the foot of Untersberg where he has been running a small company for 30 years.

Stan Wolf is married, has two daughters and by this time a granddaughter. His hobbies are flying and submerged cultures. His preference for the desert leads him to Egypt where he follows remote paths alongside the traces of the Pharaos several times a year.

Because of his adventurous events on his travels he decided to present them to a broad audience in form of a book.

www.stan-wolf.com

**novum** PUBLISHER FOR NEW AUTHORS

# The publisher

„Semper reformandum", the ceaseless drive to renew oneself, has been accompanying novum publishing since its foundation in 1997. The name signifies something unique, something that never existed before. The various publishing programme consists of books, which fascinate all employees as well as the publisher himself. The programme reflects a broad spectrum of the current book scene in Germany, Austria and Switzerland.

Thereby the multiple-awarded publishing company focuses especially on the group of first authors and can be considered as discoverer and sponsor of literary newcomers.

**New manuscripts are welcome at any time!**

novum publishing gmbh
Rathausgasse 73 · A-7311 Neckenmarkt
Tel: +43 2610 431 11 · Fax: +43 2610 431 11 28
Internet: office@novumpro.com · www.novumpro.com

AUSTRIA · GERMANY · HUNGARY · SPAIN · SWITZERLAND